The Fire Drill

Tess Shepherd

Edited by Kate Studer
Cover illustration by Dorina Nemeskéri
Cover compilation by Tami Boyce
ISBN: 9798652016081
First Edition: August 2020

Visit the author:
Website: www.tess-shepherd.com
Instagram: author_tess.shepherd

The Fire Drill

Chapter 1

Ivy listened to her handler's high-pitched, whiny voice over the phone and tried hard not to sigh out loud. But because she was on the phone, she rolled her eyes for good measure as she touched up her make-up in the bathroom mirror of her Koreatown apartment.

She wasn't quite sure how she was going to let Angelica down nicely, and quite frankly she didn't really care. It was a Friday night; worse, it was the first Friday night she'd taken off in months. Literally. She'd spent the last eight weeks working ten to twelve hours at her day job and then dedicating every Friday, Saturday, and even the occasional Wednesday evening to the Antoinette Rupetta Agency. She spoke to Angie more than she spoke to her own roommate.

"Just let me tell you how much he's offering?" Angelica asked, her voice rising in the exact pitch and frequency that made Ivy's skin crawl.

She closed her eyes, fought to remain calm, and started counting to ten in her head so that she didn't say something cruel. If Angelica didn't give her a number by the time she reached ten, she'd just hang up.

"It's seven thousand dollars, Ivy. For four hours."

Ivy moved the phone away from her ear so she could frown down at it in her palm. She must have heard that wrong.

Seven thousand dollars?

For four hours?

Raising the phone quickly, she said, "Repeat that." She didn't bother with niceties; if Angelica was going to make her work on her night off, she could at least make it known that she wasn't happy about it. Not. One. Bit.

1

"You heard me," Angelica countered. Ivy could tell by her smug tone that she was smiling on the other end of the line.

"Why me?" She asked the same question that she did every time that she was asked to escort a new client for the Antoinette Rupetta Agency. What did he want from her? Why was he willing to pay well-earned money to have her on his arm for a single evening?

In her experience, the answer varied. Drastically. She had learned early on that the less you knew about the client, the safer you were. She had also learned, very early on, exactly how big a role she was prepared to play in a strange man's life. Oh, she wouldn't do herself the injustice of denying she had sex with clients, but only when the chemistry was right and she actually wanted to, not because he thought that his bill included the favor—because it didn't. Legally. The way Ivy saw it was simple; she dated more than normal girls and as a direct result, she had more sex.

She had worked for long enough now that she only accepted new clients under three conditions: If he needed a date for a formal, above-the-table function; if he wanted to stock his business, be it a bar, club, or restaurant, with attractive women who, naturally, drew men with money to spend; or, she thought she could personally benefit from the experience, which, if she were honest with herself, didn't happen very often.

"He was very specific," Angelica was saying. Her high-pitched voice distracted Ivy, bringing her out of her reverie. "Down to height, appearance, mannerisms…" Angelica paused, deliberately drawing out her next point in that particular way that Ivy had learned to ignore. "…college education."

Ivy sighed and plopped her chin in her hand. She looked at herself in the mirror. All that effort put into getting ready. *Wasted.*

"What's his background?" As much as she didn't want Angelica to think that she'd accepted the offer, she was curious as to who was prepared to throw away seven *thousand* dollars for a single date.

"Let me see," Angelica said as she pretended to rifle through paperwork on her desk. Ivy rolled her eyes again, familiar with the routine. Not that Angie didn't deal with a lot of paperwork; the Antoinette Rupetta Agency only used paper contracts, which were one hundred percent legal, but printed and FedExed to clients overnight priority with paid return shipping. Nothing digital except the client's profiles. Even payments were made to a bank account that was simply named ARPEA.

"Ah! Mmm, interesting."

"Angelica. *Please.*"

As if sensing that she was losing valuable ground, Angelic switched to her no-nonsense business tone without missing a beat. "His background check came back squeaky clean. He's been a repeat client of ours for about five years with no complaints filed by any of the girls." She paused, took one breathy sigh and added, "My my, he is—"

"Angelica." Taking a deep breath, Ivy swallowed her impatience. "What does he do? More importantly, what will *I* have to do? Does he know that sex isn't in my contract? These are the questions I want answers to."

Angelica gave a small half-sigh and Ivy could hear her tapping her nails on her black, lacquered desk over the line. "He's in banking," she said.

"What kind?" Ivy prompted. "Investment? Retail? Credit risk?"

"Investment."

"You're sure?" she countered, summing all of her patience to regulate her tone.

"Yes." The answer was immediate. "He's a managing director at Black Finch Capital's office in Downtown LA.

He isn't married, never has been. No criminal record. Needs a casual date for a formal, work event."

"But?"

"He specifically requested an educated date. It was his only non-negotiable. And to be quite honest, Ivy, you're the only one available who fits the master's degree requirement. Jessica fit the profile to a T and had even been out with him before, but she left us a few weeks ago…found herself a boyfriend worth losing the cash money over. Apparently."

Ivy raised her eyebrows in surprise but remained silent. She knew Jessica; they had worked a few bar and nightclub openings together. Jessica was a six-foot blonde who literally could have been a Victoria's Secret model. In fact, Ivy was pretty sure that the only reason Jessica wasn't a Victoria's Secret model was because she was in LA, trying to become an actress instead.

So, the takeaway was that the client had requested a tall blonde with baby-blues. A textbook 34-24-34. *Typical.* She wondered if he'd be disappointed that he ended up with her when he saw her. No, *if* he saw her.

And why was she procrastinating? Both she and Angelica knew that she wouldn't say no to seven thousand dollars. Even if she only took home four of it after Antoinette took her cut, the money was worth it for a few hours of work. "Send me the file."

She tried not to wince when Angelica's chirpy voice squeaked, "Yas! I'll send it over now, along with the non-disclosure. Stay fabulous, Darling!"

When the phone disconnected, Ivy felt a vague urge to throw it against the wall, and she gripped it tightly in her hand to counter the impulse. *You could have said no.*

She closed her eyes for a moment and took a few deep breaths. This would be good for her. Four thousand dollars in a lump sum would take a chunk out of her credit card debt; it would even reduce her monthly interest. Fractionally.

She opened her eyes and found herself staring at her reflection in the mirror again. She tried to erase the fatigue reflected in her wide, emerald eyes, practiced a flirtatious but unassuming smile back at herself, grimaced, tilted her head, and tried again with marginally better results.

Damien was going to be pissed.

She'd been promising him that they'd make plans to go out for months now. But, between her day job and, well, her work, she'd just been too busy. And now she was going to cancel. Again. *Great.* Nothing like a pissed-off best friend to get the night off to a good start.

She sighed and rubbed her temples to try and ease the fatigue that had settled there before hopping down from her perch on the bathroom sink. With one last resigned shrug, she slipped out of her spiked, black heels and stretched behind herself to unzip the short, red dress that she'd specifically bought for the occasion.

Damn it. She had looked great—not just good—great. Which was not something that came easy to her; sure, she was tall and pretty... in an unusual kind of way, but she had to try really hard to look *incredible.*

"Hey, did you fin-" Damien paused in the bathroom door, his eyes flicking down her lingerie-clad body before moving back to her eyes. "You were dressed a moment ago."

She looked at him, couldn't help the grin that spread over her face when she noticed his tight, black leather pants, accented only by a pair of suspenders and big, chunky military-grade boots. She plastered on her best regretful smile, which luckily for her, she felt in the bottom-most corner of her soul. "I'm sorry. It's a big contract."

"Seriously? You're bailing on me? Again?" He pouted, crossing his arms over his chest in a gesture she knew was defensive, not confrontational.

Nodding, she moved past him into their tiny hallway, carrying her red dress forlornly. She tried not to look into his big, blue, disappointed eyes as she turned and said, "I wouldn't go if it wasn't a big deal. But it's the biggest lump sum I've ever been offered to work."

Even Damien, her disapproving best friend had the grace to look shocked. "More than the gay son of the oil tycoon who wanted to introduce a girl to grandma before she died?"

"Shit, Damien. It's nearly double."

"Fuck." His eyebrows disappeared under his shaggy mane of hair, as he padded into her bedroom behind her, his boots clomping over the old carpeted floor.

Because she was comfortable with him and because he was one hundred percent gay, she sat on her bed in her black, lace lingerie and pulled her laptop onto her folded legs before opening it. She may as well suss the man out before she decided what to wear. And, if she had to admit it, she liked to be prepared, liked to know as much as possible about a client before she committed to an outfit. It was amazing how much you could tell about a person given only a few simple facts.

While her computer booted up, she glanced up at Damien. He stood just inside her doorway, his thick brown hair curling ever-so-slightly above his milk-white, bony shoulders, his blue eyes assessing her. Not judging—assessing.

"How much longer are you going to do this?" he asked, a small frown creasing his brow. "It's been a year already."

"Fifteen months," she clarified. As if she wasn't the one counting the days.

She logged on to her computer and opened her email so she could read the file Angelica had sent her. Before he could respond, she added, "And you know I can't stop. Not until..." She trailed off when the words lodged in her throat, suffocating her.

Damien sighed. "I know." Sensing her reluctance to talk about it further, he changed the subject. "So, if you get off at a remotely reasonable hour, could you please come find us?" Before she could refuse, he added, "It's only nine now and we'll be out until morning."

Because she knew it was true, she chuckled. Because she doubted she'd want to track them down at a dark, sexy, sweaty nightclub at one in the morning after making small talk with a stranger for four hours, she added, "We'll see."

She double-clicked the email from Angelica, spent ten minutes hurriedly reading the questionnaire that the man had filled out before opening the picture attached.

"Holy. Shit." Damien said it for her, leaning over her shoulder so that he could get a better look. "He is...not bad."

"Not bad? Really? That's the extent of your vocabulary to describe this man?" she asked, pointing to the screen. When he craned his neck over her shoulder, she turned it more fully towards him.

"Words fail me."

She grinned before turning the screen back so that she could study it. The man in the image was beautiful—that was the only word for it—with high, sculpted cheekbones and a square jaw. His blonde hair, although cut short, curled slightly and she imagined that if he grew it out, it would turn into a full head of ringlets. He didn't smile, despite the professional headshot; his mouth was set in a firm line that was matched by a pair of cold, blue eyes. She thought he looked like the stereotypical golden boy from a World War II movie; the one who's in love with the heroine and gives her a black and white photograph of himself before going off to war.

"He looks super serious," Damien said, seeming uncertain. "Why would he need a date? He must have women falling at his feet..."

"You never really know." Although even she had to admit that even she was curious. Other than the slightly cold eyes, he was truly gorgeous. "Sometimes it's simply for convenience. Like they were given too short notice about the event but don't want to go alone. Sometimes it's just for fun. I even had one guy hire me because he knew that his ex-wife was going to be in attendance at an annual charity event that they had always frequented together." At Damien's soft gasp, she added, "Bastard didn't even warn me."

"What did you do?"

"Played it out; ended up moseying up to the ex-wife and finding out that Steve, let's call him Steve, actually wasn't a bad guy. Just lonely. And still very much in love with his ex."

"People are so weird."

"Mmhmm." She scrolled through the file one last time, and then closed the laptop as she thought about what to wear. She only had an hour before she was supposed to meet him at the bar in the Ritz Carlton Downtown Los Angeles, which really meant that she had twenty minutes to get ready.

"Help me pick an outfit?" she asked, hoping that the request would bring Damien a little closer to forgiving her.

He smiled, his blue eyes laughing at her weak attempt. "Don't I always?"

Chapter 2

She stepped into the Ritz Carlton's bar, acutely aware of all the male eyes that gravitated in her direction. Aside from a pretty blonde woman in her mid-forties who just shook her head, a small smile on her face as her husband lapsed into silence mid-conversation, all were eyes trained on her.

Her stomach clenched uncomfortably, and Ivy fought the urge to tug her dress down. Banking her nerves, she scanned the bar. *You have to play nice.* Those were the rules, and by God, as much as she didn't want to be there, she'd suck it up for a few hours.

From his picture alone, she knew that her client wouldn't be hard to spot. He had to be six-feet tall at least, and judging by the high resolution digital, his shoulders were closer in width to a linebacker's than the typical investment banker's.

She took a few steps forward, squinted a little into the dark room, trying unsuccessfully to scout him out. She sighed when she didn't see him, figured that he was probably late, and rolled her neck in irritation. She'd get a single drink at the bar, she decided; wait for him to arrive and play a nice, polished—or was it educated?—girl.

When she subtly squeezed between a small man with glasses, who barely reached her shoulder, and a tall, leggy blonde who was leaning on the bar but had no intention of ordering, the bartender instantly made a beeline towards her. She heard the man at her side give a defeated sigh. Out of the corner of her eye, she saw him slip his fingers underneath his glasses so that he could rub at tired eyes as the bartender skimmed past him—or given his height, maybe over him was more accurate.

"What can I get you, Miss?"

Ivy smiled her most charming smile. It wasn't dazzling, far from it, but it was enough to have the tall, young bartender grinning back at her. "Could I have a Balvenie? Neat. And whatever my friend is having," she finished and looked at the man at her elbow.

He hesitated, sent her a wide, grateful smile, and added, "A vodka soda and…I guess I'll take a Balvenie too," he said. "Neat."

The bartender smiled and tipped his head in a friendly gesture, before stepping back to pour their drinks.

She briefly glanced at the man by her side, took in his thinning hair and small, pale hands. She noticed him look at her awkwardly, his big, brown eyes flicking from her face to the bar, and asked, "I hope you don't mind. Sometimes, it's just easier to get their attention if you double up your order the first time," she said, trying desperately to alleviate the man's obvious discomfort. "Now, when I come back later, he'll come straight to me."

She smiled kindly, waited for a full ten seconds for the man to reply. Eventually, he said, "I appreciate it,…?"

"Ivy Watts," she replied and shook his outstretched hand.

"Bruce Standard."

She was surprised by his firm, professional handshake. She already knew that he was wealthy by the cut of his tailored suit, but the handshake was a solid giveaway. Bruce Standard's money had been earned, not inherited as she originally would have guessed. It was the type of handshake that made the recipient aware that Bruce Standard had done a lot of business, and of course, shaken a lot of hands.

"I was honestly going to leave. It's hard enough getting attention when you're five-six as a man, but at a paying establishment…" He trailed off, his head moving in a brisk shake of disbelief.

"I wouldn't take it personally," Ivy replied. "I've been in here a few times, so I'm sure he recognized my face." It wasn't a lie, per se. She had been in the Ritz Carlton more than a few times for one thing or another- just not in the bar.

"Ah," Bruce nodded.

"Are you visiting Los Angeles, then?" she asked, noting his New York accent.

"Yes," he replied, nodding in thanks to the bartender when he placed their drinks on the bar in front of them.

Ivy palmed over her credit card subtly before Bruce Standard had a chance to ask for the tab. "I'm in town for a few weeks…" He glanced down at Ivy's tight, black dress and three-inch heels, before clearing his throat and adding, "with my wife, Deborah."

She grimaced inwardly and barely refrained from pulling her dress down. Again. *Goddamnit, Damien.* She should have just trusted her instincts, should have said no when he'd insisted on the tiny number. She'd only agreed when he'd argued the dress being all-black compensated for how short it was.

Liar.

"I figured," she said, picking up the conversation again. When Bruce raised his eyebrows, she smiled. "I don't know many men who'd order a vodka soda, or at least I don't know many men who would order a vodka soda in public."

He hesitated for a second, and Ivy thought she'd blown it. Then Bruce threw back his head and laughed a big laugh, a laugh that was surprisingly deep for his small, slight frame, a laugh that brought a genuine, and relieved, smile to her own lips.

When he sobered, Ivy chuckled and out of the corner of her eye, saw a small, dark woman working her way through the crowd, her short legs moving quickly, as if she was trying to walk-run from someone she didn't want to speak to. She noticed that the woman's near-black eyes were focused on Bruce uncertainly as she made a beeline towards him. When she was just within hearing distance, Ivy shot her a warm smile and said, "You must be Deborah."

The woman stopped dead in her tracks only a few feet away and glanced from Bruce to Ivy.

Ivy forced the blood out of her cheeks, refusing to acknowledge the blush swirling underneath her skin, making her feel warm and itchy all over. Instead, she grasped the woman's hand between both of hers and said, "It's so nice to meet you. Bruce was just telling me that you're visiting from New York?"

She nodded, glanced uncertainly at her husband, and, when he smiled, said, "Yes. I'm sorry I didn't catch your name?"

"Ivy Watts," she repeated and dropped Deborah's hand. "I was just waiting for a friend and your husband and I were lamenting over the service."

"Ivy is actually entirely to thank for the fact that you have a drink at all," Bruce said, passing the vodka soda from the bar to his wife. "She was kind enough to order for us."

Ivy signed the tab and slipped the credit card back into her purse. "It was my pleasure meeting you both," she said. Seeing the perfect opportunity to excuse herself, she added, "I hope that you enjoy your time in Los Angeles. I'm going to go and find my date."

"Thanks again, Ivy," Bruce said and joined his hand with his wife's. "All the best."

She smiled and sauntered away from the bar, hoping that her client would have arrived by now. Casting another look around the room, she noticed the heavy maroon drapes and the dark, walnut tables for the first time. Even the seats of the bar stools and chairs had plush, maroon, art-deco cushions. She could imagine Sinatra standing up against the bar, sipping his bourbon before he crooned to a room full of ladies and gents all adazzle in their finest.

The thought made her smile. How romantic would that have been? To have lived in such a time? The beautiful dresses, the sexy clubs, the great music.

"The dress is a little short, don't you think?"

Ivy froze, felt a single chill shoot up her spine. She blinked and, although she had never met David Van den Berg before, she easily paired the cold, matter-of-fact tone to the ice-blue eyes that she had seen in his picture. For some reason, they matched perfectly. The word 'hostile' popped into her mind.

She plastered a smile on her face and turned around slowly. *Don't be rude Ivy*, she told herself. *He's the one paying you.*

Be nice to the client.

Be nice to the client.

Be nice to the client. She repeated the words in her head, a mantra of sorts, to bolster her morale.

She met his gaze, tried not to look away when his piercing blue eyes assessed her. She ignored the fact that he was gorgeous, ignored the slight tremble that had started in her hands, and said, "It is, but you didn't specify a dress code so I went with something that could be both formal and casual." She extended her hand. "I'm Diana." The name, one that she had decided on when she'd started at the Antoinette Rupetta Agency, slipped out of her lips as easy as a white lie to a sibling.

He didn't accept the offered hand, didn't even acknowledge that she had extended the greeting, so she dropped it.

While he continued to assess her, she took the opportunity to do the same. He was taller than his picture had made him out to be, maybe six-two or three; she had pegged the shoulders though—they belied his desk job and boasted a dedicated gym routine. The picture had definitely

13

captured the cheekbones and the cold, blue eyes, which suited his frigid personality.

She shifted uncomfortably when he didn't say anything. Most of the men that she accompanied were flustered and embarrassed the first time they met her, not brazen and rude like David Van den Berg. "Are you done?" she asked, drily. "You're going to attract attention."

"Oh, I think the dress has accomplished that already," he returned without hesitation.

She felt the heat flood her cheeks before she could bank it, tried, unsuccessfully, to meet his eyes. This was not going to be a good night.

"Would you like me to go and change? Give you a refund?" *Please say yes*, she thought as she looked at him. The money was not worth having to spend all night in his company.

"No. There's no time, and considering you were the Agency's last resort, I doubt I could get a replacement this late." He delivered the last insult with a casual glance at his watch. "Speaking of which, the car should be here by now."

She bowed her head slightly, stepped to his side when he made an "after you" gesture with his arm, and followed him from the bar.

They were both silent as they came to stand at the hotel's passenger drop-off zone, neither of them interested in making small talk. Ivy shifted from one foot to the other as she tried to think of something she could say to interest him, or at least keep those cold, blue eyes from looking at her with condescension because every time they did, she felt a solid weight slide into her stomach.

Nothing came to mind.

"This is us," he said when a black Range Rover pulled up in front of them.

Ivy nodded, stretched out her hand when the car came to a stop exactly abreast of her and drew it back quickly when David did the same, their fingers brushing for a single moment. She clasped her hands together, embarrassed.

He cleared his throat and opened the door for her.

She nodded in thanks and hopped in as elegantly as she could, lamenting the short, tight dress the entire time. She and Damien were going to have a serious conversation about wardrobe functionality when she got home.

She smiled at the driver and said, "Hi," when David shut the door on her.

The driver flashed her a grin in the review mirror. "Evening, Miss. I'm Morgan. Let me know if you need anything," he said before sobering instantly when David got into the car on the other side. Morgan, unlike her, obviously knew the routine.

The car pulled out into the street, and she couldn't help but sigh as David took out his phone and checked his email before he started typing a reply. This was absurd, she thought. "Are you going to tell me anything about the event that we're going to?" she asked. She looked out at the passing streets, noticed they'd turned north towards Westlake.

She turned when he didn't reply, saw that he was still typing his email, his fingers flying across the screen, and she waited patiently for him to finish. He must have clicked send because he turned to face her suddenly, blue eyes cold and direct, and asked, "What do you need to know?"

"What is it for?"

"Work."

"Specifically?"

"It's a company-hosted event for employees. There's a general expectation that everyone has to be there, so it'll run the gambit from analysts to SVP's. I plan on staying for an hour, maybe two if the CEO has flown out."

"And your position would be?"

"Managing director."

"Investment Banking?"

He nodded. "Didn't you read the questionnaire?"

"Yes," she sighed, "but sometimes it helps me get a sense of how much you want me to talk about your job. How many details I should know."

"Don't talk about my job. That's not why I hired you."

"Noted," she returned coldly before she could reign in her inner diva. "So, show up, smile, don't be charming, speak only when spoken to, and God forbid people actually think I'm your date." He glanced at her, eyebrows raised, and she finished with a saccharine smile. "Easiest money I'll ever earn."

"Look," he began, his tone placating, grating, "there's an expectation that I'll bring a beautiful woman. I don't have time to date so escorts it is. This is a Fire Drill. That's why you're here. Just have fun, don't get drunk or embarrass me, and we'll be fine."

She nodded. *Fine by me.* If he wanted to be insufferable then she'd smile, play nice, and by God when this evening was over, she'd take his money and never have to see his miserable face again.

David rolled his shoulders, trying ineffectively to loosen some of the tension that sat in the middle of his back. The fact that he had to make an appearance at this work event bothered him. He had already put in a twelve-hour day, and now, on his Friday night, they'd rustled up an event out of the blue, even hired a venue and had the gall to call it a party. If they hadn't mentioned that the CEO might be flying in for the occasion, he would have boycotted the evening entirely.

But, knowing that he'd had no choice but to attend had put him in a sour mood before he'd seen Diana. Oh, she'd definitely made it worse, but he could have at least made an effort if he hadn't already been wanting to throw something.

He glanced at her, noticed that her hands were folded in her lap just above the line where her dress met smooth, flawless thigh.

She stared out of the window.

He didn't try and make small talk.

He'd specifically asked for someone who could pass as a woman he'd date; an educated, slender blonde who'd know to wear at least a knee-long dress to an investment banking event. Not a leggy brunette with curls to her waist, an unreasonably wide mouth, and emerald eyes as wide as quarters. For Christ's sake, add in the little black dress and high, strappy heels and she looked like an…escort? Or a model. No, an actress, he decided. *Definitely an actress.* More like Eva Green playing schoolgirl than a blonde bombshell off the Victoria's Secret runway.

Okay, so she was a smoke show. *And* she was going to draw attention, which was precisely what he'd been trying to avoid.

She sighed softly as the car pulled up to the door of the Camelot House and David couldn't help but feel a twinge of shame. It was a *twinge,* but it wasn't fleeting. He'd been rude. Worse, he knew by the way she'd blushed earlier that he'd embarrassed her. His grandmother would have been ashamed of him and knowing it settled an unfamiliar weight in his mind.

When the driver came to a stop, he reached for his door handle.

"Thanks, Morgan," she said, flashing a dazzling smile at the driver.

"You have a good time, Miss." The driver looked at his surprised expression in the review mirror, and added a polite, "Sir."

He shook his head and went for the handle. When had she even had time to befriend the driver? He stepped into the warm Los Angeles night and walked around the car. Diana had already opened her own door and David had a glimpse of a slender, bare leg before she scooted all the way out and came to stand beside him. He felt the same gnawing awareness in his stomach that he had when he'd first spotted her in the bar, deliberately ignored it, and glanced down at her. She was tall, he realized for the first time. With the heels, she only had to tilt her chin slightly to meet his eyes.

When she did just that, turned wide, sad eyes on him, he felt the knot in his stomach tighten. He had really offended her. The thought left a metallic bitterness in his mouth. He hadn't meant to; it was just who he was. He didn't have the time or the energy for these things.

He extended his elbow for her, saw her raise her eyebrows, the slightest bit surprised before she threaded her hand through it. He felt the feather-light weight of her palm through his suit jacket and resisted the urge to place his left hand over her fingers. "Shall we?"

She nodded silently, took the first step towards the wide, teak doors, her shoulders back, her eyes looking forward. He saw the moment that she locked in her persona, saw when she plastered on a smile that made her full lips curve prettily and her eyes widen perceptibly. He nodded when a pair of doormen swung the wooden doors open theatrically and walked through the arched doorway with her, resigned to force a smile on his face and enjoy as much of the evening as he was able.

The archway opened into a cobbled interior courtyard that even David would admit looked charming. White fairy lights were strung across the red-brick façade and intertwined with the thick, green ivy that climbed the walls. A wrought iron bar with a black granite top had been welded in the far corner, its extravagant legs curling up and outward in a finish that made the bottom of the bar look like a rolled scroll.

Although they were fashionably late, the courtyard was still relatively quiet, with only a handful of people standing around, mingling. He glanced at the faces, filed away the names of the people he knew. Almost certainly, he was looking at a group of analysts who'd arrived right on time, happy to use the party as an excuse to escape the office early on a Friday evening.

One of the analysts that he knew, Drew, a tall freckled boy with bright orange hair and dark rings of fatigue under his eyes, looked up and saw Diana. He blushed a brilliant shade of red and dropped his gaze when he realized that David had seen the open-mouthed stare. He could have grinned at the bright, splotchy blush that burned from the boy's carrot-top hair all the way down his neck, before disappearing under his dress shirt, but refrained because he knew that it would have embarrassed him more.

"Would you like a drink?" he asked when he noticed that she stood silently beside him, waiting for his cue. He didn't wait for her to reply but made for the bar. Diana—he didn't think the name suited her—followed wordlessly, her high heels clicking softly on the cobbled stones of the interior courtyard.

"What will it be?" the bartender asked, his eyes sweeping over her.

"A Balvenie. Neat, please."

David glanced at her surprised. "Whisky neat? Really?"

She tilted her head and met his gaze, not bothering to keep her smile in place when she said, "Really."

He smiled at her barely contained hostility. Oh, he was pretty sure that she did not like him. The thought usually would have made him smile, but for some reason, he was more disappointed than humored. Probably because this time, it was entirely his own fault.

"For you, Boss?" the bartender asked. "Scotch and soda, please. I'm not quite as brave."

The bartender laughed good-naturedly and moved away to grab the Balvenie off the back of the bar. David turned to survey the courtyard. He noticed that more people had already started filtering in and that others were walking out of the courtyard and through, into the event space. Once they had a drink, he'd take her through to see what their events manager had done with the place.

He had not been to Camelot House before. It was a square, red-brick building in the Westlake neighborhood that, at least from the street, looked unimpressive and quite tired. But that was where the normalcy ended. He hadn't expected the self-contained fantasy world he'd wandered into once he'd stepped through the doors. Judging by the oohs and aahs of the people still walking through, he wasn't the only one who thought so.

"Balvenie neat, and a Highball."

"Thank you," she said, smiling kindly at the bartender. He grinned in return, his face lighting up with happiness.

David barely refrained from rolling his eyes. "Do you want to go and see the event space?"

She looked up at him, her green eyes wide, a small smile dancing across her lips. "I really do."

Ignoring the way his eyes kept gravitating back to her lips of their own volition, he walked through with her, back across the cobbled courtyard, and through the second set of double doors that led inside the building. He couldn't help but notice how her long legs kept stride with his despite the ridiculously high heels; she even took the cobbles without breaking speed or stride.

The interior had been done in a similar style to the courtyard, except instead of cobbles, the floor was an intricate herringbone of rustic hardwood. Elegant wooden tables were dotted throughout the room, with wrought iron centerpieces dripping displays of ivy and lilies. He'd have labeled the space as the parlor of a millionaire's ranch house before he'd have labeled it a venue.

But it worked.

He finished surveying the room and turned to his date, noticed that she was taking in the décor in much the same way that he had, her eyes wide open and expressive. He wondered if she knew that everything she felt was so clearly reflected on her face. He wondered if she cared that she gave herself away to the world.

"What do you think?" he asked.

She looked up at him, surprised. "You don't have to make small talk with me, David. You were very clear."

He sighed. He was trying to apologize, and she was making it very difficult. "Alright, then. I guess we should make the rounds? Say hello to the people I need to and then get out of here as soon as possible."

"You have four hours of my time," she said, quietly. "Where were you thinking of going afterward?"

He wasn't sure, but there was something in the way that she said it that made him wonder exactly what she was trying to ask him. He had been thinking about going downtown for a drink and seeing where the night took them. She looked...nervous, maybe even a little scared.

The way that she shifted from one foot to another made his hands itch to reach out and hold her still, but he didn't trust himself to touch her. "What are you trying to say, Diana?" he asked. "Please be candid."

"I won't have sex with anybody that I can't even hold a conversation with," she whispered, a sweet smile on her face as a young couple walked past.

He felt a brief moment of surprise. Sex was, after all, part of the reason he'd hired her. He'd never force his attention on a woman who didn't want him, but he had never heard of, or hired, an escort who wasn't prepared to have sex with him. More than that, he'd never hired an escort who hadn't initiated it herself. He was a gentleman, despite what Diana NoLastName thought of him. It was just that, well, sex was an expectation of the industry.

Prostitution was illegal. Companionship was not. Paying for sex was illegal. Paying for a woman to escort you to a party, having a mutual like for each other, and having sex afterward was not. That's the only reason that escort services legally existed.

"I can drop you home if you'd like," he said, hiding his irritation easily. Oh, he wasn't irritated at her, or the fact that he had spent seven thousand dollars on two hours of her time. He had Money. He was irritated because she genuinely didn't like him—and it was completely his fault.

"We can go grab dinner or something," she said quickly. When he glanced at her sharply, she added, "Or I can refund you half of the cash?"

"And, why, might I ask, would you do that?" His voice was calm, calculated.

She took the slightest step back from him, and he saw a small sliver of fear cross her features. *Shit*, David thought. *What the fuck is wrong with you? Moron.* "That came out wrong," he added.

He held up a palm, closed his eyes for a moment, and took a deep breath. "Look. I have had a really shitty day and I...I was in a bad mood before I picked you up. I'm sorry," he said honestly, telling her more than he would have told any other woman. "I'm an asshole, but I'm not mean or violent and," he leaned close enough to whisper, "I don't expect you to go home with me if that's what you're worried about."

"It's not in my contract," she said, her voice coming out in a nervous whisper as she glanced around to make sure nobody was listening.

"I know how it works. If we'd actually gotten along, I might have had higher expectations."

She grinned unexpectedly, her full lips curving up prettily. The flash of humor that spread over her face hit him in the stomach with a surprising jolt, a jolt that had his mind shouting, *'What the fuck was that?*

"I'll still refund you," she said, "for every hour less we spend together."

He shook his head. "Don't. As an apology for my behavior earlier."

She smiled. "Dinner then?"

"I don't think that's a good idea." He saw her flush in embarrassment again, winced at how he'd sounded. *Great. Job. David. Way to make a woman feel special.*

He saw her engage her spine and stand tall, her eyes, which had been laughing at him only moments before, now appeared calm and cold. "Perfect," she replied. "Then just drop me at home, please."

He nodded, not wanting to apologize twice in the space of an hour. He wondered if he could fit his entire leg in his mouth instead of the foot that was currently lodged there, halfway down his throat and making it very difficult to breathe. He'd drop her at home and next time he needed a date, he'd book one of his regulars in advance instead of waiting until the last minute.

He spent twenty minutes leading her around the room and introducing her to his business associates. He had to hand it to her, she was good at her job. She smiled sweetly, almost shyly, spoke well, and seemed to be able to talk about anything to anyone. David was just starting to unwind, just beginning to relax, when he saw Gordon approaching out of the corner of his eye. He sighed. *Of course.*

Gordon Smith was also a managing director, also in investment banking, and also in line to become a Partner at Black Finch Capital. Unlike David, Gordon was short, fat, and balding, and seemed to constantly overcompensate for his appearance by being a general asshole. He was needy, over-amorous, and completely off-putting.

He turned to Diana, noticed that she was deep in conversation with an associate who had recently joined the company. Not wanting to distract her from her conversation, or be too obvious, he dropped his hand and gently took her palm in his own, interlacing his fingers with hers. She tensed briefly, glanced at him with a practiced smile and leaned closer, picking up on his cue as the associate kept talking.

"Gordon Smith. Disgusting and aggressive but relatively harmless. Don't let him bother you." He smiled and brushed his lips across her cheek in a subtle gesture that anyone would have taken as a casual kiss, and then dropped her hand.

He saw her angle her head so that she could see Gordon approach, saw her eyes flit over him quickly, assessing, right before she picked up the thread of the conversation that she'd been having.

"Van den Berg!" Gordon practically shouted when he was close enough. David cringed when he saw Diana jump slightly at the loud sound of Gordon's voice echoing through the room. "There you are!"

"Gordon." David nodded. He stepped to the side so she wasn't completely blocked by his body and added, "May I introduce Diana. My date. And you know Phillip Brookes?"

He watched as Gordon completely ignored Phillip and raked his eyes over Diana. She didn't flinch when his gaze narrowed in on the point where her dress ended, and her thighs began. *Good for her*, David thought.

"It's nice to meet you. Gordon, did you say?" she said, extending her hand.

Gordon took it and planted a wet kiss on the back of her palm, before saying, "Jesus, David! Where have you been hiding this one?"

"We're only newly dating," she said casually before he could reply himself.

"Ah, I *see*."

The way he said it made David's skin crawl in disgust, and he noticed that Gordon still hadn't released her hand. To his surprise, he felt angered by it.

"Have I seen you before?" Gordon asked, his eyes narrowed exaggeratedly. "You don't work in the Starbucks on Grand?"

David saw her eyes snap slightly, not enough for anyone to notice, but he could see that she was pissed.

"Or, were you the centerfold in last month's Playboy?" The words were said in jest, a poorly-mannered man's attempt at humor, maybe even intended as a compliment to a beautiful woman.

David opened his mouth to say something, then shut it just as suddenly when she touched his clenched fist and, when he relaxed, interlaced her fingers with his in warning, just as he'd done earlier. "I'm a junior associate at Fitch and Mathers." Without hesitating, she added, "Although I'm sure that Playboy pays much better."

Gordon opened and closed his mouth once. Twice.

David grinned, even as he felt a single jolt of shock travel through his system. If she was lying about being a lawyer, she was damn convincing. Even Phillip coughed into his hand, his face reddening as he tried to hide his chuckle.

"What is your practice area?" Phillip asked kindly, his brown eyes failing to hide how smitten he was.

"I have my Masters of Laws in patent law," she said, returning his smile, "but I enjoy dabbling in other areas when I can and when the firm allows."

"Wow." Phillip shook his head. "That's impress..." he trailed off, paled, and stuttered, "Sir. It's nice to meet you." He stuck his hand out, past David's elbow, causing him to shift one step closer to Diana.

David frowned and turned to see who he was talking to, felt his stomach twist when he saw Bruce Standard, the company's CEO, standing behind him, his short figure almost completely obscured by David's own shoulders. Bruce leaned forward to shake Phillip's still outstretched hand, followed suit with Gordon and David when they turned to include him in their circle.

Beside him, Diana blushed prettily as a small woman came to stand beside Bruce. But before he could make introductions, she chuckled prettily, and said, "Bruce. Deborah. What are the chances I'd see you here?"

"Ivy, we were just talking about you as we stood at the bar," Bruce said, patting his wife's hand affectionately. "I couldn't get a drink."

Ivy, which David realized was probably her real name— and better suited those snapping, green eyes—chuckled again. David, Gordon, and Phillip all stood mute, staring at the trio.

"I apologize," she started, never losing stride, "Ivy is my first name. Diana is my middle name." She rolled her eyes playfully. "Disagreement over what to name their only daughter was the greatest bone of contention between my parents and so, naturally, I go by both."

Bruce laughed, a big, rolling chuckle that had the other three men grinning too. "Seems likes a fair compromise to me," he said. "But I'm going to stick with Ivy because those eyes are going to make it easy for me to remember."

David glanced from the CEO, arguably one of the most powerful men in the industry, to Ivy and back again, trying to figure out what was happening. *Bruce knows Di—Ivy? How? Was she on his legal counsel?*

"I met Bruce and Deborah at the Ritz only a few minutes before you arrived, David," she said, meeting his puzzled expression with a small smile.

David nodded, forced a smile, and tried to calm his beating heart. *This. Is. Impossible. Literally. Statistically. Probably. In every way.*

"So, you're the date who kept her waiting?" Bruce joked and turned to fully look at David, his brown eyes quickly scanning his face.

"David Van den Berg." He introduced himself. "My pleasure, Sir. And, if I may, I was only six minutes late because there was an unmapped road closure."

"In his defense," Ivy added, "*I* was ten minutes early."

Bruce chuckled and realigned his glasses on his face. "My wife and I would love to get dinner with you two while we're here. Say, tomorrow or Sunday?"

Ivy tensed and David realized that they were still holding hands. He didn't let go this time.

"Absolutely," he replied, looking at Ivy as he did so. "If you have the time this weekend?"

Ivy smiled, although David was pretty sure he felt her twitch. "I would love too. I'm free tomorrow evening."

"Excellent!" Bruce glanced at his wife, and David noticed that even she seemed happy. "I'll have my assistant set it up then."

"Perfect." Unsure of if he should add anything more, David nodded awkwardly.

"Well, we're going to make the rounds, but it was lovely meeting you all. Ivy. David. See you tomorrow."

David watched Bruce and Deborah Standard walk off, not entirely convinced that he hadn't daydreamed the entire thing. He looked at Ivy.

She tilted her head up at him, her brow furrowed in confusion. He wanted to kiss her, he realized, as his heart pattered gently in his chest. The thought took him completely by surprise and he consciously fought to keep his face neutral. He was just amazed that she'd landed him a dinner with the CEO of Black Finch Capital.

She dropped his hand and turned, smiling, to Gordon and Phillip, both of whom stood staring at her, Phillip with a look of pleased surprise, and Gordon with one that could only be described as hateful, his small, beady eyes glinting dangerously. "It was so nice to meet you both. I think we've got to get going though. Right, David?"

He nodded. "See you two at work," he added, before following her out of the building.

It was only when he paused and turned sideways to let Ivy go ahead of him, that he saw Gordon staring after them. His colleague's short arms were crossed over his chest, resting on his protruding belly, his features were twisted in anger, and the look of hatred on his face was so blatant that David felt a cold tendril of unease snake through his stomach.

Turning his back on Gordon, he followed Ivy through the cobbled courtyard, and tried—unsuccessfully—to smother the crawling discomfort shooting up his spine.

You're just being paranoid. He kept telling himself that he was overthinking it and, by the time the car pulled up, he'd managed to convince himself that he had largely imagined the hostility in Gordon's eyes.

He opened the door for Ivy, felt his mind blank when she smiled up at him, her green eyes laughing. "What did you do to Gordon?" she asked as she slid back onto the seat, her lean, pale thighs dangerously exposed to his gaze.

Deliberately forcing his eyes back to her face, he raised his eyebrows. "I have absolutely no idea," he replied before closing the door and walking around to the other side of the car.

He'd dropped her at home as he'd promised, without so much as making a move. Instead, he'd left with a simple, "I'll contact Antoinette and see that I have your time for the next few days."

Ivy had watched the Range Rover pull into the street, kept her eyes on it until it disappeared into the late-night traffic. She wasn't quite sure why she hadn't objected, wasn't quite sure why she hadn't told him that she had plans on Saturday and Sunday night, plans every Saturday and Sunday night where he was concerned. She knew she didn't have to go out with him again, knew that he could easily tell Bruce and Deborah Standard that something had come up and he'd have to cancel. So, why, she asked herself for the thousandth time, had she said yes?

She didn't even like him.

Maybe it was because of how his hand had stiffened in hers when he'd seen Bruce, the CEO of his company, standing behind him? He'd been nervous, and for just a moment, she'd seen an actual human part of him through the stiff facade. Or, maybe it was because she was making a thousand dollars an hour to tolerate his company? *Yeah, I'm gonna go with that one.*

She walked up the steps to her apartment, unlocked her front door, and pushed it open with a loud sigh. She paused just inside the door, surprised to see Damien and his boyfriend, Louie, snuggled on the couch. An episode of *True Blood* played on the TV as they cuddled together underneath Damien's big, quilted comforter.

They looked up at her when she closed the door. "Holy shit! Your legs look amazing, baby," Louie said immediately.

"I picked it out, of course," Damien seconded, referring to the dress.

"And I looked like a hooker at an investment banking event," she quipped. "So, thanks."

Damien grinned at her. "You were a hooker at an investment banking event."

She rolled her eyes when they cackled and gave each other high-fives, slipped out of her shoes, and sighed when her feet hit the soft carpet. God, it felt good to feel the flat floor after hours in heels. She wandered through to the kitchen and grabbed herself a glass for the wine that they'd opened and left on the coffee table.

"Why are you home so early?" Damien asked.

Ivy turned with the glass in her hand. "I told him I didn't want to sleep with him, and he was fine with that, but we didn't want to spend any more time in each other's company."

"You didn't want to sleep with him? Ivy," Damien waited for her to look at him, "*I* would have slept with him. And I wouldn't have taken any money either."

"Hey!" Louie exclaimed, his eyebrows raised in mock horror.

Damien rolled his eyes. "Get the picture."

Ivy giggled and fetched her laptop. She snuggled on the couch next to Damien as she booted up, and enjoyed Louie's exaggerated gasp when she showed him David's picture.

"Yeah, I'm with Damien. *Why* didn't you sleep with him?"

"I don't like him very much."

"Of course, he's an asshole," Damien concluded. "No man who looks like that *and* is a Managing Director in investment banking is single unless he's a *real* asshole!"

"Yeah," Ivy said. "He literally told me my dress was too short, and that I was a 'Fire drill'. Oh, and that my only role was to" she raised her fingers in air quotes, "not get drunk or embarrass him."

Louie nodded sympathetically.

Damien chuckled.

"You realize that you're working in an industry that is a legal loophole for prostitution, right? You can't get all high and mighty when a client tells you what he wants."

"Yeah, how does that work?" Louie asked. "Like how come Ivy can get away without having sex with these guys?"

"Oh, she has sex with them," Damien sniggered.

"I have sex with the ones I *want* to have sex with. Exactly like any normal date that goes well," she countered, a little defensive.

"Okay, but what about like if the guy hires you thinking that he's paying for sex and you don't like him?"

Damien looked at her, eyebrows raised. "A very good question."

She sighed. "There are different girls at the agency I work for...It's complicated and the boundaries are rough because there are no written rules or legal parameters..."

"And?" Damien pressed, his smirk widening.

"And the reason I'm going to stop as soon as I can," she countered. "Besides, nothing too sketchy has happened yet."

"I picked you up off the side of the road at one in the morning in Whittier just three weeks ago!"

Ivy sighed. She was tired and she really didn't want to talk about the dangers of what she did right at this moment. Worse, the guy who'd dumped her on the side of the road had seemed like a pretty nice guy until she'd asked that they wait until the end of the evening. Oh, he'd dropped the façade instantly. At least he hadn't hit her, she thought. She knew other girls who'd been hurt, hell, some of them took money to let men hit them, usually while they fucked them.

"Truce for tonight?" she said instead, trying to distract herself from her dark thoughts. "You know that I'm going to stop when I can."

"You're a patent attorney, right?" Louie asked.

She nodded. "But I'm only in my third year. I don't make enough money, and as much as I hate to admit it, escorting is quick cash. It's easy money most of the time. I go on dates with lonely men or men who just don't have the time to find an actual date. I get paid. We all go home happy."

"How much do you make as a lawyer?"

"Like a hundred and twenty K before taxes," Ivy said, unembarrassed.

"Wait," Louie said, clearly shocked. "Why do you need to escort then?"

Damien elbowed him; Ivy smiled kindly.

"Oh, something bad?"

31

"Jesus, Louie! Stop fishing!"

Ivy laughed. "It's okay, Damien." She looked at Louie, his pretty face eager, his brown eyes soft and concerned. "My dad has advanced ALS, so he's on a trach full-time. I'm just footing the bills until he dies and then," she looked at Damien so that she could make her point, "I'll stop."

"Shit," Louie said quietly, his eyes misting. "I'm so sorry." He sighed and turned back to face the television to hide his sniffling. "I was honestly expecting like student loans, or credit card debt…"

"Oh, I have student debt too," Ivy said and laughed. "From undergrad, my JD, *and* my masters."

Louie shook his head, momentarily confused. "There must be a government program that would pay for your dad's treatment though, right?"

"It's a dead horse, Louie. Leave it be. I've beaten this thing to death over a zillion times. It's a flayed, rotting carcass already."

She shook her head.

"She says that the treatment that she can pay for by escorting is near twice as good as the government-subsidized ones."

"It is," she returned.

"Props to you then," Louie said, effectively ending the conversation.

She smiled. She liked that about Louie, liked that he was non-judgmental, and saw her for who she was. He was like Damien that way, but she had known Damien longer and knew that kindness was his character trait.

Ivy didn't tell everyone that her father was dying from a disease that was slowly depriving him of his ability to breathe. It wasn't something she liked to think about, let alone talk about. The only thing she was grateful for was that her mother had died before he had been diagnosed. Watching them both trying to cope with her dad's slow descent towards death would have killed her.

"At least you'll never have to see Mr. Investment Banker again," Damien said and nudged her good-naturedly. "Asshole. That dress is fabulous."

She knew that he was, in his own way, trying to redirect her thoughts away from her father, but it didn't help. She was canceling her once a week visit to Hanley Hospice to go on a second date with said asshole.

"Oh. My. God. You're going to see him again?"

And kudos go to the best friend who knows everything about me.

"No!" Louie added, looking at her. He clapped his hands together, like a child who'd just received a puppy dog for his birthday.

She held up her hands in a gesture of surrender and added, "I had a connection with the CEO of his company, and he invited us out to dinner. I'm still being paid," she added when neither of them responded.

"Screw the money." This from Damien.

"He's not that bad," Ivy countered, more trying to defend her actions than excuse David's manners. "He's just successful and…preoccupied. I don't think he's had to consider being accommodating—or nice for that matter—in quite some time."

"Oh, he's old? He doesn't look old," Louie said. His eyes widened. "Wait, did he do the catfish thing? Where the online picture is like from ten years ago?"

Ivy laughed. "No, he's actually that hot. I don't know. He's maybe forty? Maybe a little younger."

"Well, at least he doesn't expect you to sleep with him," Damien added.

"True." Ivy pushed off the sofa. She cast one last glance at the empty wine glass and decided that her fatigue trumped her desire to sit and chat over merlot. "Anyway, as much as I've enjoyed this heart-to-heart, boys, I'm going to crash."

"Laters, baby," Louie said with a wink.

Ivy showered and changed in record time, the stress of the night finally hitting her. Once she had slipped into her panties and an oversized tee-shirt, she pulled back the covers, welcomed the familiar scent of her bed, and, as she drifted off, she felt a small ball of relief slide through her. David knew her real name. He didn't mind that she wouldn't have sex with him, and he had hired her for tomorrow, which meant only one thing for Ivy—she didn't have to make small talk, or worry about avoiding sex with another complete stranger that Saturday night.

Maybe seeing him again isn't the worst thing in the world.

Chapter 3

This was going to be a very expensive thirty-six hours, David realized after he'd hung up the phone with Antoinette Rupetta herself. The four hours from the night before, plus the six hours he'd requested of Ivy's time later in the day were going to set him back a solid fifteen thousand dollars. He winced. Yeah, he could afford it, but that didn't mean he was happy about his decision-making.

He tapped his fingers on his granite counter and looked out at his view of the Hollywood Hills. As much as he hadn't wanted to see Ivy again, or so he told himself, the truth was that her small interaction with Bruce Standard could have altered the trajectory of his entire career.

Just like that.

If he made an impression tonight, a real impression, he could be set in his career. He could have everything that he'd ever worked for. He knew that he was good at his job, knew that he was competent, but at the top of the game, luck and the depth of your network played a huge part in who made it big. And who didn't.

The thought made him restless, made his stomach flutter uncomfortably. What was he going to do with the entire day? He couldn't just sit around and wait for the dinner. He'd go crazy. He was already as prepared as he could be. If he tried to do anything more to prepare, he knew that he'd just end up a nervous wreck.

After a glance at his watch, he tallied the time as six hours before Ivy arrived for the prep session that he'd insisted upon. Not that she hadn't been fine the night before, but David was nervous, and he knew from experience that making sure Ivy was prepared beforehand would settle his mind by the time the dinner started.

Besides the fact that he wanted to prepare her, he knew it might also be a good idea if he and Ivy knew some basic facts about each other. They were, after all, supposed to be dating and, as much as Bruce apparently liked Ivy, it would not end well for him if anyone found out that he occasionally hired escorts. The practice might have been relatively common amongst the single, successful bankers, but it was also too close to illicit to be easily accepted by the corporate hierarchy—including HR.

For some reason, the knowledge made him nervous, made him question the fact that he'd ever started hiring escorts in the first place. Originally, it hadn't been intended as a long-term game plan for every social function. He'd just needed a date for an event and hadn't had the time to find one. But then, he'd started hiring girls from Antoinette and, at least to him, it had started to *feel* like dating.

He picked up a girl, had a good time, took them home if the chemistry was right—didn't if it wasn't.

He thought about Ivy, wondered if she was disappointed that she had to go out with him again. *Probably.* He hadn't exactly been kind to her. For the first time that he could remember, he'd been curt and blasé to a date. Rude, even. Strumming his fingers on the counter again, he looked out over the Hills and tried to forget the hurt that he had put in her eyes the night before.

He had six hours before she was supposed to arrive. He could go and visit his parents, he thought, and then just as quickly dismissed the notion. His mother didn't like him to drop by unannounced or uninvited. His father, if he were home at all, would drill him about the meeting with Bruce Standard and probably make him more nervous than he already was. Besides, six hours was cutting it a little too close for a casual jaunt to Santa Barbara.

Nevertheless, the thought of being on a sunny beach or on his surfboard appealed. He did the math and figured that he had time, maybe not to drive down to Santa Barbara, but definitely to hit Manhattan Beach and catch a few small swells. Eager to preoccupy himself, he trotted through to the bedroom, paused briefly to change into a pair of boardshorts and a tank top, before making his way to his garage.

He pushed open the door, scanned the room for his surfboard, and, once he'd located it in the far-right corner behind his parked Jeep, hoisted it onto his shoulder so that he could strap it onto the car.

He kept a Porsche sitting in his driveway too, but he used the Jeep for weekend driving, for when the sun was out, and for when he wanted to feel like he lived in California. The Porsche, he had bought specifically for driving to work in Downtown Los Angeles, where having the nifty 911 was as practical as it was an industry expectation.

He picked his way through a few boxes and loose bric-a-brac that he'd been telling himself he'd tidy since he moved into the house five years back and hoisted the board onto the top rack of the Jeep. His mission accomplished, David smiled; the thought of driving with the top down, sitting in the cool water as the sun beat against his back, the thought of actually catching some waves, was lightening his mood.

Probably be downright cheery by the time she shows up.

She glanced up at the house, smiled, and shook her head when Damien whistled from the driver's seat of his car. Ivy would have punched him playfully, but even she couldn't deny that the house was...gorgeous.

She didn't really know how to describe it.

It was a big, white, Hacienda-style house, nestled into the hillside and boasting an insane view of the Hollywood Hills. It was a millionaire's mansion, but also surprisingly cottage-like with red, clay tiles on the roof, and pretty curled railings on the balconies. A long set of red-brick steps had been laid into the hillside, snaking right up to the front door. It was too small to warrant a comparison to the huge Santa Barbara estates that favored the same Spanish-style of building, but it came close.

"Are you sure you want to go?"

The fact that Damien looked concerned made her smile, but she didn't want to feel sorry for herself. Not tonight. So, instead, she gave him a hug and a chaste kiss on the lips through the window of the car, grabbed the dresses hanging on the hook in the back, and made sure to snatch her gym bag with all of her shoes and make-up in off the back seat.

"David said he'd send me home in the car, so you don't have to pick me up, okay?" she said, crouching into the window to look at Damien one last time.

He nodded. "I'll have my ringer turned up to full volume in case you need me. Just call."

"You're the best friend a girl could ask for."

"Ditto."

She took a step back and watched him pull out of the driveway, gave him a final wave, and then looked down at the pile of crap she'd have to carry up the long staircase that trailed to the front door. She sighed. At least she was wearing sneakers this time.

Draping the dresses over her arm, she hiked the gym bag strap over her shoulder before she bent her knees awkwardly to try and pick up her handbag. She had not thought the logistics through, and she strained to reach the purse while keeping her other bags on her shoulders.

She heard him before she saw him, turned around awkwardly so that she could face him and pretend she still had some of her dignity as she crouched on the ground, trying to pick up all of her belongings.

He raised a single eyebrow as he tried, unsuccessfully, to hide a wide grin.

"Well, you were so insulted by the first outfit that I opted to come prepared this time." She tried hard not to notice that he looked like he'd just stumbled off the cover of a surfer mag, his short, blonde hair curling slightly, his muscular, tanned arms folded over his chest as he laughed down at her. "Aren't you going to help?"

He smiled and trotted down the last few steps that separated them. "Ivy," he said simply in greeting, as he slid his hand under the gym bag strap and lifted it off her shoulder as if it weighed nothing.

She ignored the shiver of awareness that jolted her stomach when he called her by her name and, as soon as he had the gym bag, she knelt again and picked her purse up off the ground. She had not anticipated the movement bringing her exactly to his crotch level and rapidly stood to avoid thinking about the fact that she had looked longer than was proper.

"Okay." Casting a look up the long staircase that led to the house, she took a deep breath. "Let's do this."

He nodded and waved her in front of him, following immediately behind her on her right-hand side. Unlike most of the guys she knew, he had deliberately avoided looking at her ass on the way up.

Maybe he just doesn't like your ass.

She landed at the top of the stairs just as her legs were starting to burn from the effort. She wasn't sure why, but she felt nervous all of a sudden. Her heart knocked against her chest rapidly, as if it were trying to alert her brain to danger.

She glanced at him quickly. She wasn't afraid of him, or at least, not physically afraid of him. He was intimidating and judgmental, but not violent. Violent men smelled different to her; they used their eyes differently too…as if they were trying to scare you before they even touched you, as if they got off on seeing the moment the fear crept into your eyes. She had been hired by violent men before. David's eyes were closer to irritated. Impatient.

He pushed open the door with one long, tanned arm, and waited for her to step inside first. She hesitated slightly, not obviously, but long enough for him to notice. He cocked his head and looked at her as if he was seeing her for the first time.

She blushed, embarrassed by his assessing blue eyes, and stepped inside the house.

"I'm sorry to occupy so much of your time. Preparing for this will help me out."

He carried her bag into the tiled foyer, placed it by a long, curved staircase that was inlaid with hand-painted Spanish tiles. Ivy squinted so that she could see the individual homesteading scenes that had been carefully painted on them, each different but just as exquisite as the next. She wasn't certain from this distance, but she was pretty sure one of the tiles even had a few chickens painted on it, their little legs poised at different angles as if scratching the ground. She knew that they weren't traditionally Spanish like the rest of the house, but she thought they were gorgeous.

Looking up, she noticed him staring at her, his lips curved in a small smile. "I'm sorry. I love those tiles," she said, pointing. She forced the blood from her cheeks, aware of the fact that he made her blush far too often. "And, it doesn't matter," she added. "You are paying for my time."

She saw his smile fade a little, sighed when he nodded curtly, the faint thread of friendliness that had been there before, rapidly dying.

Good job, Ivy. Off to a stellar start.

"I can show you the guest room later when you need to get ready. For now, let's just think about what we want to know about each other before we meet up with them tonight."

She nodded.

He turned from her and led the way through the house. Ivy couldn't help but walk slowly behind him as she took in the interior. The foyer opened to a gorgeous kitchen on the left with stainless steel appliances and pastel green cabinetry, before spilling into a large, airy lounge that boasted pale hardwood floors, plush, upholstered sofas with griffin-claw feet and an off-white center table that looked like it had been refurbished by a very-well-paid professional.

A full bar sat in the far corner of the room, nestled in such a way that people sitting on the high, wingback bar stools could look out at the view while they sipped their cocktails. And boy, did he have every alcohol, liqueur, and mixer, as well as the required paraphernalia, to make any cocktail a guest could want.

"What?" he asked.

"Who designed this space?" she asked. It spoke southern revival meets bohemian beach boy. She would have thought him more the white tile and black leather type.

Stark.

Clean.

Cold.

"I paid a friend to do it."

"It's really impressive. Unusual, but…impressive."

"She knows me well."

"It shows," Ivy finished, ignoring the part of her that wondered who the girl was, wondered if they'd slept together and if it hadn't worked out. Whoever she was, she clearly knew him on a very personal level.

"Can we get this show on the road?"

Nodding, she followed him through the lounge. He pushed open the glass door and stepped onto the balcony. Ivy couldn't help but pause when she took in the view. It was truly spectacular. She felt the hot summer sun beat down on her skin, enjoyed the contrast of the slight breeze that ruffled the longer strands of her hair. She turned to face him, the smile on her face fading when she saw that he was scowling down at her.

What had she done now? She sighed and moved over to the glass table where he had set a bottle of white wine and glasses alongside two notebooks and a jar of pens.

"Am I going to have to take notes?" she asked, surprised, and if she had to admit it, slightly nervous. He seemed like the type who'd test her afterward too.

"Ah, not if you don't want to." He rubbed the back of his neck. It was the first time she'd seen him act awkward. "I learn faster if I write things down, but you don't have to."

He sat in the chair facing the house, his back to the view. Ivy took the one opposite him.

He picked up the wine and poured himself a glass, raised his eyebrow, his hand hovering over the second.

She shook her head. "I'm a bit of a lightweight and we're probably going to be drinking tonight. I'd hate to embarrass you again," she said, not trying very hard to keep the snideness out of her tone.

He sighed. "Suit yourself."

"Could I have some water?"

He looked at her, narrowed his eyes, and then pushed back from the table and disappeared inside.

A few minutes later he came back, a tall glass of iced water in his hand. He placed it very gently on the table in front of her and then went to sit back down. Ivy waited until he had tucked in his chair, and then moved the glass of water out of the way without taking a sip.

He scowled.

"Where do we start?" she asked innocently, pretending that she didn't enjoy having the upper hand every now and again—even if it was over a glass of water. He didn't have to know that her inner queen was trumpeting a full glory march. She didn't know why she had suddenly started taking so much joy in teasing him; it just felt like the only time that she was on even footing with him was when he was too shocked by her to retaliate.

He glared down at the paper. "How about what you know about investment banking? Bruce Standard won't expect you to know much, but even a little bit helps with the flow of conversation."

She nodded and thought about it. "I don't know much about the industry itself per se, except the cultural basics. Pretty much you're paid to work yourselves into premature middle age. I have the basic financial know-how and took finance and econometrics through the 300 level in college. Undergrad. So, proficient—but stale."

He looked at her, his blue eyes slit skeptically.

"What's EBITDA?"

"Earnings before interest, taxes, depreciation, and amortization," Ivy said. She paused, holding up a hand in warning. "To be honest, I'm surprised that I remembered that."

"Okay."

"Okay, what?"

"I don't think anyone would expect you to know that, so I think you're good on the investment banking front."

"Wait, so no prep session?" she asked, hopeful.

"Well, we should still know the basics about each other, right?"

"Sure, although we could have just told them that we're newly dating, which would have been true and," she paused, "a lot cheaper for you."

He sighed and closed his eyes. Ivy wanted to smile, but didn't; she was enjoying his discomfort too much and didn't want it to show.

"Look," he eventually said, meeting her gaze. There was a thin sheen of panic reflected in his eyes. "I know that you wouldn't choose to be here with me right now. I get that and I'm sorry."

She tilted her head and looked at him. He seemed genuinely apologetic.

"But this could potentially be the single biggest opportunity that I've ever had, may ever have again." He looked at her, forced her to hold his eye contact. "Do you understand that?"

She felt a worm of regret settle in her chest. The truth was, she'd never stopped to consider that this was basically the equivalent of her being invited out by Gregory Fitch and Andy Mathers themselves. She'd be losing her mind with nerves and fear if their situations had been reversed.

"Okay, I'm sorry. You're right."

He sat back in his chair. "I just don't know what I can do to prepare," he said, truthfully. "I can take any tests, run any models, mingle with clients...all of it. But this is like...I don't know."

"A casual dinner with someone who could make your career?"

"Yeah."

"David, you need to calm down," she said firmly.

He looked up at her in surprise.

She blinked at his cold, shocked stare but maintained eye contact. "You're a six-three, blond-haired, blue-eyed Managing Director. You'd have to be pretty shitty compared to everyone else to not progress to Partner. Literally, the laws of nature forbid that people who look like you are anything but successful"

He opened his mouth to speak but she steamrolled him. "You know I'm right. More than that, your competition is Gordon and all the other men like him. Just be yourself and you'll be fine."

He smiled.

She chuckled and added, "Maybe don't be yourself. Be more...friendly. Like Jordan Belfort on less cocaine."

She had a brief moment where she watched his lips curl, saw the way the smile lit up his eyes, and made them seem paler than possible. *Jesus, that's unfair.* She felt her stomach tighten, wondered for a brief moment what it'd be like to kiss him, to be kissed by him.

She bet he was an amazing kisser.

He cleared his throat.

Ivy jumped, realized that she had been staring at his mouth, fantasizing about his lips on hers. There was no way she could have hidden the flush that burned her face.

Oh, God.

"Your eyes give everything away."

He said it so quietly that she wondered if she'd misheard him. But when she looked at him and saw her attraction reflected back at her, she swallowed. She had not meant for this to happen. She didn't even like him. Did she?

He reached forward and grabbed the wine, filled his glass up again, and then asked, "You sure? It'll be good."

She wasn't exactly sure if he had intended the double entendre, but even she couldn't deny that she knew it to be true. Sex with David would be good. She shook her head.

"So, seeing as how the IB lecture is off, why don't we get changed and go to a bar beforehand?"

"I don't know," he said. "Drinking before a dinner like this seems…irresponsible."

She looked at him, looked pointedly to the glass in his hand. "I think that's the problem. I think you have to stop looking at this dinner as the make-it or break-it event in your career and look at it as more of a business dinner with friends. It'll eradicate the nerves and take away some of the," she waved her hand at him, "stiffness."

"My…*stiffness*, at least right now, has nothing to do with Bruce Standard."

Ivy shook her head and tried to stifle her chuckle. "You know what I mean. You're too…rigid, David. Just relax and try being the friendlier version of yourself."

45

He nodded. Stood. "Fine, but I do have a list of questions for us. Basic stuff, but enough that it'll seem like we've had more than two conversations."

She nodded. "What should I wear?"

"What?"

He seemed surprised, pale even, as he looked down at her. "I told you, I brought a variety of options, so we don't have a repeat of last time."

"Okay, well try them on and I'll tell you, I guess?"

"Sure."

"Guest bedroom is upstairs to the right. There's an en suite shower if you need it."

"Thanks." She moved back through the glass doors, into the air-conditioned house, picked up her bag and marched up the stairs without looking back. She was pretty sure that David was watching her, and to be quite honest if she turned now, she might have invited him up.

He sat in the lounge, waiting for Ivy to come down in her first dress option. He'd already showered and changed, hurried so that they could still go and get drinks without feeling rushed before dinner. Now, as he waited, he wasn't sure if he'd made a mistake.

He had known he was attracted to Ivy since the first time he'd seen her standing in the Ritz Carlton, her slender legs exposed to mid-thigh, her thick, mahogany hair spilling down her back in gentle waves and curls. A blind man would have been attracted to her. She was a beautiful woman with a striking face and a body that should have been illegal.

But he hadn't liked her. Had he?

Shit.

He hadn't liked her when he'd dropped her home last night. And no, he told himself, thinking about her as he'd fallen asleep, about the way her eyes looked up at him and

46

the way her slender hand felt in his, did not count as like. It counted as lust.

So, when had he started liking her? Liking her as a person, not as a woman he was paying to put up with him? Was it when he'd found out she was a patent attorney and not merely an escort?

He wasn't quite sure why that mattered, but it did, which, of course, instantly made him feel misogynistic. So, what? He'd misjudged her. Hell, he decided, either way, he wasn't quite sure if he actually liked her or if all the lust was clouding his brain. Maybe, he thought, it was both?

He thought back to when he'd seen the car pull up to his driveway, ignored the little voice in his mind that told him he'd been waiting for her to arrive, standing in his lounge and staring down at the empty road. When he'd seen her step out of the car, her arms laden with her belongings, he'd used it as an excuse to meet her outside.

He wished he could have snapped a picture of her as she realized that she'd miscalculated her carrying capacity, her body perched precariously as she squat on the floor, trying to reach for her bag. The look she'd given him when she'd realized he'd seen the entire event had been incinerating. But that hadn't stopped the blood from vacating his brain and traveling south.

Okay…so he was *very* attracted to her. But she'd already told him she wasn't interested in him. In fact, she had pretty much said she didn't like him at all. And, that was that.

The sound of her coming down the stairs made him take a deep breath and force his mind into a state of calm. He could do this. He could be polite and kind and not make a move on a girl who didn't want him to.

"Okay, so this is my first option, but I'm not sure if it's too fancy," she said. "I realized you haven't told me where we're going."

He turned when he heard her heels on the hardwood, felt the world stop as all of the blood in his head dropped and came to pool in his lap. *So much for that.*

The long dress was red, not diner-booth red, or fire-hydrant red, it was the red of rapidly drying blood, dark and silky. It hugged her slender frame like it was made for her, tight enough that he knew, even from where he sat, that she couldn't possibly be wearing underwear. The thin straps that met behind her neck highlighted her collar bones and showed off her toned shoulders and pale skin. She had pulled her hair back, away from her face, but tied it so that it still fell in a glorious mass behind her.

She shifted uncomfortably under his gaze. "You don't like it? I have three others. Let me g-"

"Ivy." She stopped walking away with the single word, turned to face him again, her big, green eyes wide and uncertain. "It's beautiful." *You're beautiful.*

When she smiled nervously, he stood and walked over to her, gave her his hand, and affected a small bow.

She chuckled and put her hand in his. "That good?"

He moved towards the door without replying, very aware of the fact that he needed to regain his composure. After seeing her standing there, her red dress dripping off her curves, he was having a small amount of trouble walking in a straight line.

"Oh," she said, completely oblivious to his reaction, "should I leave my bags here for now? I don't want to bother you once dinner's over..."

He felt a small pang of disappointment and tried, unsuccessfully, to stifle it. "I can have Morgan send them back tomorrow. He knows where your house is."

She smiled, relieved. "Thanks."

She picked her handbag up from where she'd left it by the door, and stepped past him. He caught the scent of her as she moved, noticed that the back of her dress was missing entirely, or rather, was held up by two thin, red ribbons that crisscrossed over her back before meeting in a simple bow in the middle. As he watched her go down the stairs in front of him, he couldn't help but wonder if a single tug on one of those long strands would unravel the whole ensemble.

Because he worked downtown, Ivy let him pick the bar. Or rather, he handed her into the Range Rover with quick, efficient movements before telling Morgan where to take them. If she wasn't being paid exceptionally well to comply, Ivy would have felt miffed by the fact that he hadn't even asked her. She went out downtown. Not often, but she had been taken to plenty of sophisticated places in Los Angeles and she could get around just fine without him.

"Is everything okay?" he asked. "You're quiet."

She smiled. "Perfect. Where is this place? I don't think I've been there before."

He shook his head. "It's a surprise."

She squinted at him long enough that he chuckled and held up a hand. "A good surprise. I promise."

"Morgan?"

The driver grinned at her in the review mirror. "It's nice to see you again, Miss."

"He's not going to kill me, right? Bury my body in the woods? Or make *you* bury my body in the woods?"

Morgan tried very hard to keep his chuckle to a polite rumble, but Ivy could see his eyes crinkling in the mirror.

Turning back to David, she noticed that he was looking at her as if unsure of how serious she was being, his blue eyes both curious and uncertain. "I'm kidding, David," she whispered.

He nodded one short, quick movement that seemed businesslike and abrasive at the same time. "I figured." He glanced at Morgan as if he wanted to say something, but didn't want the driver to overhear. "I'm not...used to being made fun of by someone I'm paying," he said quietly.

Ivy felt her face fall into a smooth, clear mask of calm. She wanted so badly to sigh and nudge him gently with her elbow until he smiled again. He was so much easier to talk to when he smiled. He was like a dog that was being loved by a kind human after years of abuse and wasn't quite sure if the person was going to beat him or give him some food and leave him be.

"That came out wrong. Again." He shifted in his seat when she didn't reply. "I…"

"It's alright, David. You're right." When he looked at her surprised, she added, "I have this weird urge to bug you and I have no idea why. I'm not usually this…blasé around clients who are paying me."

"You're not?" His left eyebrow raised as if he didn't quite believe her.

"No," she said with a small chuckle. "I'll reign it in before dinner, I promise." She crossed her fingers over her heart in a sign of good faith and then turned to look out at the city.

She felt a hot blush warm her cheeks when she realized he was right. She would never have talked to a high-paying client, a stranger, like she talked to him. More than that, she knew that he had high hopes for the evening, and she was probably putting him into a full-blown panic. She had always prided herself on being professional before, but there was something about David. Something had switched the first time he'd genuinely smiled at her; it was as if now that she knew what he looked like when he smiled, she wanted to pry it out of him with a joke or by teasing him as often as possible.

She felt a single chill creep up her arm when he brushed his hand over hers, fought every nerve to keep it planted on the seat at her side. She turned to him, not quite meeting his eyes, her practiced smile in place.

"I was going to add that it's nice…to have a conversation with someone who doesn't care about what I think."

She met his eyes then, surprised. He looked genuinely embarrassed by having told her that much, and she realized that giving her that admission had been his form of an apology. She patted his hand twice, a gesture that she found too maternal and forced. "I'm a little nervous too. I tend to regress when I'm overthinking something."

He nodded. "Understandable. It's a big opportunity."

She didn't have to tell him that she wasn't nervous about the dinner, that he was the one making her stomach flutter around inelegantly—because *that* would have been inappropriate. So, instead, she looked back out at the city lights flying by and felt the silence in the car wrap around her. Why did it seem like there were always so many unsaid things between them?

As they sat side-by-side, it was as if there was an elastic band pulling them together even as they both tried their hardest to stay apart. She wanted to make him smile, even as he withdrew icily from her attempts. He kept trying to be kind, even though she misunderstood him constantly. It was goddamn tiring, she realized, to care so much about what a complete stranger thought of you.

Chapter 4

The warm night enveloped him as he stepped onto the sidewalk and gave Ivy his hand so she could scoot out after him. He thanked the driver…Morgan, and told him when and where to pick them up, before closing the door quietly and turning towards the private club.

He knew that Ivy thought he was taking her to a bar, but he couldn't drag her around on the streets of downtown Los Angeles looking like she'd just stepped off the cover of Vogue.

The private club—which he was a member of—on the other hand, boasted a lounge that could put any five-star hotel to shame, and, for selfish reasons, he could both have her all to himself and boycott the duty of having to defend her honor from unsolicited catcalls and advances. He also, after all, had a list of questions they needed to go over and a quiet room in which to do so would prove useful.

He gave her his elbow rather than take her hand again, and led her to the wide, double doors before pushing them open and stepping inside. He glanced down at her, saw her tilt her chin just the slightest so that she could meet his eyes. Her lips curved into a smile and, for only a moment, he wondered what she would do if he leaned down and nipped her full, bottom lip.

"Impressive. I've never been here."

"I'm glad I could surprise you." He walked her through to where the elevators sat, tucked away in the back of the room.

"Good evening, Mr. Van den Berg," the hostess said with a small nod as he walked by.

David nodded politely.

As they waited for the elevator, he couldn't help but take in Ivy's wide-eyed delight as her eyes focused on the room. He looked around, seeing it for the first time again.

The interior was dark and cool, with maroon carpeting that would have looked garish in the light, but that somehow managed to look luxurious in the dimly lit room. Innate mahogany paneling crept up the ten-foot walls and built-in bookcases with a mix of dustless, leather spines peeked out from the floor-to-ceiling shelves. He wasn't sure what you would call the style, but the aesthetic was ancient and classy, with only a smidge of pretense.

"This is gorgeous," she said as they rode the elevator up to the eighth floor. "I always wanted to come here but never made the time." She looked up at him. "How is the gym?"

"Honestly?" he asked. "About as antiquated as the furniture. But that's a big part of the reason I like it. The patrons tend to be on the older side, and it means that you can avoid a lot of the riff-raff." Leaning towards her slightly, he added, "I'm too old and impatient to wait for my turn with the weights while the person using them is taking a selfie on every set."

She laughed and stepped out ahead of him when the doors opened up to Le Bibliotheque. "I once went out with a man who practically professionally photographed every single dish that he ate." She hesitated for a moment, then laughed. "Which usually I don't mind, but it was a thirty-course Michelin-starred dinner so we took a *long* time. Even the waitstaff was chomping at the bit to see us leave."

He didn't reply even though she had glanced over her shoulder at him when he'd stepped up behind her. He had been focusing all of his attention on her exposed back, or, to be more accurate, on stopping himself from placing his hand on her exposed back. He could imagine the exact feeling of her soft, smooth skin under his fingers.

Frustrated with himself, he moderated his tone. "We can get a drink and then go over those questions."

"Sure."

If she noticed his sudden discomfort, she didn't say anything. She moved towards the bar, her eyes taking in the dark, navy-blue carpet, the wall of books, and glass-topped teak furniture. He knew that the bar was impressive, with its art deco style, and steam-punky light fixtures and lamps.

"Why is nobody here?" she asked, glancing up at him.

David looked down at his watch. "It doesn't open for another ten minutes."

"Oh, should we go wa—?"

"Good evening, Mr. Van den Berg." David looked up to see one of the regular bartenders as he stepped into the room, carrying a bottle of reserve whiskey. The man nodded to Ivy, said, "Ma'am," and then walked behind the bar. "I apologize. I was just restocking. What can I get you two?"

Ivy hesitated before ordering. David rattled off his drink order and then moved over to a big sofa, knowing that she would follow. He sat and was surprised when she chose to sit next to him on the big, blue couch rather than in one of the nearby accent chairs. Their knees were so close that if he'd moved his leg just a fraction, they would have touched.

He smiled and thanked the bartender when he bought their drinks over and placed them on two leather coasters on the table in front of them.

Once they were alone again, David asked, "Okay, ready for questions?"

She smiled, nodded as she took a small sip of her drink and chuckled when he drew out the list and a pen from his left breast pocket.

"Where were you born?" he asked.

"Pasadena, California," she replied. "You?"

"Orange County, California."

"Where do your parents live now and what do they do?"

55

She didn't reply right away, and when he looked up, pen ready, he saw her expertly retract the sadness from her eyes and send him a practiced smile. "They're both dead. You?"

He stilled for a moment. He didn't want to make it worse, didn't want her to feel embarrassed. He glanced up at her. "I'm sorry."

"It's okay. I'm used to it. What about yours?" she asked again, trying to change the subject.

"They're retired in Santa Barbara. My mom didn't work after she had me. My dad was in banking too."

She looked at him and he wondered if she'd noticed the flat tone. "Only child?"

He nodded.

"Me too."

He looked back down at his list. "Alma mater and, while we're at it, degree?"

"Undergrad at USC, JD at Stanford, and then Master of Laws in patent law at USC again."

He whistled under his breath. "That is quite an academic stack."

She laughed. "Yeah, tell that to my student debt."

There was no bitterness in her tone when she said it, but he wondered if that was the reason she escorted on the side even though she had a fully-fledged career. He thought about asking her, looked up, and met her eyes. The question passed between them without him having to ask and David hated the fact that a brief flash of disappointment crossed her features.

She inclined her head. "Part of the reason." She said the words easily, even though he could see she was offended. He had realized, after only a few conversations with her, that she wasn't very good at hiding what she was feeling. He wondered what the other part of the reason was, but didn't ask. He was embarrassed that he'd thought it already and knew that she would have offered it if she'd wanted to.

"Okay, what about you? Alma mater and degree?"

"Undergrad in economics at Stanford. MBA at Wharton."

She whistled as he had only moments before. "Blue blood."

He chuckled. "Depends on who you ask."

"It always does."

He leaned back on the sofa, looked at her. Why did he feel more comfortable around her within the parameters of a casual conversation than a formal, task-oriented job? She had a knack for breaking through his carefully constructed public persona and left him feeling panicked and…scared. Nervous. Hell, he realized, he hadn't been nervous around a woman since Trish Duke in the ninth grade.

"Favorite place to vacation?" he asked, diverting from the actual list.

She raised her eyebrows, then frowned as she thought about it. "Pass."

"You don't have one?"

"I'm a practicing attorney. I haven't had time for one since I left high school, and before that, it was mostly small vacations around the US. If you put a gun to my head, I'd say Camp Wakamehu in Washington because my parents and I went there a few times together."

"Okay," he said, instantly trying to divert away from her deceased parents. Again. "Favorite fantasy vacation location?"

"Sicily."

"Why?" he asked.

"There is this little Sicilian restaurant that I go to in South Park, nothing fancy, but the owner…"

"The real deal?" he asked, noticing that her eyes had glazed over.

She nodded. "Exactly. You?"

"South of France."

She nodded but didn't ask why.

"Do you have any questions for me, then?" he asked.

"That's all you had?" she chuckled. "I was expecting a full interrogation."

"I figured we could actually talk for a while," he replied, smiling. He hadn't realized until he had started asking her questions, but he was genuinely curious about her. Every time she answered, he wanted to push her for details, and it had nothing to do with the fact that he was pretending to date her. He wanted to have an actual conversation with her.

He hadn't had the time to be genuinely interested in a woman since college. God, he wondered, could that be true? He'd dated a decent amount, but eventually, even that had taken too much time, and then he'd had the money to start hiring escorts. And that had been that.

"Why patent law?" he asked, more to divert his thoughts.

She took a small sip of her drink as she thought about it, her eyes far away. "I don't really know," she started. "When I was wondering what the heck I wanted to do with my JD, it just kind of…stood out. I found it interesting."

He smiled at that. Imagine someone picking a career because it was interesting. "That's as good a reason as any," he replied, voicing his thoughts.

"But?"

He looked up, surprised by the fact that she had read his thoughts just by looking at his face. He chuckled. "I just…" He thought about how to put it kindly. "If I could have chosen a career for interest's sake, it wouldn't have been law or banking."

She laughed. "Well, money always has something to do with it. But you never asked me why I went into law, you asked me specifically why I went into patent law."

He leaned back on the sofa, comfortable. "True. So, money mattered?"

"Of course it matters; it makes the world go round."

She settled back into the chair too, crossed one leg over the other so that one slender foot, clad in a strappy, black heel, peeked out of the bottom of her red dress. David had a very real moment during which he imagined what it'd feel like to run his hand up her smooth skin, from her ankle to her thigh.

"What about you?" Her question snapped him back, and he forced his face into a neutral, or at least not-mortified, expression. "You said that your dad was in investment banking? So…was it an inherited or desired career?"

He thought about her question, liked the way she had phrased it so easily, liked that she understood there was a difference. When he'd been a child, he had never been asked what he'd wanted to do, by his father or anyone else for that matter. It had almost been a given fact that he'd follow in his father's footsteps. David didn't resent it, because there was also a part of him that could acknowledge that even if he had been given the option, he wasn't so sure that he'd have chosen any differently.

"Both," he decided eventually. "Definitely both."

He had finally loosened up enough at the private club to tell her a bit more about himself, and Ivy felt a small whip of victory when they both left the lounge—aptly named Le Bibliotheque for all the bookcases—smiling. Oh, they weren't friends yet, but at least they weren't snapping at each other; it made her job so much easier.

Morgan pulled up to the curb almost instantly, and she frowned. She had been so relaxed that she hadn't realized that David had stuck to a near-perfect schedule. It was like he had known exactly how long it would take her to finish her drink. The knowledge made her wonder what the inside of his brain was like and if he had trouble sleeping at night. He seemed like the type that would toss and turn, only fully rolling over once or twice in his bed to glance at the clock and see how far away the morning was so that he could get up for his run, or whatever he did to stay in such good shape.

She shimmied into the Range Rover without a hand, choosing to hoist herself in using the interior handle instead of the open door because it was easier. Less elegant, certainly, but easier. When David climbed in the seat beside her, she turned and smiled. It seemed like they had spent a lot of time driving from one place to the next.

He groaned and rolled his neck, like a fighter about to step into a cage, sending his pristinely laundered suit into a bunch at his shoulders. "Okay. Here we go," he said as Morgan pulled into the traffic.

Ivy remained quiet.

What she wanted to say was, 'Don't freak out now! You're finally relaxed enough to pass for human'. Somehow, she didn't think that would go down too well. The thought brought a smile to her lips. *See*, she told herself, *you're learning.*

She looked at him again, noticed that he'd crossed his arms and that the effort was straining his suit where his broad shoulders pulled the fabric tight. Maybe this was his process? Maybe he was the type who had to get all worked up and then just let it all fall away when the actual event started. She knew people like that; it was as if they fed off their own nervous energy somehow. But because she wasn't sure and because she'd hate to rile him more, she chose to keep quiet and leave him to it.

She looked out the window at the streets; energy seemed to pulse off the asphalt in every direction. Blondes that would make David roll his eyes pranced in tiny shorts and belly tops, skateboarders in baggy jeans and dirty shirts zoomed by and, judging by the girls' hysterical giggles, said something that caught their attention. A woman pushing a stroller ignored all of the buzz as if her life depended on it, her eyes tired but strangely set, looking forward, focused as she pushed her child through the sea of people.

Ivy watched the little flashes of life pass by on the sidewalk, never disappointed by the variety. Los Angeles had a way of bringing the most unlikely of people together, forcing them to cohabitate and, if not get along, then at least exist side-by-side.

"Do you have any other questions before we arrive?" David asked her quietly.

She turned to him, saw that his eyes were squinting out at the rapidly approaching sidewalk as Morgan pulled over. She didn't think about it, she just leaned over and caught his face in her hand, turned his surprised eyes to meet hers, and said, "Stop. You're going to drive yourself crazy. We've got this."

She wasn't sure if he agreed or if he was too surprised by her to say anything snarky, but she took it as a win and gave him a quick, chaste kiss before hopping onto the sidewalk.

"Thank you, Morgan," she said before she closed her door.

She stood on the sidewalk, alone, and realized that she had just given David Van den Berg a Damien-style kiss. On the lips.

Whoops.

She cleared her throat as he came around the car to stand beside her, pretended to completely ignore the fact that she was embarrassed as hell, and asked, "Ready?"

"Not quite." He took her mouth so quickly that she didn't have a second to think, or even respond. Instead, she stood stock-still while his lips crushed down on hers. He must have felt the rigid set of her body because he drew back after only a few seconds, let out a single, loud breath and ducked his head as if he were embarrassed.

"David," she said as he started to move away from her towards the door. She reached out a hand and grabbed his arm, tugged him gently enough that he didn't think of fighting her. When he turned his cold, blue eyes on her, she noticed that none of the happiness and warmth that had been there just half an hour before remained. She took a step towards him, closed the space between their bodies enough that it was suggestive.

"You don't hav-"

She kissed him then. It was a gentle kiss, soft and deep, so deep that it made her sigh inside. *How could someone so strong and hard, cold even, have such a soft, welcoming mouth?* He kissed her back, gently this time, responding to the pace she'd set. When his hand fluttered at her back, before coming to gently rest on her exposed skin, she let him. When a tall, lanky teenager whistled as he walked by on the sidewalk, she took a step back and grinned up at him.

"You just...took me by surprise, that's all."

He didn't say anything. He didn't even nod. Instead, he dropped his hand from her back and interlaced his fingers with hers before glancing at the gold-gilded restaurant door. "Here we go."

She walked at his side, ignored the fact that her lips were tingling, and smiled a thank-you when he opened the door for her. She stepped in, took another single step forward when he came up behind her, so close that his chest touched her bare back, sending a long shiver of awareness down her spine.

He spotted the hostess first and Ivy let him lead her through the large foyer. She was distracted, still trying to figure out how they'd fallen straight down the rabbit hole and into Wonderland. The floor in the large entryway was checkered black and white marble that gleamed under the light of an enormous chandelier and dripped crystals in elegant fronds. Thick, luscious indoor house plants were expertly positioned throughout the spacious room, some on tall, elegant stands, some hanging from intricate railings—all resplendent.

She focused on the hostess's desk in front of them, couldn't help but compare the large, granite standing desk to a judge's podium, expertly placed to condemn the riff-raff and moderately wealthy to the sidewalks of Los Angeles.

"Good evening," the hostess, an expertly made-up blonde, said, smiling politely. "May I have a name for the reservation?"

"We're meeting Bruce and Deborah Standard," David replied.

The hostess looked up from her reservation list immediately. "Mr. Van den Berg?" she asked.

He nodded.

Ivy wasn't sure if it was Bruce Standard's name or David's, but the woman had obviously been prepped for their arrival. She came around the large, granite standing desk and swept her arm in front of her, before adding, "Right this way, please."

David and Ivy followed through the elegantly designed restaurant and Ivy couldn't help but take in the brightly-lit interior with awe. She was certain that David wasn't looking, but she wanted to ask him if he noticed the twenty-foot, domed ceiling, or the actual fruiting orange tree in the middle of the restaurant, or the fact that the staff members were all dressed in coattails—men and women.

"Your waitress, Ivana, will be with you momentarily. She smiled when David held out Ivy's chair for her. "Would you like flat or sparkling water to start?"

Ivy said, "Sparkling please," at the exact same moment that David said, 'flat'.

The hostess didn't skip a beat. "I'll bring those right away."

Ivy watched her glide off, stage left, and when David sat down beside her, couldn't help but ask, "What is this restaurant called?"

He grinned back at her. "The Conservatory."

"Fantastic. It's perfect."

He smiled kindly, but glanced anxiously at the doorway as if he were watching, waiting for Bruce Standard to arrive. She wanted to tell him that Bruce was shy and awkward, not imposing and braggadocious, but she didn't have the heart. Not when he was so clearly trying to mentally prepare himself for 'The Dinner' as he'd called it so many times in the last six hours.

When he paled slightly and let out one last, short breath, she turned just the smallest bit and saw Bruce and Deborah Standard approaching out of the corner of her eye. She wondered if on-the-dot punctuality was an investment banking resume requirement.

They stood, almost in unison, and Ivy gently bumped him with her shoulder. To her surprise, he nudged her back. She wasn't quite sure why, but it was at that moment that she stopped worrying about him. David, despite the fact that he thought this was the single-most-important moment of his life, would be perfectly fine. He'd clearly been raised for these types of performances. The thought made her think that maybe the nerves were from a childhood where such things had been expected from him, his performance rehearsed and, judging by the rigid set of his shoulders, criticized afterward.

"David! Ivy!" Bruce approached them, a big, friendly smile on his small, round face as he outstretched his hands. He grasped both of Ivy's first because she was closer, and then reached across her to shake hands with David. "We are so glad that you could meet up with us on such short notice. Aren't we, Debbie?"

Ivy smiled down at Deborah, who was significantly shorter than her own five-nine frame and leaned in to give the smaller woman a hug. "It's nice to see you again, Deborah," she said. "You've met David, of course."

David took the cue and gave Deborah Standard's hand a friendly shake. "Hello, again."

She smiled shyly and answered, "It's very nice to see you both," before the hostess, who had been hovering nearby, swept in to tuck the chairs underneath them.

"Do you know why I like this spot, Ivy?" Bruce asked as he leaned both of his elbows on the table as if he were eating at home.

"Because you can order a drink in record time?" Ivy asked. She saw a tall, waitress with jet-black hair and sharp, blue eyes making a beeline for them as Bruce pointed at her and chuckled in approval. "I'm sure Ivana here can help us with that," she added as the waitress came abreast of their party.

Underneath the table, David brushed his hand over her thigh, just once, but it was an oddly comforting gesture, one that told her that, like her, he had realized the evening was going to be fine.

She nudged him with her leg in reply, deliberately ignored the faint tremor of awareness that traveled up from the point of contact, and settled a heavy weight between her thighs.

Chapter 5

He clearly couldn't believe that they had pulled it off.

"I mean, that went insanely well. Don't you think?" He didn't wait for her to reply before he added, "I think even Deborah was having a good time by the end of the night, although it's hard to tell with her. She's so shy. Doesn't seem to talk much at all."

"She's sweet," Ivy managed as he lapsed into silence beside her. "So, what now?" she asked. "Do you think anything will come of it?"

He shrugged his shoulders. "Honestly, it's impossible to say. I'm just happy I didn't humiliate myself."

She chuckled, rolling her eyes for good measure. "Something tells me that these dinners are second nature for you."

"I couldn't have done it without you, Ivy." He stopped then, looked at her, his eyes calm but cautious. There was something there that he was trying to hide from her, something he was feeling that he didn't want her to see.

Because she wasn't close enough to nudge him playfully, she replied, "At least you got your money's worth."

"More than."

She glanced at him, surprised by the compliment. He wasn't usually overflowing with them.

He reached across the car and took her hand in his, the gesture forcing her to meet his eyes again. "I genuinely mean that. I know that we didn't get off to a good start, but I appreciate the fact that you helped me despite it."

What did one say to that, she wondered? She had been thinking that the dinner had been a success, sure, but she had also been thinking about the mind-blowing kiss that they'd shared on the sidewalk.

He clearly was not.

Still, she wasn't sure why the thought disappointed her; she'd literally told him twenty-four hours earlier that she wouldn't have sex with him. And she realized that was the problem—she'd changed her mind. But because he clearly did not anticipate taking things further, Ivy patted his hand and replied, "Of course. You did pay me though, so no thanks necessary."

She felt him draw back from her slightly, felt his eyes turn cold on her skin. How did he do it, she wondered. Alienate himself so quickly and efficiently from others, like that?

"Ah, I'll have Morgan drop your bags tomorrow?"

She smiled, felt the edges cracking a little. "That would be great. Thanks."

"Can he come any time?"

"Yeah," she thought about it, "I'll be home all day. So," she looked at Morgan in the review mirror, "whenever suits you, Morgan."

He smiled at her, nodded, and said, "I'm as-needed and can be available any time Mr. Van den Berg requests our car service."

All three of them lapsed into silence and remained quiet until Morgan pulled up to her apartment building twenty minutes later. Because she didn't want to face David again, because she was scared that he might reject her, or worse, sleep with her because she was an escort, not because she was a woman that he might be interested in under different circumstances, she hopped from the SUV the minute it came to a rolling stop. "Thanks for being such a great date," she said and smiled into the car.

David was frowning.

He didn't say anything.

He just looked at her as if she'd sprouted two heads. She turned to Morgan. "Thanks for being such a great driver, Morgan."

"Any time, Ivy," he replied with a grin, his dark brown eyes flickering to David.

She closed the door, didn't stand on the sidewalk to watch the car off this time, but turned back for her apartment. She heard the Range Rover pull away quietly, sighed to herself, and climbed the concrete stairs to her apartment wearily.

She'd undress, have a nice hot shower, maybe read a book or start a show on Netflix. She'd never finish the whole season, because, well, things came up. But she'd start it. And she would, under no circumstances, feel any regret for not taking advantage of David Van den Berg. Hell, she thought as she turned the key in the lock, she wouldn't think of him at all.

Starting now.

There were very few times in her life that Ivy felt truly alone. She had her grandparents in the area, great friends, an amazing roommate and, even if she hadn't had all that, she enjoyed her own company, enjoyed solitude.

Tonight was different.

The apartment was deserted; it even looked deserted, thanks to the once-a-week cleaner she and Damien split the cost of, who had left the apartment so clean it looked damned close to institutional.

She trudged to the fridge, kicking off her heels as she did so, and leaving them in the middle of the carpet to add a sense of mayhem to the room. She opened the door and sighed. It wasn't that there was no food; Damien always kept the fridge well-stocked. She just wasn't hungry. She'd finished a four-course meal only an hour before and the idea of eating, despite her melancholy, was unappealing.

Moving back over to the sofa, she flopped stomach-down onto the soft, comfy cushions her grandma had made to cover the ugly brown couch, which she and Damien had dubbed, Sally.

Ivy was irritated and she didn't know why. Or rather, she knew why and couldn't do anything about it. Maybe she'd text Damien and see where they had ended up? It was a Saturday night, barely ten-thirty. She could meet up with them, grab a few drinks, loosen up, and then come home when she was finally tired enough to sleep.

And that was appealing for an entire ten seconds before she let the idea slip away. She knew that by the time she'd changed out of the formal, red dress, caught an Uber to wherever they were partying and had a drink in her hand, she'd just want to come right home again.

Groaning, she pushed herself off the sofa. She'd stick with the shower and Netflix. Chances were that the residual anxiety, or whatever it was that was making her irksome, would seep out of her pores once she had unwound from the evening.

The shower worked. Taking off the tight dress and thick makeup had helped loosen her up too, so that only thirty minutes later, she sat back down and took a sip of the red wine she'd poured in a last-ditch effort to revive her previous good mood. She tucked her feet under her legs and started her laptop up. There had to be something that she hadn't watched before, something that would pique her curiosity but not compromise her already-fragile mood.

She scrolled, mentally saved the options that weren't terrible, and eventually settled on a romantic comedy that she hadn't seen before. It would do. No emotional investment. No mental stimulation. No disappointment when she couldn't finish it. Just a loose, whimsical plot with a guaranteed happy ending. *Perfect.*

She hit play, let the opening credits run as she stood to turn the lights off. Once she'd reduced the entire apartment to darkness, she curled back up on the sofa and finally felt the last residual tension drain from her body. She snuggled into the comforter that she had pulled off her bed and settled into the cocoon, content to ward off the frigid air of the air-conditioned apartment, which Damien kept at a cool sixty-five degrees.

There was a knock at the door.

Ivy paused the movie right as the lead actress walked onscreen. She hadn't imagined it. Someone had knocked. Damien kept his apartment key with his car key so there was no way it was him. She listened, hearing only the traffic outside.

The knocking sounded again, even quieter this time.

She wasn't sure why, but she felt a moment of pure, unbridled panic. She wasn't expecting anyone. Forcing herself to calm down, she sat up straighter on the sofa, and called, "Who is it?" loud enough that they'd hear. If it was a burglar, scouting out if anyone was home, they'd most certainly leave when they heard her. Right?

Ivy was shocked to realize that it was the first time she'd really felt like a single woman in Los Angeles.

"It's David."

She jumped off the couch in one fluid movement and yanked the door open quickly, making him jump in fright. "You nearly gave me a heart attack! Why the hell would you knock on my door like that? Jesus, David, I thought I was going to be killed!"

He looked down at her, a half-laugh, half-confused look in his eyes. "Sorry," he said and rubbed the back of his neck. "I…I got Morgan to drop me at home and then drove my car straight back here. I wanted…to drop your things…and say thank you."

Ivy felt her heart crawl into her throat, felt her stomach twist with nerves. He'd come back…to say thank you?

"Ah, do you want to come in?" she asked, feeling the first twinge of embarrassment. She'd just scolded a very

71

successful, very good-looking investment banker like a third-grade teacher would have.

"I don't know if that's a good idea," he said. He handed her gym bag through the door but didn't take a step closer.

She raised her brow. "So, you just want me to say, 'sure thing' and be done with it?" She leaned against the doorframe, slightly irritated, stuck her hand out for the bag, and nearly dropped it when he let it go. She'd forgotten how heavy it had been. She heft it just inside the door, let it drop with a loud thud inside the corner of the apartment without taking her eyes off him.

"I know that you said you wouldn—"

She didn't give him a chance to finish what he'd been about to say. Instead, she grabbed a fistful of his dress shirt and tugged him until he came to stand inside her apartment.

Because she wanted to, not because he'd paid her to, she ran her hands up and under his shirt, felt his hard, flat abs and the heat of his skin under her cold palms. Her body tightened when her hand came to rest over his frantically beating heart. He didn't move. He just stood there, as if he wasn't quite sure what he was supposed to do.

"What's wrong?" she asked, her hands still on his chest. "You don't want me?" She spoke the question quietly, felt her pulse quicken slightly when he didn't reply right away.

Finally, he exhaled on a long rush of air, let his head roll back slightly as if undone, and then grabbed both of her forearms and gently moved her hands away from his chest and out from under his shirt.

She felt the blood rush to her cheeks as tears burned her eyes. She'd embarrassed herself. He'd genuinely come to say thank you and she'd tried to seduce him. Worse, she'd tried to *jump* him. Literally. It didn't help that her body was still aware of how close he was, or that her palms were sweating with nerves.

When she looked away, he cupped her cheek and turned her face back towards his, forced her to meet his gaze again.

"Ivy, at this moment, I want you more than…probably more than anything I've ever wanted before."

"But?" she asked, his simple admission tightening every muscle in her body.

"I don't…" he trailed off, dropped his hand from her cheek.

"Is it because I'm an escort?" she asked. Surprisingly, she would have understood that, wouldn't have judged him for having that standard.

"No," he said. "Not for the reason you're thinking at least." He was quiet for a moment. "I don't want to have sex with you if you think that I'm only doing it because I paid you. I…I guess I'd like to take you on an actual date, potentially more than one. I'd love nothing more than to undress you," he said, his eyes dark with honest lust. "But, I'd like it to be by choice. For both of us." He paused for another moment and then added, "If you want to sleep with me because I paid you, then I'm not interested."

She stared at him. Mute. She wasn't quite sure how to respond to that. If she were honest with herself, she'd admit that she was surprised. Sex, she could deal with. Dates…well, it had been a while since she'd been on a date with a man who wasn't hiring the Antoinette Rupetta Agency for a very specific reason. She hadn't had a boyfriend since undergrad, hadn't dated seriously since her master's.

"I can see I've thrown you off," he said. He took a step back towards the door.

Ivy took a step towards him. "I'm just…you took me by surprise. Again. I want to sleep with you, and not because you hired me to." She looked at him, saw him waiting for her to go on, and added, "Why? Why does it make a difference? You've paid other girls to sleep with you. You've technically paid me, and I know that you would have slept with me that first night if we'd hit it off."

He nodded. "I'd say that the truth is closer to the fact that I've had sex with other women whom I've paid to go out with."

"Meaning?"

"The dates were necessary, what I paid for. The sex was optional, wanted, on both sides. I just…never really went out with a girl who didn't come on to me instantly—until you that is. And now…" He rubbed the back of his neck, "I want to give you time so that you know this is different for me."

She felt a deluge of emotions flood her when he lapsed into silence: Happiness, that he'd felt whatever was happening between them too; fear of the intensity of her need; and wariness because she couldn't stop herself from questioning the happiness and the fear. She shook her head to clear her doubt, finding her own cynicism funny, one might even say hypocritical.

He smiled, not the ice-cold professional smile, but the kind of embarrassed David smile. "What movie were you watching?"

"*In Her Shoes*. With Cameron Diaz. But, I haven't started it yet." She leaned forward and interlaced her fingers with his in a way that already seemed intimate…familiar, but made sure to keep her distance because she didn't want to embarrass herself a second time. "Stay?"

He hesitated for only a moment before stepping fully into the apartment and closing the door behind him, inadvertently throwing them into complete darkness aside from the white glare from the laptop screen.

Ivy was distinctly aware of how close he was, of the feeling of his rough, calloused palm covering hers, of the leather and oak smell of his skin. "We don't have to watch anything," she said, suddenly embarrassed. He was a forty-year-old man; the last thing he probably wanted to do was watch a chick flick with her in her podunk Koreatown apartment.

74

"That sounds fine," he replied. He took a few steps towards the sofa and Ivy, her hand still in his, suddenly felt the world tip as he tripped just before he reached it and landed in a heap on the floor, inadvertently pulling her down with him.

She sat silently on the floor beside him for a full ten seconds as she thought about what to say. When nothing came to mind, she chuckled and reached forward blindly to try and find what he'd tripped on. When her hand latched onto the stiletto that she'd discarded as soon as she'd arrived home, she sighed and tried to force the flush from her cheeks despite the pitch-black room. "Believe it or not, I'm not a slob," she said. She tried not to smile as she thought about what must be going through his mind.

He chuckled and reached out a hand to pull the other shoe out from under his leg. "I'm not judging," he replied. "Although a few inches to the right and this would have emasculated me," he added, handing her the shoe.

She pushed herself to her knees, fumbling on the small side-table for the light switch so she could flip it on. When she did, she squinted against the bright light, looked across at David, sitting on her apartment floor, and couldn't help but grin. He sat in his perfectly tailored clothes, his arms resting on his knees as he shook his head, laughing. Still on her knees, she moved the shoes under the side table, out of the way, and then cast a glance back at him. "Threat neutralized."

He smiled and pushed himself to his feet, offered her a hand, and pulled her up beside him, the momentum bringing them chest to chest. She tilted her head and looked up at him, felt her breath catch in her throat when their eyes met.

He frowned and took a step back.

She tried not to show her disappointment. Why was he being such a gentleman now when all she wanted was, well, him?

She left him standing alone in her lounge as she grabbed a second wine glass from the kitchen. When she returned, he was sitting down, his left foot crossed over his right knee, his long dress socks peeking out from under the hem of his pants.

She wanted to walk up behind him and run her fingers through his thick, blond hair. She wanted to kiss his neck and feel his pulse beat frantically as she did so. But somehow, she didn't think David was ready for that, so instead, she said, "I have a Nebbiolo open, but I think I have a riesling in the fridge and a pinot in the cupboard too if you'd prefer."

He looked back at her and Ivy had to fight the urge to sweep her hair out of her face. She felt self-conscious all of a sudden; this was the first time that he'd seen her without makeup on. She knew it was a solid downgrade, was well-aware of the fact that her pale skin showed the black rings under her green eyes to be much worse than they really were.

"Nebbiolo is perfect," he said, not taking his eyes from her face.

He watched her as she filled his glass, tried not to spill it on him when she handed it to him, her hand trembling slightly with nerves.

When she finally sat back down next to him and picked up her own glass, she couldn't help but notice that his skin was hot through his clothes, couldn't help but realize that thinking about his skin was not helping her current state.

She wasn't sure that she had ever felt so aware of a man before, wasn't sure that she was entirely comfortable with the charged air that vibrated between them or the way her stomach was flopping around uselessly inside her.

"What are you thinking about?" he asked, a small frown creasing his brow. "Your eyes are far away."

She could have lied. But she didn't want to. "I'm still wondering why the date first? You know I want you, and we've been on dates already."

He nodded. "I more just want you to know that I'm not sleeping with you because of the money."

She put her glass down gently, met his gaze as she moved closer to him. "Well, technically, your time ran up over an hour ago," she said. When she saw his eyes widen, she wasn't sure if it was with lust or surprise, but she knelt on the sofa and slid one knee over his lap so that she straddled him.

He reached behind her and put his wine glass down on the coffee table, rested big hands on her hips, and watched her silently as she brought her lips to his, took his mouth gently, her tongue taking the time to taste him before dipping deeper into the kiss. She lifted her hands, first to his face and then to his hair, where she finally got to run her fingers through the thick mass of it before fisting them there.

He kissed her back, tightened his grip on her unconsciously as he nipped at her bottom lip, then trailed hungry kisses down her neck.

When she felt him, long and hard underneath her, her body tightened in anticipation, her nipples ached, and she felt her breath hitch when a tremor of nervous anticipation traveled through her belly. Reaching for the hem of her tee-shirt, he tugged it up and over her head, and sighed when her breasts spilled out.

Ivy raised her arms to cover herself, uncharacteristically embarrassed for a brief moment when she realized she was topless on top of a successful, very well-dressed man. Her knee-jerk reaction surprised her, forcing a hot blush into her cheeks.

David shook his head and gently caught her hands, pinning them by her side. "You're beautiful, Ivy. Don't be shy."

She didn't fight him when he took first one and then the other nipple in his warm, wet mouth. She didn't think she'd have been able to even if she wanted to. She moaned softly when the feeling of his tongue sent small tendrils of pleasure through her body. "Wait," she said, her voice husky with lust.

He paused immediately, then pulled back.

Ivy met his blue eyes, felt her stomach form a hard knot when she recognized the black need reflected in them. "My roommate could come back at any moment," she managed, thinking about what Damien would say if he saw her now. "We should take this to the bedroom."

He closed his eyes and took a deep breath, exhaled on one long sigh and asked, "Are you sure?"

She smiled, moved her pelvis so that she rubbed up against the hard length of him just the tiniest bit. "I'm pretty sure I was the one who initiated this," she said, a small smile on her lips.

He grinned then. Ivy felt a blossom of nerves unfurl in her chest at the dangerous look in his eye. He stood to his full height, taking her with him easily, her legs wrapped around his waist. She chuckled when he exaggeratedly looked around for shoes on the floor before taking a step towards the bedrooms.

"Mine's on the left," she said and nipped his throat playfully.

He opened the bedroom door and flicked on the light switch in the corner before shutting it behind them.

Ivy glanced around, felt a small sigh of relief pass through her when she saw that her bedroom was in an acceptable state. There weren't even any clothes strewn on the floor, which, she'd admit, were an occasional, albeit temporary, hazard in her bedroom.

He walked over to the bed, moved over it so that she could untangle her legs from his waist and plop onto it, his body now over hers. She met his direct gaze, struggled not to blush when he dipped his head and trailed open-mouthed kisses over her chest, leaving little licks of pleasure where his mouth touched.

Needing something to do with her hands, she reached for him, started unbuttoning his shirt when he paused, propped over her, a wide smile on his lips. She finally reached the last button, pushed the shirt as far back on his broad shoulders as she could, and ran her hands up his chest, enjoying the way his abs tensed where she touched.

He lowered himself down beside her gently, and she couldn't help but sigh when his hot skin met hers, couldn't stop the purr from rising in the back of her throat when one big, rough palm stroked down her body. He kissed her again, his tongue teasing, taking her deeper as his right hand trailed a lazy path from her hip, up her side to cup her breast.

Ivy felt her stomach clench with need, moaned against his mouth when his fingers circled her nipple, barely touching her sensitized skin, only just enough to send a delicious shiver from the point of contact, down her stomach, to collect between her thighs. When he shifted, moved his hand to her other side, she arched off the bed, trying to get closer, trying to press herself more firmly against his hand.

He shifted so that his head was over her chest, moved close enough that she could feel the slightest whisper of his breath against her skin, the warm brush of it pulling her nipples tighter. His hand moved down the flat of her stomach as he took one small peak, then the other, into his mouth again.

Ivy felt her body respond, felt the way her thighs trembled as his hand worked its way down, and underneath the waistband of her pajama shorts, felt the way that her nipples ached as his mouth and tongue did impossible things to her chest. She didn't need to hear his groan or his tortured, "Fuuuck," as he slipped a single finger between her folds, to know that she was hot and wet.

When his finger slid over her clit, gently exploring, she gripped his shoulders, sank her nails into the bunched muscles there. Through the rush of blood in her ears, she could hear her pulse jackhammering in her throat with a resounding thud, could hear her breath coming in small, frantic gasps.

Her body pulled tighter, a coiled spring at the edge of its tension, and she ground her hips instinctively, begging him to hurry. Somewhere in the back of her mind, she was aware of the fact that she was afraid of the intensity of…everything, afraid of the fact that she'd never quite felt *this* before.

When his finger slipped inside of her, she lifted her hips slightly, her body instinctively showing him what she wanted. He swore, a strangled, "Fuck. Ivy…" and dropped his head to rest between her breasts.

He was still for a moment, and she felt her stomach tighten, felt her legs tremble. *Don't stop.* "Please, David," she begged, hating the fact that her voice was hoarse but needing to tell him what she wanted.

He raised his head to look at her, and she saw the predatory glint flicker in his eyes before he slowly added a second finger to the first and then slid in and out of her with long, fluid strokes, his thumb moving over her clit with brutal efficiency.

She could feel him beside her, could feel the length of him pressing into her hip, but all she could focus on was the fact that she was about to shatter into a thousand pieces. And when he drew her nipple back into his mouth, circled his tongue around it, she did just that: Shattered.

The orgasm tore through her, and her hips rose off the bed as she moaned his name. He slowed his pace instantly, alternately inserted and withdrew his fingers as she found the fragments of herself and tried to piece them back together. Her fingers still gripped his shoulders, and, beneath the pulsing waves of her own release, she became aware of the fact that he was impossibly taut, tight, his muscles bunched, like a big cat, full of adrenaline and ready to pounce.

He stood suddenly, tugged his shirt off the rest of the way and took a few one-legged hops as he yanked his dress shoes off, before unzipping his pants and slipping out of them.

Ivy watched him as she yanked off her own pajama shorts. She noticed that he didn't toss his clothes on the floor as she had, that he draped them over the chair that was tucked into her small desk. She also noticed that she had seriously underestimated how fit he was under all those clothes.

His broad shoulders tapered into a long, lean torso with defined abs, all sun-kissed and golden, his legs long, lean, and strong. She felt her body respond to him, felt her heart flutter a little when she glanced down his torso to his thick erection and then back up to meet his eyes, a small, knowing laugh in them.

This time, when he lowered himself down onto the bed beside her, Ivy felt all of him, naked, tense, hot to the touch. Hard. She ran her fingers down his chest, raked her nails softly over his abs, her hand trailing lower until she closed her palm around him. When he trembled at her touch, she felt a small lick of satisfaction. Slowly, she moved her hand up and down the hard length of him, used her fingers on him until his eyes were closed, his jaw clenched shut, his breath coming in pants.

Feeling her body pull impossibly tight again, she placed one hand on his face, waited until he looked at her through unfocused eyes. She couldn't wait any longer. She didn't want this to be slow and gentle. She wanted *him. Now.* "I want you inside me," she whispered.

He groaned, bowed his head for a moment. "I didn't bring any condoms. I…wasn't expecting…this. Anything, really."

Ivy felt a wave of pleasure wash through her. She wasn't sure why, thought it might have had something to do with the fact that he'd genuinely come over without expecting anything, but chose not to analyze it just then. "I have an IUD. And I'm clean." She cleared her throat, momentarily awkward. "Regular testing is a requirement with Antoinette. But…" Reaching over, she opened the drawer to her bedside table, pulled out a condom from the pack that she kept there. "I'm also always prepared."

He looked at her, took it from her hand before she could tear the foil. He sheathed himself quickly, then moved over her in a single, fluid motion, held himself just close enough for her to feel him. "I'm always safe." He shook his head. "But I had a full physical a month ago and I'm clean too."

She looked up, met his ice-blue eyes as he slowly inched inside of her. She forced herself to keep his gaze, bucked her hips to take the rest of him, and wrapped her legs around his waist when he exhaled on a sharp breath and thrust inside of her with one smooth stroke.

Ivy closed her eyes against the rising pressure, matched the movement of her hips to the pace David had set. As he moved inside of her, with her, she raked her nails over his broad, muscular back, felt his body tremble at her touch. She wasn't going to last, and as much as she tried to deny it, she couldn't hide from the fact that she couldn't remember feeling this way, this fear, excitement, and pure joy with anyone else. Couldn't remember having experienced this maddening need and frenzied, wanton coupling before David.

When she would have moaned, he stifled it with a kiss and when her body fought for release, he increased his pace. She felt herself tighten around him and a single thought echoed in her mind: *Impossible.*

"I want you to look at me, Ivy," he said, his voice husky and raw.

She opened her eyes and met his gaze, fought against the greed already clawing through her, begging for more, begging for him. She could hear her own heart, beating thick and strong in her ears, sighed in pleasure when he leaned down and took her mouth.

Because she knew that she couldn't hold out much longer, and because she wanted to give to him too, she put a hand on his chest. He looked confused for a moment, so Ivy gently nudged him away and, when he lay on his back, she whispered, "My turn."

She felt a small whip of satisfaction when his eyes glazed over. She straddled him, let him feel her against his skin for a moment before she guided him to her and sank slowly down, taking all of him.

He gripped her hips tightly, as if trying to anchor himself, groaned when she moved on top of him, with him.

She loved the feeling of him, of all of him inside her. She threw her head back as she rode him, felt her own body pull tighter with every movement. When she looked down at him, saw him watching her, she raised a single hand, and gently played with her own nipple. The feeling of him, of her own hand, and of his gaze burning into her skin brought a soft moan of pleasure to her lips.

He swore, thrust his hips faster, taking both of them closer. Just when Ivy thought she couldn't take anymore, he rose up, flipped her over, and, thrusting hard and fast inside her, he pushed them both over the last rise.

Chapter 6

He looked at her while she slept and couldn't quite shake the feeling that he had made a mistake.

She looked so...beautiful, although that didn't quite capture all of her. She was on her side, both of her hands pillowing her face, her thick eyelashes casting full shadows on her cheeks, her long, chocolate-colored hair spilling in a dark mass on the pillow behind her.

He thought she looked angelic, almost child-like as she slept, and the thought disturbed him. She was so much younger than him and yet...she had completely destroyed him. He ignored the tightness in his stomach at the memory of her rising over him, her thick hair falling forward over pale skin and full breasts.

He wanted to reach out a hand and touch her cheek, wanted her to open her eyes, and look at him like she had just an hour earlier. The thought made him frown, made him deliberately pull back the palm that hovered just an inch away from her face.

Because he felt a thick ball of panic lodge in his throat, he gently pushed himself off the bed, making sure not to wake her. What had he done? He'd slept with Ivy, not Escort Ivy, but Ivy Ivy. The differentiation, the fact that he knew them to be two parts of her, made him turn and look down at her again.

He felt his heart trip in his chest, felt an unfamiliar tightness spread through him when she sighed in her sleep and snuggled deeper into the blankets as she inched towards the warm spot he'd just vacated.

Shit.

This wasn't supposed to happen. How had he developed feelings for a girl he'd known for just over twenty-four hours? Was that even possible? He moved to where he'd draped his clothes over a chair the night before, and changed quietly.

He couldn't fall for Ivy Watts. *She...she could literally kill me.* She could ask anything of him, and he'd say yes. The thought made him frown, made him wonder if she'd do the same for him. He shook his head. He got the feeling that she wouldn't stop escorting for him. Not that he'd ever ask her either.

He sat on the chair in her room and wondered what he was going to do as he put on his shoes. Could he date her, knowing that she was seeing other men? Probably sleeping with them too? He already knew the answer to that question. If what he'd felt for her had been casual, purely sexual, he could maybe handle other men in her life; he did, after all, deal with other women in the escorting business.

But something had changed. Somehow, she had crossed the line without him even being aware of it, and now he knew that he could never endure seeing her with someone else. Knowing that when she wasn't with him, she was with another man would be torture.

When his fists tightened at the thought, he sighed and dropped his head, clasping his hands between his knees. He knew what the right thing to do was; wait for her to wake up and explain why he couldn't stay, why he'd changed his mind since only a few hours before. Explain that he couldn't know she was dating other men and be fine with it. Because he'd fallen for her. Maybe he hadn't fallen in love, but he'd fallen in something that he didn't care to analyze, and the knowledge scared him. *She* scared him.

Worse, he knew he wasn't going to wait for her to wake up because he knew she'd be hurt by him, hurt that he'd slept with her under the presumption he wanted more, and then cut her out of his life. And he didn't want to see her hurt. At least if he just left, she'd be angry. Strangely, he knew that he could handle her anger.

He pushed himself to his feet, felt for his car keys in the pocket of his pants, and then, as quietly as he could, let himself first out of her bedroom, and then out of her apartment without once looking back.

As he drove home just before one in the morning, David felt a niggling guilt creep into the back of his mind. He pushed it aside, narrowed his eyes, and focused on the road. Ivy would be better off never knowing why he'd left.

In fact, she'd be better off without him in general.

Chapter 7

It had been three weeks and Ivy finally decided to take another job. Three weeks since David had slept with her and then left in the middle of the night without an explanation or even, she was loathe to admit, a goodbye.

Honestly, she could have hated him if she hadn't been so mad with herself. He had hired her for God's sake, literally paid her to accompany him on a few dates, and, per the norm, sleep with him if things worked out. And she'd gone and fallen for the golden boy routine. She'd thrown herself at him like…well, like an escort being paid to do just that. And for that, she could never forgive herself.

She'd humiliated herself.

And still, she wasn't sure which was worse, the fact that she'd fallen for it, or the fact that she'd waited a whole three weeks before going on another date, in the hope that he'd call her. It was pathetic. *She* was pathetic.

So, instead, she ignored the small stab of sadness that pressed into her chest and tied the laces to her white sneakers. She'd go and see her dad, talk to him about nothing in particular for a few hours and then go on her first job in nearly a month. She'd smile and act like she was having a good time, and pretend to be interested in everything that her date had to say.

At least, she reminded herself, he was a regular. A kind, slightly pudgy divorcee from Beverly Hills with a sweet disposition, a shy smile, and a brain for antiquities that would have put Indiana Jones to shame. Fred was harmless, intelligent; he was a man who liked to have a pretty girl to talk to when he had to attend the gallery openings and exhibitions he was always a preferred guest at. Ivy sighed and stood. Hell, she might even try and have fun.

She opened her bedroom door, was about to knock on Damien's to say goodbye when she caught his and Louie's muffled laughter coming from his bedroom. She smiled and made her way out instead, leaving them to each other.

It didn't take her long to drive to Hanley Hospice, especially on a Saturday. The end-of-life care facility was located in a quiet neighborhood in Pasadena, which, on a weekend, was only a twenty-minute drive from her apartment.

She parked the car in one of the visitor parking spaces, locked the door out of habit, and glanced up at the facility as she meandered towards the entrance. It was a big, white building; a sprawling village-type, multi-family complex that had been bought and converted to a hospice care facility by the Hanley Group.

The tall, white walls and red, clay roof tiles looked oddly comforting in the unfiltered Pasadena sunlight, almost like an old, austere, and well-loved family compound where she could imagine children playing on the grass while adults barbequed by the pool. The aesthetic was one of the primary reasons she'd chosen Hanley Hospice for her father, second only to the fact that it was in Pasadena and close enough for all of his lifelong friends to visit.

She stood for a moment outside the main entrance, which comprised two huge oak doors that lead to the interior courtyard, and cast one last appreciative glance at the façade of the building before gently pushing the heavy right-hand door open. She knew from experience that the fairytale would end as soon as she stepped inside.

Hanley Hospice was not a place where families let their children run around while they barbequed; it was where people sent their loved ones to die when they had the money but not the time or training to look after them.

She let the door swing closed on its hinges behind her, walked quietly into the courtyard, her steps pattering lightly on the red, brick floor. Even the quiet tap tap tap of her soft-soled shoes sounded too loud to her ears compared to the eerie hush that filled the hospice. Veering right, she walked into the Guest Reception area where she knew she'd have to sign in and wait until one of the regular nurses took her through to her father's room.

She smiled at the elderly lady at the front desk. Her name was Amanda; she worked the desk every Saturday from ten in the morning until six in the evening when the hospice closed its doors to visitors. Ivy knew Amanda well after over a year of Saturday visits to the hospice.

"Ivy." Amanda's eyes brightened when she saw her approaching. "How are you?"

Ivy smiled, noticed that Amanda had styled her white hair differently since she'd last seen her, opting for a short, stylish pixie cut over the shoulder-length bob she'd had before. "I'm good. How are you?"

She shrugged. "I can't complain." Chuckling, Amanda leaned closer as if she wanted to share a secret. "I have a new gentleman friend. Ike Matenzo." She didn't pause to catch her breath before adding, "Oh, Ivy, this one makes me feel nineteen again."

"You *look* nineteen again with that hairstyle. It's amazing," Ivy said, genuinely. The hair made Amanda look a solid ten years younger than Ivy knew her to be.

Without pause, Amanda replied, "I'm eighty-four. I'll take looking like a seventy-year-old at this stage." She looked over her glasses at Ivy. "What about you? Seeing any nice young men these days?" Ivy sighed, grimacing when she noticed Amanda raised her eyebrows at the sound. "Trouble in paradise, dear?"

Ivy shook her head. "Nothing of the kind. I'm just…taking some me-time."

91

Amanda snorted, raised one hand in a 'hold-on-a-minute' gesture. "Trust me, girly, you can have all the 'me-time' in the world when you're my age, but until then, you need to put yourself out there, have fun!" Pausing, she looked pointedly over Ivy's high-waisted jeans and cropped top. "How long do you think you're going to look like that?"

Ivy laughed despite herself. "You know, you're absolutely right." Smiling, she leaned over the desk to write her name in the guest log. "I'll remember that the next time a nice-looking man comes my way."

Amanda looked at her out of the corner of her eye, and Ivy had the distinct impression that she was contemplating something serious. "You know," she began, casting a quick glance around to make sure that nobody was around, "I have a grandson."

Oh no, Ivy thought to herself. *Please, God. No.* She wondered how to tell a woman over eighty that dating wasn't her issue. Or, rather, it was her *only* issue.

"He's a bit older than you, but he's a good man. Works like a dog. And let me tell you something, Ivy—that boy is the spitting image of my Daniel. Tall. Blonde." She lifted her arms and fluttered them over her upper body in a way that was clearly supposed to indicate muscles. "Strong."

Ivy laughed and held up a hand, hoping that she could stop Amanda from any other arguments in her grandson's favor. "Thanks." She paused when Amanda tilted her head to the side, and just looked at her silently. "If I can't find a date in the next few weeks, I'll consider it, okay?"

Amanda nodded, a small, mischievous gleam in her eye. Then, she sat back and cleared her throat. "Oh, there's Laurie, come to take you to see your dad."

Ivy turned and smiled at Laurie, one of her father's regular caregivers. "I'll see you soon."

She followed behind Laurie when she made for her dad's private room, not feeling the need to talk as they meandered through the deathly-quiet halls. She could already feel the weight of the visit, slowly working its way into her throat, suffocating her. She felt like turning around and leaving, but instead, she tucked her hands into the pockets of her jeans and looked at the back of Laurie's head.

"Do you want me to go in with you?" she asked when they came to stand outside the door. When Ivy didn't answer right away, Laurie added, "He's had a rough week, Ivy. The...the trach isn't helping much anymore. We're...we're not sure that there's much we can do except ease his pain."

Ivy felt the tears burn her eyes even though she'd had three years to prepare for this eventuality. "I understand," she said. "Is he awake?"

Laurie nodded. "I know that this is hard for you." She placed a hand on Ivy's arm, gave a light, reassuring squeeze; it was a practiced gesture, but one that Ivy knew Laurie meant from the bottom of her heart. "You should come to the support group sometime; it'll help...just talking about it, about your fears...It'll help."

Ivy smiled through her blurred vision, nodded even though she knew that she'd never actually go to the support group. She didn't want to feel others' pain compounded with her own. She wanted to be left alone in a quiet, dark room so she could sleep undisturbed.

She cleared her throat, gave Laurie one final nod, and quietly opened the door. The bed was positioned in the center of the room, the clean, white and blue bedding lying stark against the tan walls. Her father lay on his back, his face turned to the wall, his neck at an awkward angle that made him look unnaturally crooked. She moved around to the side of the bed that he faced so that he could see her through eyes nearly fully-closed.

He didn't say anything. He had stopped talking months ago, had refused the Eyegaze Edge that Ivy had offered to buy because he didn't feel the need to waste money on communications technology so close to the end.

93

She took his paper-thin hand in her own, tried not to drop it when his dry, leathery skin touched hers, sending a ripple of unease through her stomach. "How have you been, Dad?" The words were barely a whisper.

Because she wasn't expecting an answer, but because his eyelashes fluttered in acknowledgment, she began talking about her day, about the new cases she was working on at Fitch and Mathers, about Damien. She talked only about good things as the sound of his breathing apparatus whined quietly in the background.

Eventually, as she always did, Ivy ran out of things to talk about, and instead, held his hand as he drifted off again. As she watched him sleep, she felt her heart break for the thousandth time, only this time it wasn't with sadness for his condition, this time it was all self-pity. She knew that very soon she'd be losing her only remaining parent.

She stayed for a little under two hours, stood and stretched when Laurie knocked on the door and let herself in. Ivy returned her sad smile, gave her father's hand one last squeeze, and made for the exit.

She didn't usually pause by Amanda's desk on the way out, but she happened to glance up and see the elderly woman wave her over.

"Now I know that this is a little desperate, but once I had the idea in my head, I just couldn't let it go," she said as Ivy approached the desk.

Ivy frowned.

"I've put my grandson's name and number on here for you." She passed Ivy the piece of paper, a neatly cut piece of pink letter card stock.

Ivy was too tired to refuse. She took it, said, "Thank you, Amanda. I'll think about it."

As she turned to leave, Amanda added, "I think you two would be good for each other, Ivy. It just…makes sense."

Ivy gave her one more smile before walking into the courtyard and pushing open the big doors. She walk-ran to her parked car, needing to put distance between herself and the hospice, needing the clear air and space of solitude. Yanking open the door, she hopped into the driver's seat and revved the engine, pulled out before realizing that she still held the pink piece of paper in her hand.

Curious, she opened it.

When she read the neatly written name, hand-written in Amanda's pretty cursive, she couldn't help it, she laughed until her sides hurt, until her eyes watered and her breath came in short, gasping cackles. She laughed until she was gasping for air. The only reason she was eventually able to pull herself together at all was because she was blocking the hospice's driveway and a white sedan had pulled up behind her. God knew the driver probably thought she'd lost it.

Maybe she had.

She pulled out into the street, turned towards Koreatown. She wondered what would disappoint Amanda Van den Berg more; the fact that Ivy wasn't going to reach out to her grandson, or the fact that her grandson had already slept with her—and never called her back.

He pulled into the long, winding, gravel driveway that ended in a loop—complete with fountain—in front of his parent's door, parked the car, and steeled himself for what lay ahead before stepping out into the Santa Barbara sunshine.

David would stay for a few hours, be polite over the lunch his mother had organized, and then leave; maybe he'd stay the night downtown with his childhood best friend, Meg, and her husband, James; he could wake up early in the morning to catch some waves. Either way, the less time spent in his parents' company the better.

With a final sigh, he got out of his Porsche 911, stood for a full minute so that he could look up at the large estate home. He'd admit to himself that even though it was obnoxiously large for just two people, the Spanish-style home was enviable. It's wide front doors, large, square windows, gently sloping roof, and cobbled floor made it look like a big, welcoming home. A place for family—like something the Von Trapps, all seven children included, would have felt right at home in. Which, to David, was laughable.

The front door swung open in a wide arc before he reached it. His mother stepped outside, her perfectly made-up hair glinting blonde in the sunlight, her pristine makeup taking at least ten years from around her eyes; although, David knew for a fact that Dr. Madison had taken another ten off with a few nip tucks.

She was dressed in a lemon-yellow, knee-length skirt that emphasized her perfectly sculpted physique, with a white blouse tucked in, simple yellow flats in the same color as the skirt. He wondered, as he walked towards her, if they had come in a matching set.

"David." Her voice was soft. Flat. Instead of giving him a hug or taking his hand, she leaned forward slightly, offering him her cheek.

He gave her a quick peck on either side—as was expected. "Mother, you look lovely. As usual."

She ushered him into the foyer and David couldn't help but feel relieved as the cool air wrapped around his skin. The two and a half-hour drive from downtown Los Angeles had not been relaxing or smooth—it had been tiresome and congested and David felt like he needed a swimming pool and a gin and tonic to put him in a better mood.

"You're the first one here, except for your Grandmother. So, why don't you go and freshen up before the other guests arrive?"

He nodded and without another word, turned to move up the left side of the winged staircase to the guest bedroom where he kept an array of extra clothes for situations such as these. He didn't care that his mother had referred to him as a guest. He had definitely noticed, but he didn't care.

Not anymore.

He changed quickly, didn't bother to shower because any time dawdling meant extra time he'd have to spend with his family. Minus Grandma. His Grandmother was the salt of the earth, but how she had birthed his father was something of a mystery. Grandma was cultured and spunky, hilarious if you got a few drinks in her and downright rude if you pissed her off—irrespective of the number of drinks she'd had. The thought made him smile. If he'd known that she'd be here, he would have offered to drive her. He frowned because, usually, she would have called and asked him to.

Once he'd shrugged into another button-down, pulled on a pair of jeans, and retied his shoes, he gave himself a cursory glance in the mirror.

Shit, he looked old, he thought as he turned away from his reflection. He was forty-two and still didn't have much to show for it; a steady career trajectory, expected compensation, but nothing remarkable, nothing personal.

He'd always thought that by twenty-eight he'd been on the cover of Forbes, or at least, swinging hundred-million-dollar deals for the firm. Instead, he was forty-two and an MD. Sure, he might have been a year or two younger than the average MD, but that didn't make him remarkable. He was just another labradoodle in the world of investment banking.

The thought irritated him, because it reminded him that he had dinner with the CEO only a month ago. And because that brought a whole horde of other memories that he'd rather forget, David made for the door. He'd say hello to grandma, wolf down his food, and leave having done his familial duty.

"Oh, my goodness!" Grandma was waiting at the bottom of the stairs when David came trotting down.

"David, I could have sworn when I saw you marching down those stairs with hell in your eyes, I thought, for just a second, there's my Daniel." She sighed. "You look so much like your grandfather that every time I see you, I'm transported back."

"That sounds awful," David teased and leaned down to fold her into a hug. Her familiar scent, roses and talcum powder, wrapped around him like a comforting blanket.

"Are you kidding?" she asked, pushing him out to arms-length, her lavender eyes sparkling. "What a lucky lady, to never need a photograph to remember the one true love of my life!"

Chuckling, he took her tiny, fragile hand in his own and led her from the foyer towards the receiving lounge. "How are you, Grandma?" he asked, always concerned by how thin her gnarled hand felt in his own. It seemed so small, so…near-gone.

"As chipper as always," she said with a smile. "I've got a new sweetheart," she added. "Ike Matenzo. He drove me today, so you'll get to meet him. I think you'll get along."

"How is it that you're eighty-five and still manage to have a more vibrant love life than I do?" He shook his head. "It's literally unbelievable."

"I'll have you know I'm eighty-four," she replied with an exaggerated flounce of her head, which, he noticed, had been cropped into some new style that made her look like an aged Elizabeth Taylor. "But," she continued, "I think it has more to do with the fact that I actually make an effort whereas you're, well, a bit of…"

"A social enigma?"

"…A workaholic hermit."

Because he knew that she was trying to get a rise out of him, he didn't gratify her observation with a response. Instead, he led her to the receiving lounge, made a beeline for an old gentleman who was seated on a big, leather chair, his spectacles perched neatly on the end of his nose. The stuffed, leather chair made him look ridiculously small in contrast.

Ike must have seen them because he gripped the arms of the chair and pushed himself to his feet, the effort showing in the tense set of his fingers against the leather. David didn't try and help him or wave him down back into his seat. If he were eighty, he'd still want to be able to stand and greet people.

"Ike?" David asked as he released his grandmother's hand. "I'm David. It's a pleasure to meet you."

Ike shook his hand firmly, met his eye with a look that said that he was clearly still in charge of his faculties. "It's a pleasure, David," his deep baritone traveled across the cavernous room. "Amanda has told me a lot about you."

David leaned a little closer. "Mostly lies. She turns a blind eye to all of my faults."

Ike chuckled, good-naturedly. "As any good grandmother should."

"David!" his mother called from the doorway. "Could I get your help with something?"

David tried his hardest not to look irritated and failed; Grandma winked. "Ike and I will be fine alone, dear."

"Are you sure?" He felt guilty for abandoning them without even the niceties of small talk, felt irritated at his mother for pulling him away.

She nodded, a small, knowing smile on her face. As David turned away, he heard her say to Ike, "Never understood what my son saw in that woman."

He tried to swallow his grin because the feeling was mutual. Most days he wasn't one hundred percent sure that his mother had given birth to him.

Maybe she hired an egg donor?

Maybe a stork dropped me at the doorstep?

In the back of his mind, he thought he could remember a time when they'd been close, maybe when he'd been too small to remember, but either way, such things had passed.

"What can I do?" he asked when he came to stand beside her.

She frowned at him. "You look tired. Or sad? Is everything alright?"

He nearly took a step back from her but caught himself just in time. Camilla Van den Berg did not talk about emotions. *It's a trap.* She had to be plotting something. "What is it?" David asked, too weary to play along.

She frowned, the lines on her forehead barely creasing despite her sixty-five years. "Patricia Carmichael just arrived with her parents. Show her a good time."

David wondered exactly what his mother's idea of a good time was, but refrained from asking for specifics. He'd be polite...for exactly one hour and thirty-seven more minutes before he made a hasty retreat.

He nodded.

Camilla turned on her heel and led the way.

He followed.

Patricia Carmichael suited her namesake, David decided, after only twenty minutes in her company. She was a petite blonde with blue eyes, ivory skin, and a near-perfect mouth that pouted on cue. When he saw her, he couldn't help but compare her to Ivy with her ridiculously thick, untamable hair, her wide, emerald eyes, heavy lips, killer legs, and secret smile.

Because the thought made him uncomfortable, perhaps even a little sad, he pushed it aside and tried to focus on what Patricia was saying. Something about Syrian children, which he was pretty sure she'd watched on the news only that morning. He'd seen the same segment, down to the statistics that she was now expertly regurgitating in a perfectly cultured monotone.

He nodded politely, tried to keep his eyes focused on her face and not on the fact that Ike was swaying with his grandma on an impromptu dancefloor that they'd made room for by pushing Camilla's expertly-placed Restoration

Hardware coffee table aside. He would have liked to have seen his mother's look of horror, but as he homed in on her standing on the opposite side of the room, he realized she was too preoccupied with her guests to notice.

The picture of his grandmother dancing with her beau made him smile, made him feel like he'd missed the point somehow. He looked down at his third gin and tonic in accusation as if the drink alone had made him miserable.

"Will you excuse me?" he asked Patricia, moving aside before she had a chance to break her exceptionally long monologue. He really wanted to leave now, wanted to be alone with his drink and his thoughts.

He made a beeline for the veranda before she could reply, ignored the volley of daggers that his mother's eyes sent his way when she noticed Patricia Carmichael floundering alone in the large living room, and let himself out into the warm night air.

He drank in the night, felt the fresh air fill his lungs with much-needed perspective. God, he couldn't do it, he realized as he ran a single hand through his hair. He couldn't stand one more minute in there and pretend like he was having a good time. It was bullshit. All of it. He was over forty years old, for God's sake; he shouldn't have to play these games anymore.

"Finally caved, huh?"

David spun around, faced the shadows in the darkened garden. "Dad?" he said, certain of who the voice belonged to, but unsure of exactly where it was coming from.

His father stepped out of the shadows, his hands in the pockets of his linen slacks.

David began to apologize. "I didn't know you were out here. I was ju—"

Michael Van den Berg held up a hand, quietened his son with the gesture. "I get it," he said simply. "What do you think I'm doing?"

101

David nodded uncertainly. "I haven't actually seen you tonight," he said, realizing that it was true. How had he completely missed greeting, or at least having a conversation with his own father?

Michel shrugged. "I was finishing some work in the office and only came down about twenty minutes ago," he offered in explanation. "The Carmichael girl looked about ready to marry you, so I didn't want to disturb."

David shrugged.

"Not your type?"

He sighed. "It would appear as if I don't have a type," he said, giving little thought to his father's opinion. He was tired, he realized. Tired of the games that he no longer had to play.

"I doubt that." Michael came to stand beside him as they looked into the black night. "You just need to be a bit more…open."

David couldn't help it; he laughed. "This coming from the man who told me that emotions wouldn't get me anywhere in life?"

Michael took a step back, had the decency to look offended. "I didn't ever want you to be alone, David. I just wanted you to make good decisions. Good choices. I…" he paused uncertainly, "I wanted to impart my hindsight on you somehow."

David sighed because he knew that he was in a foul mood and was taking it out on his father. Sure, Michael Van den Berg had been absent, but he'd never been cruel or hard. Strict, of course, but never cruel.

"I'm sorry. It would seem as if I'm not much for polite company tonight."

Michael crossed his arms over his chest, his broad shoulders bringing the suit up a few inches at the bottom. "Is it a woman?" he asked, and David could see the curiosity in his blue eyes, even in the dark night.

He focused on his father's face, noticed the greying hair, the ice-blue eyes, and the firm jawline. Despite the grey, he could have been David's older brother.

He ignored the question. "How are you, Dad?"

Michael nodded. "As good as it gets. You?"

"About the same."

"But?"

"I just...I don't know what's wrong with me. Potentially a mid-life crisis."

"So it *is* about a woman," Michael concluded, this time with a small chuckle.

David didn't say anything. He was trying to forget Ivy, really trying to unimagine her waking up alone, unimagine her the moment she'd known he wasn't going to call.

She hadn't called him either, he realized with a pang. She hadn't called to check-in, to figure out if he was interested, to ask where the fuck he was. She'd just assumed that he'd never meant what he'd said to her. Surprisingly, and despite what he'd done, that hurt.

"I fell in love with a woman I'd known for less than two days." He turned to face his father as the words spilled out, horrified by what he'd said, more, by who he'd said them too.

Michael just looked at him, his eyebrows raised. After a beat of silence, he nodded, rocked back on his heels, and whistled. "Must be some girl."

David nodded. "I left. Haven't called her since."

He felt the stab of regret, still unfamiliar with the pain of it. God, he wished he'd handled that better, handled her better. He wished he hadn't been so afraid.

"Why?" his father asked suddenly, his voice unbelieving. When David didn't reply, Michael asked him again, "Why did you leave?"

He thought about what to say, thought about how to phrase it delicately. His mother's crystal laugh distracted him, drew his gaze back to the lounge where people he didn't know filtered about, making polite conversation as they tried to fit in with Camilla Van den Berg's ideal party crowd.

"Ahhh."

His father's affirmation left him feeling guilty, made him feel ashamed for thinking the thought so loudly, at least loud enough for it to be obvious to his father.

"You're worried that you'll end up like your mother and me?" he asked simply. Unbegrudgingly.

David didn't reply. He would have died happy if the world had just swallowed him then, if a stray lightning bolt hurled from Zeus himself and stuck him down on the veranda of his parents' Hacienda-style mansion.

"It's alright," Michael said quietly and reached out a hand. He placed it on David's arm. "You may find this hard to believe, but Camilla and I weren't always like this. We loved each other once. Actually," he chuckled, "sometimes I think we still do."

"Dad…I didn—"

"No, really. It's okay. Our relationship is obvious to anyone who's met us. We just got lost along the way, you know? So wrapped up in doing well, making VP, making MD, making Partner, saving for a lavish retirement. Somehow the…" he tapped his heart a few times, "connection faded."

"I wouldn't change anything," David said, trying to remedy the situation he had hurled them both into. "I like who I am, who I've become. And Mom and you…you're the reason that I'm me."

"Oh," Michael laughed. "I wouldn't change anything either. Neither would your mother" He nudged David. "And that is precisely the problem. But also, precisely why we work together."

David nodded, rubbed the back of his neck awkwardly. What did he say to that, exactly?

"So, this girl? What makes her so special?"

David sighed. "Nothing. Everything…I don't know. I couldn't explain it if I tried. It's purely illogical."

"Sounds like an investment I'd pursue."

"Yeah, me too. But I'm well in the weeds with this one. The situation is unredeemable."

"Really? Jesus. What did you do?"

David sighed. He really didn't want to talk to his father about Ivy. "Nothing that can be remedied. Trust me."

Michael shrugged. "Well, if you're not prepared to try, maybe she wasn't worth it after all, eh?" He turned back towards the house, sighed loudly, and asked, "How about another drink to numb the pain?"

"I'll come in just a moment," David said and turned back to face the grass, not quite ready to talk to Patricia again.

Just as Michael took a step towards the huge, glass doors, towards the lightened room and tinkling laughter, his grandmother stepped outside, leaning her tiny frame on Ike. "There are my two favorite boys."

David tried to smile, tried to ignore the fact that he just wanted to be back in his own home, preferably alone.

"Hi, Mom," Michael said and, as David had done earlier, he wrapped her in a hug, his arms completely covering her from view. "Sorry I haven't said hello yet. I got caught up."

Although she nodded, David caught the glint of steel in her eye, couldn't help but feel sorry for his father even if he was glad that her judgment wasn't directed at him. She was a scary lady when she wanted to be, and David had been on the receiving end of her criticism more than once.

"I'll go and greet my guests now," Michael said sheepishly. David noticed that he at least had the dignity to look ashamed as he ducked inside the house.

Amanda turned to him, her frown transforming into an affectionate smile so fluidly that David blinked.

Ike laughed. "You're good," he said simply.

She chuckled and raked a hand through her short hair. "Eighty-five years of practice."

"Eighty-four," David corrected her as she had done to him just thirty minutes earlier.

Ike laughed and moved forward to look out at the huge yard. "Well, Amanda, you didn't exaggerate. This is splendid."

"I know." She looked at David then. "Sometimes I just wished that my son had more than a big house to his name."

Ike didn't reply. David grinned because he knew where she was going, knew that she wasn't being coy. She was parenting. Filling in where his own mother and father should have a good twenty years earlier.

He took her hand and led her closer to Ike, waited for the man to turn so that he was included in the conversation. "I will make a concerted effort to live more and worry about my career less," he said and crossed his heart over his shirt, as, he remembered, he'd seen Ivy do once.

She laughed. "I just don't want you to end up like Michael. Do you understand?"

He nodded.

"I want you to have what Daniel and I had. What Ike and Faye had," she added, turning to Ike and giving his hand a squeeze. "People *matter*, David."

"I know, Grandma."

A small part of him wanted to tell her about Ivy, wanted to tell her that he had already made the biggest mistake of his life, lost the only girl he'd met that he'd wanted to pursue. He didn't. She was eighty-four years old; she had enough to think about without taking on his sadness, without taking on his regret.

Besides, he felt ridiculous. He'd already told his father that he loved her, which was insane. He'd only met her twice, or did it count as three times? Either way, love was impossible given the parameters. Well, it was *at least* improbable.

"What is it?" she asked. She raised a hand to touch his cheek. "You look old, David."

He laughed, a short bark at the honest way that she said it. "Wow, Grandma."

She shrugged. "It's the truth." She waved her hand in his general direction. "Seeing you this stressed flares up my angina."

Ike shifted from foot to foot and David had the sense that he was tired. He turned towards the house without commenting, and gave his grandmother his arm so that Ike wouldn't have to, "Shall we?"

She smiled, unoffended, and, taking the cue, looped her arm through his, making sure to keep abreast of Ike as they walked inside, each of them prepared to play nice for a little while longer before making excuses—for very different reasons.

Chapter 8

Ivy plastered on a smile and met her client's eyes. They were a soft hazel, a warm brown that seemed sincere, even though she knew that he had just broken up with a nearly-famous model and, almost certainly, wanted to pretend he was unaffected. Blasé. Moving on.

He could have been a model himself, Ivy thought and gave him a quick once-over. He was tall, maybe six-one or two, with a swimmers' build; lean and rangy. His shoulder-length chestnut hair fell in gentle waves and made him look more like a Spanish actor than the Kansas-raised McKnight Consultant she knew him to be.

"So, have you been here before?" he asked, clearly looking for a way to break the tension as he focused on the menu.

She sighed and picked up the same menu, tried not to roll her eyes. "I have," she said. "I came with a girlfriend last year."

Oliver looked up at her, let out a long breath. "I'm sorry. I…I've never done this before."

She put the menu down without looking at it, ready with the speech that she has rehearsed, delivered, and refined for eighteen months now. "You're doing great. Just relax and pretend that we're childhood friends going to grab a drink before we meet our spouses for dinner." *Cool the patronizing tone. Jesus.*

He smiled as if encouraged. "My childhood best friend…You sounded just like her then. She gets so high and mighty about anything she had a solid opinion on. It was— *is* downright irritating."

She laughed, genuinely pleased by the comparison. "She sounds like someone I'd hang out with." She raised her hand subtly to catch the waiter's attention.

"Yeah, she's everyone's favorite."

When he fell silent, Ivy glanced at him, noticed the faraway look in his eyes. "She's special?"

He nodded distractedly and gave her a half-hearted smile. She didn't reply, choosing instead to give him time to sort his thoughts. Finally, he looked at her and leaned forward, placing both of his elbows on the table. "Can I tell the truth?" he asked, his brown eyes wide and concerned.

She nodded.

"I'm in love with my childhood best friend and she doesn't know. She still calls me 'Bro' and walks around in her underwear in front of me like we're five years old."

Ivy tried hard not to giggle at the look of pure horror on his face.

He smiled when she pursed her lips together, grinned outright when her shoulders started shaking. "I can see that you find my predicament entertaining?"

She laughed, then shook her head as if denying his accusation. "I…." She wiped her eyes. "I just…don't know what to say." She held up a hand, caught her breath. "Why are you trying to make the model angry if you're in love with the childhood friend?"

He sat back in his chair. "How did you know that Valentine isn't the childhood best friend?"

She smiled. "Just a hunch."

He glanced at the waiter as he approached. Ivy watched him order. He was an expert. He ordered the wine first—an expensive French vintage, which he specifically asked to be decanted—then moved on to two light appetizers, one pasta, and one protein. He ate well; that was for sure.

When he looked back at her, she felt her mood lighten. He was in love with someone else and, clearly, wasn't interested in her. That made her job easier. She'd be the shoulder to cry on. The ear to lend. And then she'd go home and curl into bed with a couple of sleeping pills and lucid dreams.

"So, what are you going to do about it?" Ivy asked, genuinely interested in the love triangle. "You say that you love the homegirl, but you're dating other women? Escorts?"

He flushed a little, broke eye contact, and looked towards the open kitchen where the staff buzzed incessantly. "I can't sum up the courage to tell her," he said. "I've been in love with Hannah since I was a kid."

"And you don't care about the model's feelings in all this?"

He had the dignity to look offended, but still sighed, defeated. "She doesn't care."

Ivy nodded, aware of the fact that the couple's break-up had been very public and very...final. "But...why? I mean, if she doesn't care, then why all the effort?"

He smiled. "I don't know. It's...expected. If I have a new girl, the media will assume that there's no story. No heartbreak. Maybe they'll post one story about how we've moved on, but then it'll die down. Finally, be over." He looked relieved at the prospect.

"Wait. The model knows about this?" she asked, indicating between them.

He nodded and laughed, held up his hands. "I'm sorry. We just thought it'd be easier if you didn't know." He rubbed his chin. "You're just way more intuitive and easier to talk to than I'd anticipated."

Ivy couldn't help but grin. She rolled her eyes for good measure. "As long as you're paying me, I don't care."

"Truth again?" he said. "If I wasn't madly in love with someone else, I'd be trying my hardest right now." When she grinned, he added, "But I hope that we can still have a good time?"

"Are you kidding? A good-looking man who wants to pay for my dinner and not sleep with me is my best-case scenario."

"That's reasonable," he said on a laugh.

Feeling uncannily comfortable with him, she asked, "Do you mind if I ask a personal question?"

"Shoot."

"You're young, successful, good looking…" she trailed off as she tried to think about how to phrase her thoughts.

"Why didn't I just actually date someone? Instead of hiring you?" he filled in for her.

She nodded.

"It seemed wrong to date someone who I had no intention of actually staying with, whereas you…you knew the parameters beforehand, you won't judge me, and, if I'm being totally honest, I'm assuming the hole Antoinette has left in my pocket can be corked with a big wad of discretion."

"Of course." Ivy smiled. "We'd be out of work very quickly if that wasn't a given. Escorting is still surprisingly taboo."

"Which makes zero sense to me," he replied, waving his hand in front of him to show his frustration. "I understand that you're not a prostitute…"

She conceded his point with a nod. "I'm luckier than a lot of women who need the money."

"Exactly. But *if* prostitution were legal, we'd be giving the power back to the women."

"Eradicating pimps."

"Men might get married later in life. Women would have more time to focus on their careers."

"Legislation would help keep women in the business safe, would regulate the standard of their working conditions."

"Allow them to access health care without fear of criminal charges," he said, his eyes glinting. "So why haven't we done it?"

"Because our lawmakers, law enforcers, and yes, even the people who run the companies that make our bras and tampons, are predominantly male.

"Men are pigs."

Ivy couldn't help it; she laughed, bringing a flashing smile to Oliver's handsome face.

When the wine arrived, the waiter poured the smallest amount into the glass in front of Oliver. He swirled it, raised the glass to his nose for a quick sniff before taking a sip. He smiled at the waiter, nodded, and the man filled Ivy's glass before topping Oliver's.

Ivy did the same with her wine. She was pleasantly surprised by the pinot noir. It was medium-bodied and fruit-forward; although, not what she usually would have ordered for herself, she liked it. She said as much to Oliver.

"You know your wines then?" he asked as the first appetizer was put in front of them.

She thought about his question, thought about the countless expensive dinners that she'd been to over the past year and a half. The experience had upped her expectations in weird ways, ways that she had never thought about before, including the quality of the wine on her shelf at home. "I would say that I know enough to have a conversation, but not pass the first Sommelier test," she finally said.

He tilted his head and looked at her, the movement making his hair fall forward ever-so-slightly into his face. She couldn't help but sigh at the picture he made, all broad shoulders and dark, sexy features.

"That's really all one needs to know about wine," he added. He took a bite of the appetizer in front of him, pushed around the last piece on his plate. "So, any advice for me?"

Because Ivy could see that he was pining, she asked, "Is Hannah back in Kansas?"

He shook his head. "We came to LA fifteen years ago for our undergrad at UCLA. She lives a few streets down from me—actually, now that I think about it, she's always lived a few streets down from me."

"Is she single?"

He frowned. "I don't know. She always has men sniveling around her, but doesn't seem to like any one staying too long." He met her eyes. "Can you see why I'm petrified?"

"I think you've got to stop trying to make her jealous," she said with a small shake of her head. "I know this little show is technically for the model's benefit, but if your best friend loves you too, she probably thinks you're just a really big asshole at this point."

Oliver laughed, raked a large, tanned hand through his hair. "So, after tonight, what? Just tell her I'm taking time to be single and…?"

"And spend as much time as possible with her. Woo her. Take her by surprise!" She laughed when he grinned. "Women love romance."

"Well…" he shrugged, "you have me convinced that I have to try anyway."

"Being scared of falling short of someone else's bar is natural. But regretting that you never tried, never truly put yourself out there is worse. *And* you'll only have yourself to blame for it."

He raised his glass. "To hoping like hell that I don't fall short."

She clinked her glass to his and was about to ask him another question when she noticed his eyes were squinting at something behind her. Ivy was just about to turn and see what he was staring at when he said, "I think that's a colleague of mine. Our firms worked together about a year or so ago…"

He raised his hand, waved when whoever he was looking at saw him. "You'll like this guy, Diana. He's really intense but also surprisingly cool." He glanced away from her again, stood, moved past her chair, and held out his hand. "David! What are the chances?"

Ivy felt the world tilt on its axis, slowly put her wine glass down so that she didn't spill it. She told herself that David was a really common name even as the hair on the back of her neck rose. Plastering a casual smile onto her face, she turned to where Oliver stood just behind her chair.

Yeah, not so lucky.

"Diana, this is David. David, Diana," Oliver said, completely missing the fact that David stared down at her as if she was a rabid wolf about to tear his throat out, his blue eyes wide with surprise.

The thought made her feel strangely calm. Because she was an adult, and a professional, she pushed back her chair and stood, took a single step so that she effectively joined them. "Hi, David. How have you been?" She held out her hand, trying not to grimace when he took it gently, sending small tingles of awareness up her arm.

"Oh, you two know each other?" Oliver asked, his big, brown eyes wide with curiosity as he glanced from her to David.

David flushed. Ivy smiled and met Oliver's hazel gaze. "Yes. We met at an event a few months ago," she said, lying easily.

David dropped her hand. "How are you?" he asked, tucking his hands into the pockets of his slacks as if he could wipe off the feeling of her. For some strange reason, she felt both disappointed and relieved that he hadn't gone in for a hug. She both wanted and was afraid of physical contact with him. She knew that if she took one step closer, she'd smell the oak and leather scent of him.

So she didn't.

"Doing well. You?" she asked, inwardly cringing at how stale the small talk was.

She noticed Oliver seemed to be catching on to how awkward the situation was because he chimed in with, "We should get a drink sometime, David. Catch up."

David nodded, said, "I'd like that," but he didn't break eye contact with Ivy.

She felt her body tighten inadvertently, hated herself for blushing when she felt the blood warm her cheeks. How was it possible that he made her feel like this even after what he'd done? She'd have thought that her lady parts would have at least had the dignity to not be attracted to him, even if he was as perfect as she remembered.

"I'll see you both around, I'm sure," he said suddenly. He smiled at Oliver.

"Yeah, I'm at the same number so give me a call."

David nodded, looked at her. "Diana. Oliver," he said simply, her fake name slipping off his tongue fluidly.

He walked away.

She breathed a sigh of relief when he opened the door and exited the restaurant, felt her stomach unravel from the knot that had been bunched there. She didn't so much as move, afraid that her legs would give out for a second, afraid that she'd burst into tears. Once she had composed herself, she turned back to Oliver, who stood at her side, staring down at her.

"What was that about?" he asked as he pulled her chair out for her.

She sat. "What do you mean?" she replied, trying to be blasé, forcing her eyes forward instead of glancing back to see if he was still there.

"Come on! David is like the...Yoda of socializing. It's an art to him, a game even. It's common knowledge that it's the exact skill that's going to get him promoted ahead of his peers. But he didn't know his head from his foot around you. What did you do to him?" he asked, leaning forward on the table eagerly.

Ivy laughed at the hungry look in his eye. "Nothing," she said. "I was ah, escorting someone at a work event of his and I think he wasn't sure how he felt about it."

"Oh." Oliver leaned back in his chair, disappointed. "I thought more along the lines of you loved each other and couldn't figure it out." Ivy felt the blood rush through her ears, stared at him as he added, "All this Hannah stuff is making me think that everyone must be going through the same thing."

"You'll figure it out," she said with a forced smile, deliberately ignoring the way her pulse kicked in her throat. "Just be you."

The entrée was put in front of them and they ate, chatted, and laughed even though each one of them was completely buried by thoughts of someone else. Ivy knew that he wouldn't notice her distraction through his own and let her thoughts wander back to David.

He looked good, she realized. He looked like he hadn't lost any sleep over the past two months. The knowledge that he'd probably moved on without another thought made her slightly angry. She had spent weeks waiting for him to call; she hadn't even taken work in those weeks because she knew he wouldn't want to share her time with other men. She'd lost sleep over him, she realized with no small amount of self-disgust.

Well, no more. She'd move on. She'd erase him from her mind completely. Besides, she added, she only had to do this for a couple more weeks. Then it would all be over. She could genuinely just be a patent attorney by day. And sleep by night.

God, sleep sounds so good.

Oliver had fallen silent, and the waiter swooped in to clear away their plates. "So, what's your first step going to be with Hannah?"

He grinned. "I'm thinking start slow and see where it takes us. Take her to a Dodgers game or something we'd usually do together."

Oliver dropped her at the bar where she was meeting Damien, made sure to get out of the car and hug her goodbye. "Thanks. Especially for coming out with me on a Wednesday night."

Ivy tilted her head and looked up at him. "It was nice to meet you, Oliver." She smiled at him. "I hope things work out with Hannah."

"I hope things work out with David," he replied and took a step back, grinning at her wide-eyed surprise. "Come on, that sexual tension was hard to ignore," he added as he walked around the hood of his Audi. "And, not that you know me or trust me, but I promise that David is the best type of guy. You deserve that."

Ivy looked after him as he pulled away from the curb, trying hard not to frown. How could it have been that obvious to a stranger? She had played it off so well. Or, so she'd thought.

She sighed and turned down the street, her vision narrowing on the single door of the bar only fifty feet away. It was a basement bar; one of those cool, trendy, underground spots that was obscured, or rather completely unmarked, from the street. Ivy tucked her purse under her arm, focused on the dark sidewalk as she picked her way over the broken, uneven pavement in her spiked heels.

She had only agreed to meet Damien there when she and Oliver had wrapped up dinner before nine. She could have one night-cap with her best friend before Ubering home for the night. Besides, it was only two days until the weekend, and she had no dates lined up for either Friday or Saturday so that she could finally catch up on some much-needed sleep.

Ivy saw the door up ahead, hesitated for a moment, wondering if she had the right spot. Unmarked was one thing, but this place looked totally abandoned. And shouldn't there be a bouncer outside? Or maybe he stood inside to add to the post-apocalyptic effect?

She shrugged, took a step forward, and hesitated when she felt someone come up close behind her. For only a second, she thought it was Damien, half-turned to greet him right before a sharp shove sent her falling forward towards the curb.

She saw the edge of the raised curb rushing towards her face, tried to untangle her hands from the straps of her purse as her head hit the edge of the pavement and the world went black.

"Miss? Miss, can you hear me?"

Ivy heard the voice and, even though it sounded like it was coming from far away, she knew that the man who was speaking to her knelt at her side because his hands trailed, feather-light, over her face.

She tried to open her eyes, felt a heavy thumping in her head, and opted to keep them closed for just a second longer. "I can hear you," she said quietly. She could also smell the pavement and the scent of stale beer, or urine— she didn't want to overthink it—brought bile to the back of her throat.

"The ambulance is coming," he said. "Just stay still; try not to move."

She sighed, forced her eyes open to look up at the young man who knelt over her.

Her first thought was that he had the reddest hair she'd ever seen. Her second was that he'd called an ambulance. "I don't think I need an ambulance," she said clearly. How much exactly did one have to pay out-of-pocket for a single ambulance ride anyway? She had no idea, but she was guessing it wasn't cheap.

The man chuckled, his eyes crinkling with what she would have called relief. "Either way, you're getting one. You hit the corner of the pavement," he said. "I was hoping that you hadn't broken your neck."

Ivy tensed her body, tried to push herself into a seated position, and felt the world swirl uncomfortably.

"Whoa, just relax." In the distance, Ivy could hear the wail of sirens.

Great.

"What happened?" she asked as she came to lean on her elbows. Her vision was leveling out, and she felt like she might be able to stand. She drew her legs in, trying to hide her exposed thighs from a group of onlookers who peered down at her nervously, and felt a sharp twinge in her left knee that almost sent her back down to the ground.

"We were just on the other side of the street, and we saw it all!"

"A man followed you and pushed you as he grabbed your purse," another person, a young brunette woman, said, her eyes nervously glancing down the street as if the man might still be hovering nearby. "He took off running the minute you were down."

Ivy looked around where she lay, noticed that her purse was gone. She just sighed; there was nothing she could do about that.

She managed to push herself into a seated position with the help of the man, who introduced himself as Gregory. By the time a police car pulled up to the curb, she had just gotten her feet under her, leaning heavily on his arm.

"You okay?" the first policeman asked, his hand outstretched to steady her.

She nodded. "Yes, thank you. I…I don't think I need the ambulance," she added, right as the fire department's first responders arrived, the lights on the bright red ambulance spinning in a haze of electric red, telling everybody in a five-hundred-yard radius that she had been hurt.

Fuck.

He grinned at her. "Too late."

She smiled because it seemed as if she didn't have a choice, waited for the medic to walk up to her, and support her weight as he led her back to the ambulance where he pulled out a low stretcher and told her to sit.

"What's your name?" the Policeman asked, a small notepad in his hand.

He introduced himself as Officer Chapman and Ivy gave him her details as the paramedic checked her over, told him that she hadn't seen what happened at all, and deferred to Gregory to tell the story. He nodded. "Morales," he said, calling over the over officer who had been hovering nearby, "take the witnesses' statements."

Morales nodded.

"Could you give me a description of the items in your purse?" he asked. When she nodded, he added, "We'll let you know if we recover anything, but in most cases like this, we try to prepare you for the fact that whatever was in there is gone for good."

She nodded, felt a small thread of panic lodge in her throat when the realization hit her. She'd been mugged. Worse, she'd been physically assaulted; although come to think of it, she wasn't sure that knocking oneself out on the pavement counted as assault. "I didn't have anything that I can't afford to lose," she said. Her cellphone contacts were saved on her Apple cloud and she could cancel her credit cards using her bank's emergency phone line. Other than that, she didn't keep anything important in there.

Officer Chapman nodded. "There's not much more you can do to help, so I'm going to let the medics take over from here. We'll call you if we find anything."

He left her a number that she could reach the police at if she thought of anything that she could add to her statement or had any questions, then left to go and join Morales with the witnesses.

Ivy turned to face the medic who was currently turning her knee gently left and right. She couldn't help but flush when she noticed he was at her crotch level and her little black dress had crept up her thighs to expose just the tiniest bit of her black underwear.

She winced when he turned her leg further to the right, felt her leg tense against the movement.

"That hurt?" he asked and looked up at her.

Ivy felt her embarrassment warm her cheeks. Of course, he was gorgeous, with close-cropped blond hair, expressive green eyes, and wide, strong palms. *Perfect.* She nodded. "Sorry, I just wasn't expecting it."

She shifted, tried unsuccessfully to shimmy her dress down a bit more, tensed against the pain that her movement caused.

"It's impossible to say without an X-ray, but if I went on the swelling alone, I'd say that you've partially or completely torn your ACL," he was saying. "It's a ligament in your knee that essentially connects your thighbone to your shinbone."

She nodded. She didn't know exactly what the implications of the injury were. But she knew that it wasn't good.

"You almost definitely have a concussion and are going to have one heck of a shiner," he said, still crouched at her feet.

"Can I go home?" she asked.

He shook his head. "I'm really sorry, Ivy. You need to have that leg looked at, need to be put on pain meds, and possibly even crutches. And that's without the monitoring for the concussion."

"So, hospital?" she asked with a sigh.

He sent her a small smile that lit up his green eyes. "Trauma center. And probably only for ten or so hours. It's not that bad, I promise."

She flushed, looked down at her swollen knee. "Just not the way I wanted to end the night."

"Big plans?"

She smiled. "Not really. No."

"Hey, Ivy!" Gregory called as he came trotting over to her, her black, spiked heels in his hands. "You left these on the sidewalk."

She took them from him, noticed that the paramedic was chuckling. "Thanks for the help, Gregory," she said, looking up into his kind, young face.

He blushed, the red flush spreading up his pale neck, across his freckled face to his ears. "Yeah. Good luck with the recovery," he offered and walked away with one last glance behind him.

"I think he's in love," the medic joked.

Ivy chuckled. "He'll get over it."

He stood up from his perch on the ground and she realized why he'd remained kneeling. Standing up, he towered over her. He must have been six-foot-seven with shoulders as broad as a refrigerator. "Alright, let's get going then." He tapped the side of the bright red ambulance and a small Asian woman hopped out of the driver's seat and walked to where they stood.

She looked at Ivy and smiled. "Transport?"

He nodded. "LA Trauma." He shot her a wink. "Nothing she won't come back from."

They helped her into the ambulance, allowed her to sit rather than lie on the stretcher, and even had a conversation with her as they drove her to LA Trauma. The woman, Lisa, was a five-year EMT with the fire department but had served as a nurse for four years in Iraq before that. The man, Nick, had been an EMT in LA for ten years before joining the LAFD. They both loved their jobs, but apparently, calls like hers were the easiest.

"Although," Nick said as he turned to look back at her, "usually it's a drunk sorority girl at USC falling down the stairs, not someone getting pushed in a mugging."

Lisa grunted. "Sorority girls are the worst."

Ivy laughed. "It sounds like your job is never boring," she offered, not feeling envious at all. She had heard the horror stories, knew that medics faced terrible situations amongst the silly calls like hers.

Nick nodded. "Oh, just an FYI, they'll let you call your next-of-kin from the hospital," he said. "We don't like to get into a habit of doing it from here."

"That's okay. Thanks," she replied, not willing to voice the fact that she had nobody. Oh, she'd let Damien know why she hadn't shown up and he'd come right over. She knew that much. But she had no parents to call, no boyfriend to meet her at the hospital. No one.

Do not cry. Do not cry. Do not cry.

Lifting her fingers to her face, she touched a hand to the tender spot around her right temple and eye and winced.

"So, what's the story going to be?" Nick asked, looking back at her from the front as Lisa drove.

She met his eyes, grateful for the distraction. "What do you mean?"

"Bar fight?" Lisa volunteered. "That always sounds badass coming from a girl."

"Or really tacky?" Nick said with a chuckle. "I don't know any girls that get into bar fights."

"How about...bad landing skydiving?" Lisa suggested.

Ivy chuckled. "You know, that's not bad. Maybe I'll steal it."

"Honestly," Nick said, "getting mugged outside of a club is pretty hardcore to begin with."

Lisa indicated and turned into the ambulance entrance of LA Trauma. "I actually agree. That's a pretty cool story."

"Yeah," Ivy said. "I'd probably milk it if half my face wasn't purple and I could walk without someone else helping me."

They laughed.

Chapter 9

He glanced down at the screen of his phone for the thousandth time since he'd sent her the message the day before and frowned when his notifications showed no new messages.

No reply.

Nothing.

He felt a small stab of panic and flipped the phone back over, letting it sit on the corner of his desk as he turned back to the spreadsheets on the computer screen in front of him.

If she didn't want to ever speak to him again, well, he couldn't blame her, but he'd be disappointed. He thought about the message he'd sent. It had been simple; an apology for the way he'd behaved with a brief invite out on Friday so that he could explain. Although, even now, five hours before he'd suggested they meet, he wasn't quite sure what his explanation was supposed to be. He couldn't exactly tell her the truth, because 'Hey, I fell in love with you after I'd known you for only two days, and freaked out after we had sex' sounded…crazy.

So what was he supposed to tell her? If she even showed. Which, at least at this stage, looked improbable.

Hey, Ivy, I haven't been able to stop thinking about you.

I know that we barely know each other, but I miss seeing you.

Frustrated because nothing sounded adequate, he cast a glance at the clock on his desk. Three in the afternoon on a Friday seemed like dead time to him. The office was quiet as people buckled down in a push to get as much done as possible before the weekend. Looking outside his glass, office walls, he noticed that all of the analysts had their heads bent over their dual monitors, intent on what they were doing.

He frowned and dialed his secretary.

"Sir?" she answered immediately.

"Tammy, have them open a ten-thousand-dollar tab at The Cask on Eighth Street. I forgot to ask you earlier. HR approved it already."

"Yes, Sir," she replied, unsurprised.

"Then send an email out to everyone in IB saying that Happy Hour starts at five o'clock."

"Yes, Sir. Single drink price cap? Or, all drinks covered?" she clarified.

"All drinks. Thank you, Tam."

"Of course, Mr. Van den Berg."

Once she'd hung up, he sat back in his chair, opened his email, and waited for the news from Tammy. As soon as it hit his inbox, he glanced up, after a few moments saw one, then another of the analyst's make eye contact and grin.

He smiled.

He remembered what it had been like to put in six fifteen-hour days and feel like nobody cared or noticed. It was hard. A near-impossible career path that most analysts only ever intended to do for a couple of years so that they could add it to their resumes as a calling card.

He remembered the feeling of his hamstrings cramping from sitting for ten hours straight; although, that had been before standing desks. He remembered looking at his body in the mirror and being horrified by how out of shape he had gotten, but being too tired to do anything about it. He also remembered putting in a God-awful week and then having an email pop into his mailbox last thing on a Friday saying that a free-for-all happy hour started at five. Pure unbridled joy.

Picking up his phone again, he saw that he still had no messages. He tapped his fingers impatiently on his desk and, realizing that his spreadsheet was going to go untended until he heard from her, he dialed Ivy's number. It didn't even ring. It went straight to voicemail. He frowned at the phone, wondered if she'd blocked his number. *Probably.*

He considered calling her again, even pulled her number up, and stared at it. He was about to dial when another idea came to mind. Rummaging through his desk, he found the single un-itemized receipt with a neat fifteen-thousand-dollar sum hand-written on it, flipped it over, and read the number off the back.

"Antoinette Rupetta. How may I help you?"

David leveled his voice. "Antoinette, this is David Van den Berg."

"Mr. Van den Berg," she replied, immediately switching to her practiced business voice. "How may I help you?"

"Is Ivy free tonight?" he asked. He knocked his knuckles nervously on the table when he heard her sigh over the phone, not even bothering to check.

"I'm sorry, Mr. Van den Berg. Ivy is…unavailable. Could I suggest someone else? Someone just as competent?"

He closed his eyes, tried to stifle his disappointment. "No, thank you. It would have to be Ivy." He realized how stalker-like that sounded and added, "The people I'm meeting know her."

Antoinette cleared her throat. "We're hoping that she's able to come back in a few weeks if that helps at all?"

He opened his eyes, a small shiver of alarm running the length of his spine. He had heard something in her voice. "Is…is she okay?"

"Oh, yes! Just fine!" Her voice on the other end of the phone sounded too high-pitched, too cheery. "She just had a small scare, that's all. But she was released from the hospital yesterday, so there's nothing to be alarmed about."

David hung up on Antoinette Rupetta's second offer to find a replacement and grabbed his jacket off the back of his chair.

Tammy glanced up at him as he made for the elevator. "I have a family emergency. Please make sure that the analysts behave at the Happy Hour," he said, and finished with, "Close the tab at ten," as he pushed the down button.

"Anything I can do?" she asked, her blue eyes creased with concern.

"I don't think so. Thank you." He didn't wait for her to reply as he stepped into the elevator with four other people, his jacket swung over one shoulder.

His chest was tight with panic and he had to actively refrain from taking a deep breath to try and calm himself. Something had happened to Ivy. Something bad enough that she'd wound up in the hospital. He had a single moment where he remembered her smiling happily up at Oliver Murphey, a look of genuine happiness in her eyes. Could Oliver have hurt her?

He dismissed the thought instantly. He knew Oliver. Not well and only in a business setting, but he knew him well enough to know that he'd never hit a woman. The thought made him pause, made him wonder if she'd even been hurt by a man. She could have been bumped by a car crossing the street or fallen off a ladder changing a lightbulb. So, why did he assume that one of her dates had hurt her?

He frowned, noticed an analyst standing next to him take a solid step back, adding distance between them. He forced himself to show a neutral expression, ignored the analyst, and thought about what the hell he was doing.

He was going to show up at a girl's door and demand that she tell him what had happened to her, demand to know who had hurt her. He stepped into the underground parking garage from the elevator and made a beeline for his Porsche.

She's not just any girl though.

She was Ivy. And she'd been hurt. He knew that she would close the door in his face if he showed up guns blazing. The knowledge that he'd deserve it didn't ease his anxiety, but it did make him take a step back, re-strategize his approach, think about what he'd say that might make her tell him what had happened. He did know that, despite what she said, if a man had hurt her, he'd personally see that the bastard suffered for raising a hand to her. No, he corrected, for raising a hand to a woman. Period.

He pulled onto the street, gripped the steering wheel, and sped away from his office building towards Koreatown.

Damien heard the knock again and frowned at the door. As far as he knew, they weren't expecting anyone. Louie was visiting his parents in Missouri and, well, Ivy didn't have many visitors these days. Between both her jobs and her visits to her father, the girl barely had time to sleep, let alone make friends.

He glanced towards her bedroom, making sure that she hadn't been disturbed. She hadn't left the apartment in over twenty-four hours, and to be quite honest, Damien didn't blame her. She looked like shit. One side of her face had turned a splotchy blue and purple and the residual swelling had forced her right eye closed. Her left knee was swollen so big that he'd had to help her into baggy sweatpants, and she had been using a crutch to hobble from her bed to the sofa and back, too sore and, well, too proud to go out and about, looking like the victim in a serious domestic violence dispute.

He padded over to the door, opened it quietly, and stopped just shy of stepping outside, his body blocking the doorway. He recognized the man, recognized the tall, athletic build, square jawline, and impossibly blue eyes from the photo that Ivy had shown him. He also remembered that Ivy had said she'd made a mistake by trusting him and that she never wanted to see him again.

"Can I help you?" Damien asked, feigning ignorance.

The man frowned down at him, cold blue eyes assessing his black skinny jeans with haphazardly slashed knees, his white tank top, and black converse. Damien stood his ground, didn't cower or flush. He raised his eyebrows when the man just stared at him as if calculating how much energy it'd take to physically move him out of the way. He figured not much; the stranger had a good few inches and at least fifty pounds on him, most of which was muscle.

"Is Ivy in?" he asked, finally.

Damien leaned in the doorway, watched the man's eyes narrow at the gesture. "Who's asking?"

"David Van den Berg. I'm a friend of hers."

Damien shook his head. "Uh-uh. I'm her *best* friend. I know everyone that she'd want to see right now." He took a step back inside, fully prepared to close the door in the stranger's face.

The man, David, held up a hand. "Look," he said slowly as if speaking to a slightly slow dog. "I...I went on a date with Ivy, two actually, and I...I left and didn't call."

Damien frowned. He knew that Ivy had been paid a lot for the effort, but also knew that she had been legitimately offended by David Van den Berg, knew that she had refused to tell him, her best friend, the details. He glanced at the man's face, saw the slight panic in his eyes.

He sighed. "Can I give her a message?" he asked, his curiosity piqued. "She's not doing too well, and she literally went to lie down ten minutes ago."

David shook his head. "I can wait in my car. Just call me when she wakes up? Please?"

He looked so sincere for a split second that Damien felt genuine sorrow for him. He wondered what was going on, and if Ivy knew that the investment banker had a more-than-crush on her. If Damien could hazard a guess, he'd say David Van den Berg was downright smitten. When he nodded, David turned to go. He groaned and said, "Hey!" When David turned to face him, he added, "If you're actually a friend, you should wait inside." He indicated the apartment with his head. "She might be out for a while."

David looked towards his Porsche as if unsure and then shrugged and climbed the few stairs again. "Thank you; although, you should know that she probably won't be happy to see me."

Damien nodded. He had figured as much.

He closed the door behind them, watched as David put his hands in his slacks, and glanced towards Ivy's bedroom. Interesting, Damien thought, that he knew exactly which room was hers. Although Ivy slept with the occasional client, she *never* ever brought them home.

Damien walked to the sofa, picked the blanket that Ivy had been using up, and folded it so that their guest had room to sit.

"Do you know what happened?"

Damien turned to look at him, struggled to maintain the intense eye-contact that seemed to be Van den Berg's M.O. He shrugged. "She was mugged waiting outside a bar for me, tripped and hit her head on the edge of the curb, tore her left ACL."

David looked at him. "It wasn't a date, then?"

Damien glanced up, surprised by the vehemence in the tone. "You thought that she was…hurt by a client?"

David looked away, but even in the dimly lit apartment, Damien could see the rigid set of his clenched jaw, the fists bunched tightly at his sides. "I wasn't sure."

"It's a rational assumption given the situation," he replied, trying to be nonchalant. "It was my first thought too."

David nodded, sat down on the sofa. "I'm sorry," he said, turning, "I never got your name?"

"Damien."

"Nice to meet you."

Damien nodded. "Can I get you a drink?"

"That would be great. Thanks."

"Red wine, okay?"

"Perfect," David replied.

Damien walked into the kitchen and pulled two glasses from the cabinet, filled them both halfway, and carried one to David. He would be lying to himself if he said he wasn't curious. As far as he knew, Ivy hadn't spoken to David in months, and things hadn't ended well. Yet, within thirty hours of her being seriously hurt, David had come to check-in on her, come to see if another man had hurt her.

It was fascinating. And it raised a lot of questions. Questions that Damien was dying to know the answers to.

He sat on the other side of the sofa, crossed his ankle over his knee, mirroring David's posture. "So," he asked, "why does it matter to you?"

David had the dignity to look shocked at his blunt question, maybe even offended. He leaned back into the sofa and stared back at him, clearly not used to being spoken to so frankly. When Damien didn't budge, again, he sighed. "I…care about Ivy. I just want to make sure that she's safe."

"How can you care about someone you only went on a few dates with?" Damien asked, again not bothering to mask his tone with polite overtures. "*Paid* dates, I might add."

This time, David chuckled morosely. "I have no fucking idea." He raked his hand through thick blond hair, turned to look back at Damien with complete fear in his eyes, "She stumped me from the get-go."

The answer surprised him, and Damien chuckled at the unexpected honesty, smiled when David shook his head and took a big sip of the wine.

"Last question before we revert to small talk?" Damien asked.

He shrugged. "Sure."

"Why didn't you call after you slept with her?"

David's head shot up like he'd seen a ghost, his blue eyes boring into Damien's face. "She told you?"

He shook his head. "You glanced at her door when you came in. Instantly. No question about which was hers."

David frowned at the easy answer, knew that he couldn't deny it. He sat back. "I...I don't know. I was watching her sleep and...I panicked. I freaked out." He strummed his fingers on his knee. "I've never felt this way," he said, swirling the wine in his glass. "Never wanted to feel this way for anyone. Never thought I could if I'm totally honest."

Damien nodded. "And the escorting thing bothered you? Made you question how legitimate she was?"

"I thought that was your last question," David returned immediately, but grinned to take the sting out of his words. He looked towards her closed door once more, then nodded. "The idea of her being with anyone else doesn't settle easy. And, before you ask, I've hired escorts before, even dated seriously, and no, none of them mattered. But Ivy...is different."

"So, she scares the shit out of you?"

"Pretty much," David replied and leaned back again on a long exhale. "More than anything I've ever faced before."

Damien raised his eyebrows. Scratch smitten, he realized, this man was in love. Like *in love* in love. Head over heels, even.

"It's not my place to say..." he started.

"But?"

"Do you know she didn't go on a single job after your last date?" When David shook his head, he added, "Yeah, for like two weeks. I thought she was sick, or pregnant," he laughed.

When David's head whipped up, Damien held up a hand. "That was a bad joke."

Over an hour after he had arrived, David sat next to Damien on the sofa and talked about the state of the US government. He hadn't had much faith in Ivy's roommate in the beginning but had soon had to reposition and defend his quasi-conservative ideals in an unexpected battle of wit.

The guy was bright, David realized. Really bright. He quoted legislation like a computer, recalled the exact words that politicians had spoken years ago, posed theoretical scenarios grounded in the philosophy of Marcus Aurelius, and generally left David feeling like he'd have to study for their next conversation. He still didn't quite believe that Damien, with his ripped jeans and tank top, was a professor, even if he did teach theater at a community college.

They were just about to broach the conservative tax reform when David heard Ivy's bedroom door open. His heart thumped wildly in his chest, and he cast a quick look at Damien, who just smirked at the look of panic in his eye, before standing to face her.

He clenched his hands into fists when he took in the dark bruise that mottled the entire right side of her face, from her hairline to just above her chin, he had to stop himself from walking over to her when he saw her balancing awkwardly on a crutch, a look of pure shock in the single eye that was open.

Neither of them said anything. She looked from him to Damien and back again as if trying to decide if she was still dreaming.

"Well, I'm going to go and call Louie," Damien said. "In my bedroom."

David watched him lean down and exaggeratedly pick up his phone from the coffee table, before moving past Ivy to his room, closing the door behind him.

"David?" Ivy asked when the door closed with a decided click. She looked as if she was coming out of a trance, realizing that he was real for the first time.

He nodded, took a step towards her, and stopped when her face flooded with pain. "What are you doing here?" she asked, her voice resigned. Tired.

He sighed. "I…I left you a message. And called. And then called Antoinette and she said that you were in the hospital…"

"Okay?"

"I thought…I thought that someone had hurt you, Ivy, and I… I just wanted to see for myself that you were okay."

She took a step closer, winced when her left leg touched the ground.

David felt his heart stutter in his chest, tried to refrain from moving, from touching her, but when she looked at him and her eyes filled with tears, he couldn't help himself. He closed the distance between them, reaching for her tentatively.

When she didn't pull away, he drew her in gently, wrapping his arms around her, making sure not to put too much pressure into the hug. The feeling of her nestled in his arms felt right somehow, like they'd been molded with the expectation that they'd find each other.

She started crying then, big heart-wrenching sobs that shook her entire body. He didn't know what to do, didn't know how to hold all the pieces of her together as she broke apart in his arms. When she wobbled awkwardly on the crutch, he nudged her, picked her up gently, and carried her to the sofa, sat with her cradled in his lap until she calmed down and the sobs faded.

He hated seeing her like this, hated knowing that the funny, stubborn, charismatic woman that he had met, had been reduced to the devastated girl in his arms. "It's okay," he said, not knowing what else he could offer. "You're okay."

She pulled back from him slightly, looked at him through half-open, tear-streaked eyes, a small flush of embarrassment flooding her cheeks. He could see the confusion there, he understood that she was having trouble piecing together why he'd come, and he didn't stop her when she dragged herself off his lap and onto the sofa next to him even though he hated the space that she had left behind.

For a moment, a heavy silence hung between them. Then, she whispered, "I'm sorry about that. It's been a long week."

He touched her shoulder gently, waited until she looked at him. Even with her face black and blue, the sight of her made his stomach lurch uncomfortably. "Don't apologize. Please."

She nodded slowly, her open eye still heavy with sleep. "Why are you here, David?"

He took a moment to gather his thoughts before replying. Having her in his arms again, even for so short a time, had clouded his brain. He exhaled. "I...wanted to explain."

"Why you never called?"

He nodded, trailed a finger down the mottled coloring gently, imagined her being assaulted on a dark street, and curled his hand into a fist before dropping it onto the sofa again. "I've been wanting to talk for a while, to explain why I behaved so poorly. But when you didn't reply to my message or calls..."

"You called Antoinette and she mentioned that I'd been in the hospital," she regurgitated what he'd already told her. "I'm assuming Damien told you that it wasn't a client, then?"

"He did," David replied, "but that doesn't change the fact that I hate to see you hurt, Ivy. I mean...you were assaulted. Do you understand that?"

She closed her eyes and fell back against the sofa as if completely drained. "Yes," she said. "I understand." She sighed. "It's just not exactly a priority right now."

"I just—why are you still working as an escort?" he asked, getting completely side-tracked by his own anger. Didn't she realize how dangerous it was? Was she really going to be so blasé after nearly cracking her skull open on the sidewalk? Sure, the assault had been unrelated, but it had also only occurred because she'd been on a date with Oliver.

"So that's it? You didn't call because of the work that I do? Because you don't like that I'm an escort?" She smiled at him sadly. "I didn't work for two weeks hoping that you'd call me, David. Hoping that you cared enough to try and see past how we met." She said the words quietly. "You made me feel stupid for thinking that you cared. For thinking that you wanted to date me, like *actually* date *me*."

Because he sensed he was losing ground fast, he took both her hands in his, hated the fact that she tensed at the contact. "Ivy, I'm sorry," he said. "I'm having two conversations here." He paused as he tried to gather his thoughts, sighed, started again. "I left and didn't call because, well…I was scared. Scared of who I am with you, how you make me feel…scared of you."

"What?"

She was tired, he realized. Probably on some sort of pain pills and, judging by the way she locked her palms together in her lap, he was stressing her out. He rubbed his thumb gently over the back of her hand in an attempt to relax her, felt his entire body tighten at the small skin contact, and waited a moment as he gathered his thoughts.

"I think I fell for you that night you came to my house—when you noticed the Spanish tile on my steps—and I freaked out. I'm sorry. I don't have anything else to say except that I'm sorry."

Stop talking. Now.

She didn't say anything. She just stared at him, shocked.

"And, yes, I couldn't watch you keep escorting because I didn't want to see you with someone else, with *anyone* else. So I figured that I'd cut the strings while they were still newly formed, just eradicate you from my life entirely. And yes," he hesitated, "I assumed that you wouldn't be surprised. I assumed that you wouldn't care."

You're an idiot.

He tried not to flinch when she looked at him, her face so consumed with sadness that he had to refrain from reaching for her again. "But I couldn't get you out of my mind," he added. "Not for a single moment since I last saw you."

"Do you think I like going out with random men?" she asked quietly, her voice sad. "Dressing up for men that I don't know and pretending to be interested in their lives for hours on end? Hoping that I'm not going to be assaulted when I refuse to sleep with someone I'm not attracted to?"

He sighed. "I didn't want to ask. I didn't think I had the right, especially after only two dates. Paid dates," he added, remembering Damien's words.

"You don't, but I would have appreciated a little more…faith," she said. "Maybe even a conversation about it."

He dropped her hands, linked his own between his knees. God, he wanted to touch her, he wanted to kiss her, he wanted to lie down on the bed that smelled like her and let her sleep the night away, feeling safe in his arms. He wanted to watch her drift off, feel the shape of her body against his. He wanted to be the first thing that she saw when she opened her eyes in the morning. And that, he realized, was the problem: he was completely irrational when it came to her. Nothing made sense.

So, he didn't say anything.

She sighed. "Look, I appreciate you coming, David. I really do, but I jus—"

"I'll go," he said, standing suddenly. He felt his heart race in his chest, felt his throat close with panic. She was going to tell him to leave, tell him she never wanted to see him again, and he would have deserved it.

When he looked down at her, her eyes had filled with tears again. "Please," he whispered, torn, "don't cry."

When she tilted her head up to look at him, he leaned down and gently wiped the tears from her bruised face. When she didn't pull away, he kissed her forehead gently. "I'm so sorry."

"I appreciate that." She caught his hands in hers, planted a kiss on each palm in a gesture he found intensely intimate. "I'm sorry I never explained things to you either. We could have saved each other a lot of grief."

That caught him off guard. He crouched down at her feet, felt his pants ride half-way up his calves, but didn't care. "Would you explain it to me now?" he asked. "I would really like to know."

He'd be lying to himself if he said he wasn't curious. But, more than his own curiosity, he just wanted it out of the way. He wanted to solve whatever money issue she had so that she wouldn't have to keep putting herself in these situations. The thought took him by surprise, but he knew that it was true even if he'd never thought it through before that moment. He wanted to help.

He realized that she hadn't replied, that she was staring at the empty wall of the apartment, lost in thought. Still, he didn't push her, realizing that whether she did or didn't tell him, the choice had to be hers.

"My father is dying."

She turned to look at him then, and he realized for the first time that she was probably sedated and that her left eye was half shut with the effort of waking up through the drugs. He had heard what she'd said but wondered suddenly if she was in her right mind, if she was in a drug-induced state and didn't know what she was sharing with him.

He brushed her hazelnut hair back from her face, heaved himself back onto the couch beside her, and felt a small twinge of happiness when she didn't move away, choosing instead to burrow under his arm. He thought about what she'd told him, thought about how to broach the topic in her current state of mind. "I heard you," he started.

"I know."

"I just…I want you to tell me all about it when you're feeling better," he said. "I want you to be well-rested when we go over it so that I don't miss anything, okay?"

She nodded. "Okay."

They fell into a comfortable silence, sitting side-by-side on the brown, corduroy sofa, which David realized was remarkably ugly underneath the bright throw pillows.

He thought about what she'd said, thought about the fact that her father was dying, and wondered what was killing him. *Cancer? What kind?* He wasn't a doctor, but if she was paying for his expenses, he could help her.

He wondered if it was too late to help? When he'd first met her, she had definitely told him that both her parents were dead, which, given the current information, meant it was likely she was fully expecting her father to die, and soon.

He glanced down at her, noticed that she had fallen asleep, her head pillowed on the crook where his shoulder connected. He refrained from touching her face again, stopped himself from tracing the hideous bruise that was stamped on her entire right side.

The doorbell rang. Ivy stirred at the sound but didn't open her eyes.

Damien came out of his bedroom, cast a single, surprised glance at him on the sofa, Ivy curled up against his body, and moved to get the door. He opened it fully and David squinted against the bright light that shone in. He had completely forgotten that it was only five o'clock in the evening.

"Marnie! Richard! It's great to see you," Damien whisper-shouted as he stood aside and let an elderly couple into the room.

142

"We're sorry to barge in like this," the lady was saying, her shock of white hair bobbing as she folded Damien into a hug. "She told us not to come, but how could we just sit at home waiting? And then she didn't call us today, and we got worried. Richard," she turned to the old man to usher him inside. He was about her height, with a pair of small glasses on his nose and a regal-looking cane in his right hand.

"You know you can come over anytime," Damien said. "I think she just didn't want to alarm you."

David realized that they were talking about Ivy and felt a hot blush crawl up his neck. The couple, clearly her grandparents, hadn't realized that he was there, their granddaughter curled around him.

Damien spoke quietly. "She just passed out again a minute ago," he said and pointed at the sofa.

David braced himself, felt three pairs of eyes turn to him. Damien looked like he was trying very hard not to laugh. After the initial look of shock passed, Ivy's grandmother looked like she had just discovered a new prime-time show. Her grandfather cocked his head slightly, his eyebrows raised as he took in the situation.

"We can come back later," the woman said, a wide smile on her kind face.

David held up a hand, asking them to wait, put one arm under Ivy's legs, careful not to put pressure on her left knee and the other arm behind her back. He picked her up easily, carried her through to her bedroom, and put her down on top of the bed. He cast one last glance at her, steeled his stomach for the upcoming introductions, and then left, closing the door behind him.

Again, three pairs of eyes turned back to him. He smiled and walked over to the trio. "I apologize for intruding," he began, hiding his nerves easily. "I'm David." He paused for a second, then added, "A friend of Ivy's."

Marnie beamed up at him from her full five-three height, her big eyes the exact shade of green as Ivy's, and held out her hand. "It's nice to meet you, David."

He took her small hand in his, felt the familiar bird-like grip, so similar but so different to his own grandmother's. "It's my pleasure," he replied before turning to Richard.

Her grandfather was not sold on him and David didn't blame him. He wouldn't be either. Regardless, Richard shook his hand, his grip strong despite his age.

David looked at Damien. "I think her pills hadn't worn off completely," he said. "Would you mind if I went back to the office and showered? Came back later?"

Damien shrugged. "She'll probably want you to be here when she wakes up," he said, a small smirk on his face as he threw David to the lions.

"Great." David looked at Marnie and Richard. "I'll bring dinner?" he asked. "I would love to actually take the time to have a conversation once the workday has been washed off me."

They both nodded, mute.

"Anything sound good? Damien?" David asked.

Damien grinned back at him. "King's Palace on seventh. Best Chinese takeout in Los Angeles."

"Done." He smiled at her grandparents one last time and, before he changed his mind, made a hasty retreat.

He needed a few minutes to sort his thoughts, needed some space to prepare to meet, and converse with, her family. And, he knew that she'd want to see them alone without him there at first, let them express their tears and anger without a stranger hovering.

He'd give them two hours, he decided. And then he was going to suck up the cold-blooded fear that had settled in his chest and show Ivy that he could be there. He'd be there to meet her grandparents and socialize with her best friend—and bring them all Chinese take-out apparently.

Chapter 10

She wasn't quite sure if she'd dreamt the entire thing, but when Ivy managed to open her eyes again, she was back in her bed, staring up at her ceiling. She sighed and rolled over onto her left side, winced when a sharp stab of pain traveled through her injured knee.

She heard Damien laugh through her bedroom door, heard another male voice say something back to him, and frowned. Louie was in Missouri. She sat up in her bed, stilled so that she could strain her ears to listen. *David stayed?*

She gently maneuvered her legs off the bed, fumbled around for her crutch, and realized it wasn't there; she'd left it by the sofa when she'd been talking to him. She frowned, had a moment when she genuinely considered calling Damien through the closed door and asking him to bring it, but she decided against it. If David had stayed, she wanted to maintain some modicum of her dignity, which did not include her crying for help or belly crawling through to the living area.

She slowly stood on her right leg, gingerly touched her toes to the floor, and, making sure to only put the slightest pressure on her left knee, hobbled to the door. She pried it open awkwardly, moving her body out of the way as she leaned her weight on the doorknob.

The last thing she expected to see were her grandparents, sitting on the sofa while Damien and David faced them on the barstools they'd pulled from the tiny kitchen island. A huge spread of Chinese food and two bottles of red wine, one empty and one half-full, sat on the coffee table between them. Her stomach rumbled when the smell hit her.

145

She smiled when her grandfather laughed and took a swig of his wine. She would have stayed standing in the doorway, watching the scene unfurl with fascination, had David not looked up just then and noticed her. He looked so out of place in his perfectly tailored dress clothes, the sleeves rolled up to his elbows, sitting on the barstool surrounded by her grandparents and Damien.

She watched as David's blue eyes instantly shuttered, and Ivy had to consciously refrain from raising a hand self-consciously to her bruised face.

Her heart beat frantically in her chest when he stood and came to her, his gaze never once releasing her. Her breath caught in her throat. Had he always been this gorgeous? She wasn't quite sure how, but he seemed even more so now than when she'd first seen him frowning down at her in the Ritz Carlton's hotel bar.

She stepped into the living area, took a tentative step forward, trying to ignore the pain shooting up her leg, and sighed in relief when David picked her crutch up from its position against the sofa and passed it to her before coming to stand in front of her.

"Thank you," she said. She took the crutch, deliberately avoiding his eyes so she wouldn't be blushing when her grandparents saw her.

"Are you feeling better?" he asked.

She noticed that his body was blocking her view of her grandparents and frowned. She looked up at him then, saw a brief glimpse of pure rage flash through his eyes when his hand brushed her injured cheek.

"I'm fine, David," she said quietly and leaned her cheek into his hand for a second. "And you can't protect them from my face forever," she added and laughed when he frowned down at her.

"I don't think they realize," he whispered. She got the impression, by the slight fear in his eyes, that he was not comfortable with the idea of other people's emotions being on public display.

"It'll be fine," she said with a smile and raised her eyebrows when he still didn't move.

He looked at her one last time, then sighed as if aware that the others had fallen silent behind him. He turned to stand beside her as she hobbled forward.

When her grandmother's eyes filled with tears and her grandfather leaned one hand on the sofa to steady himself, she straightened her spine and said, "Honestly, I'm fine. The worst thing about it is that I can't mix wine with my pain pills."

She leaned into David's chest for support, aware of the fact that had come to stand right behind her.

He wrapped his hands around her upper arms, gave her a quick squeeze of encouragement, and added, "But that doesn't mean that we can't continue to imbibe."

"I might have to run out and get more," Damien joked, taking the cue. He held up the bottles and pretended to inspect them.

Ivy sighed, relieved when her grandmother laughed and shook her head, the movement sending the first tear over her lashes. "Girl," she said. "You come over here and let me take a look."

Ivy knew it wasn't a question, knew that the fifty years that her grandmother had been a nurse were being put to good use as she watched Ivy walk towards her with hawk-like eyes. She stood in front of her for a second before her grandmother wrapped her in a hug. "Not too pretty, but you'll recover," she said.

Ivy laughed, rubbed her back. "It's so good to see you, Gran. I'm sorry I didn't come; I've been sleeping most of the day."

She turned and reached for her grandfather, felt a small ball of anxiety when she felt his hand tremble in hers, right before he pulled her away from her grandmother so that he could hug her.

"How does the other guy look?" he whispered.

"Down for the count," Ivy returned without missing a beat. It didn't matter that it wasn't true; it mattered that she joked back.

He nodded. "That'll teach 'em."

She let him go, ushered them both back to the sofa, and sat in between them, relieved that she'd had Damien and David to dispel the situation.

When her grandmother leaned forward and started piling a plate full of Chinese food, Ivy chuckled but didn't stop her. She could use a meal, even if it was deep-fried. She took the plate, then laughed when Damien started a political conversation with her grandfather. She listened, but she couldn't help but be aware of David, who had gone to sit down on the barstool across from her.

She could feel his eyes on her, and her pulse was not ignorant of the fact that she wanted to touch him; she wished they could have had just a moment alone to finish the conversation that they'd started earlier, to sort things out so that they could move on.

"Don't go looking for his opinion!" Damien was saying to her grandfather. "David is more conservative than you are," he said, looking David up and down with mock contempt.

Ivy looked up just as David's eyes moved off her face towards Damien. "Probably," he said, nodding first to Damien then to Richard. "But fiscally, and only because I want more efficient spending mechanisms in place if I'm going to be taxed forty percent."

Damien laughed. Richard chuckled, but nodded.

As the men's banter swirled around her, Ivy became distinctly aware of her grandmother's gaze piercing her. She turned on the sofa, so they were face-to-face. "What?" she whispered.

"You didn't tell me that you had a boyfriend," she said, her tone both accusatory and hurt. "And such a gorgeous one."

She smiled. "We're not actually dating, Gran," she replied quietly, not quite sure how to handle the situation. "We're…figuring it out."

"Well, does he know that?" she whispered. "That man can't take his eyes off you."

"That's just his thinking face," Ivy retaliated with a small smile. "He's trying to figure out how he ended up here."

Her grandmother laughed, but leaned in to add, "I have a feeling you're out of your depth."

"You have no idea," she replied, unphased by her grandmother's honest reading of the situation.

The truth was that she did have no idea. She didn't know why her heart fluttered when he looked at her, why her palms sweated when she felt him nearby, or why she hadn't thought about another man since she'd met him. She had no idea why, after he'd hurt her so deeply, she wanted nothing more than to shut out the world and be alone with him.

She thought about whether the knowledge scared her, admitted that, although she enjoyed the butterflies constantly swirling in her stomach, they also made her feel quite queasy. She wasn't the type of girl who was easily infatuated. Hadn't planned on falling in love. Had never actually been in love. She frowned at the direction her thoughts had taken. Love was a bit too extreme. She knew that she couldn't be in love with a man she'd met twice. Could she?

No, she decided with a resolute shake of her head. That was impossible. As much as she hated to admit it, she was infatuated. And why shouldn't she be? David was sweet and kind and…infuriating. Handsome—no, gorgeous. Killer body. Yeah, she thought as she sat back into the sofa with her plate of food and let the conversation swirl around her, she was just infatuated. What girl wouldn't be?

"Ivy." Her grandmother's prompting brought her back to the conversation.

"Mnn?" she asked.

"You and Damien promised that you'd get rid of this sofa as soon as you could afford to," she said, rubbing the ugly brown corduroy upholstery. "What's keeping you? Not even my lovely cushions hide the fact that's it's ready for Goodwill."

Ivy smiled when Damien gasped exaggeratedly, drawing all eyes to him. "We could never give Sally to Goodwill!"

"Sally?" her grandfather asked, his eyebrows raised in confusion.

Ivy took pity on him because she knew Damien's humor was probably lost on her eighty-year-old grandparents. "Sally is our sofa, Papa," she said with a small laugh. "We thought it only fair to dub her so after all the times she's been there for us."

"Drunken stupors," Damien started.

"Break-up crying sessions," Ivy added.

"Make-up celebrations," Damien said with a saucy wink that had everyone laughing.

"Best friend movie nights."

"Okay, okay." Her grandfather waved his hand in the air good-naturedly. "I get it. Sally deserves to at least have a chance at re-stuffing and reupholstery," he teased.

They lapsed into a brief, companionable silence before Damien started talking about Universal Basic Income and, in doing so, deliberately drew David and her grandfather into the hypothetical scenario.

Ivy sighed in relief as she ate the food off the plate in front of her, content to listen to the conversation swirl as she wondered what the hell she was going to say to David.

"I'll call you tomorrow," she promised right before her grandmother stepped out of the apartment, trailing behind her grandfather, who had been not-too-subtly trying to leave for the better part of an hour. She sat back on the sofa, exhausted. How was it possible that two eighty-year-olds had drained her of every ounce of energy she had in just two hours?

Damien sighed as he closed the door and then moved over to where she sat and plopped down on the sofa beside her, not trying to disguise the fact that he was tired too.

"That was…"

"Exhausting," David supplied from his position, standing on the other side of the coffee table.

Ivy smiled, first at David and then at Damien. Because Damien was closer, she reached for his hand, gave it a squeeze. "Thank you both so much," she said. "You were…distracting."

The boys chuckled.

She looked at David, noticed the dark circles under his eyes. She couldn't forget that his average workday was ten to twelve hours. Yet, he'd stayed and helped her entertain.

When he met her gaze, he smiled tiredly, and she felt the familiar swarm of butterflies take off in her stomach.

Damien cleared his throat. "I'm going to go to bed before you two jump each other in front of me."

Ivy chuckled, tried to hide the blush rising in her cheeks. Was their physical attraction that obvious to everyone? "See you in the morning," she said when he padded off to his bedroom, his feet bare now.

When his door closed, David moved around the coffee table. Ivy felt her pulse tick nervously with every step closer and then jump erratically when he sat down next to her, close enough that she could smell the familiar scent of him but not close enough that they were touching.

"I should get going," he said quietly.

She glanced up at him, met his ice-blue eyes. "Work tomorrow?" she asked, knowing full well that investment bankers usually put in weekend hours.

He shook his head. "No. But you should sleep, Ivy."

She nodded because she knew he was right; she could already feel a steady thrum behind her right eye and felt, more than knew, that she had missed the mark for her last round of painkillers.

"I'd ask you to stay," she said. "But I don't know how I could manage anything with this leg." She said the words unashamedly. She had already decided that she wanted him to know how she felt, wanted him to know that she wanted him, wanted to feel his hands on her again.

"I want to stay." She met his eyes again, saw the need and lust that she felt mirrored there. "No sex, just sleeping," he added.

She nodded. "If you're okay with that?"

"Of course," he said, a soft smile on his face. "You can't even walk."

She nodded, couldn't help but chuckle at the absurdity of the situation.

"I do want to talk to you though," he said.

Ivy tensed. He turned to face her more directly on the sofa. "I...I meant what I said that first time that we slept together. I want to date you."

"But...you don't want me to escort?"

He shrugged as if he felt awkward. "I don't."

Before she could reply, he added, "I can help with your dad's expenses until..." He raked a hand through his hair, clearly struggling with how to say what he was thinking.

"David," she said and took his hands in hers. "It's okay." He looked at her. "I have enough put aside for a few months of care and...the hospice doesn't think it'll be another two weeks until he's gone."

Thoughts of Hanley Hospice brought Amanda Van den Berg to the forefront of her mind. She ran a single finger over the back of his big hand, smiled when she thought of how they'd mostly been running in circles before now. "I actually met your grandmother a few months ago," she said. Realizing that she hadn't exactly told the truth, she quickly corrected herself. "I mean, I met her a few years ago, but I only realized who she was once we'd…"

"Your dad's at Hanley Hospice? In Pasadena?" He sounded surprised.

"Your grandmother tried to set us up once."

"Wait." He ran one big hand over her head, his movements impossible gentle. "*You're* her 'nice young friend from work'?"

"I guess so." Chuckling, she added, "Unless there's another one."

"Huh."

She smiled at him sadly and added, "Also, you shouldn't offer random escorts money to pay for their expenses. That's…not very smart."

He exhaled on a chuckle before sobering again. "I'm so sorry that you've had to go through all of this," he said. He turned to face her. "You're the bravest person I know."

She felt something small and hard break inside her; he had somehow cracked the walls she'd built around herself over the years so that she could manage the emotional upheaval. When her eyes misted, she looked away. She didn't want to be brave. She wanted to cry until her tears ran dry, she wanted to scream at the unfairness of it all.

He rubbed her hands between his. "Is this," he said indicating first him and then her, "what *you* want?"

She didn't have to think about it. She knew that although she didn't know if or how it would work out, she wanted to try. She nodded. "I won't escort. I don't need to anymore."

He grinned and his eyes, so blue, seemed to get even lighter. "Of course, it's mutual," he added.

"Exclusive?" she asked for clarification.

"Considering I can't function past thinking about you already, I don't think it'll be a problem."

She chuckled, leaned against him, and sighed when he wrapped one big arm around her. She loved the feeling of his muscles against her, loved the smell of whichever deodorant he was wearing.

"I would have lost money on this day ending like this," she said.

He leaned back on the sofa, bringing her to lie against his chest. "Disappointed?" he asked as he stroked his hand down her back.

"Yes." She felt him tense. "But only because I'm physically incapable tonight."

And damned if that didn't suck, she thought, especially considering that just his proximity to her was clouding her brain and making her blood run hot beneath her skin.

He chuckled. "Why don't we get your painkillers and then go to bed?" he asked.

She nodded. "They're on my bedside table so we can just head in there."

He sat up, then stood to his full height, and when she moved to get the crutch, he swept her off her feet and into his arms. She giggled despite the twinge in her knee, locked her arms around his neck, and touched her lips to his when he looked down at her, smiling.

When he didn't move, she knew that he was worried about the bruising on her face. She shifted in his arms, brought her face closer so that she could deepen the kiss, so that she could use her tongue on him. He kissed her back then, his own tongue gently responding to her with an urgency that betrayed his lust. Ivy felt his heart beat rapidly from where she rested against his chest, felt her body tighten when he strengthened his grip on her.

He broke the kiss first, sighed, and rested his head gently against hers for a moment. "Bedtime," he said suddenly.

154

She laughed when he carried her through to the bedroom, sighed, perfectly content when he put her down gently on the bed. "I have my pajamas here," she said and held up a pair of boy shorts and a long tee shirt that she had tucked under her pillow earlier in the day.

"I can sleep in this," he said.

She looked at his button-down dress shirt, black slacks, and polished shoes. "Don't be absurd." He raised his eyebrows. "We've already slept together," she said. "Just sleep in your boxers."

He grinned. "How do you know I'm wearing any?"

"Because I know that you'd never go commando to work," she replied instantly. When he frowned, she chuckled.

He shook his head, tried not to smile but failed. When he undid a few top buttons and pulled his shirt off, she felt her stomach jump. Yup, she told herself, she definitely hadn't imagined the bronzed abs and corded muscle.

He took off his shoes and socks while Ivy watched. He hesitated before taking off his slacks, seemingly embarrassed. "Don't be modest now!" she said.

"I'm...ah," he indicated to his groin.

"Oh. Sorry," she said, blushing at the shape of him through his pants as she pulled her shirt off before unhooking her bra and letting her breasts fall loose. She grinned up at him, aware of the bruising down her right side, but also aware of the fact that his eyes couldn't quite decide where they wanted to stay. She pulled her tee-shirt on to cover herself, left the sweatpants on because she genuinely didn't want to attempt removing them with her sore knee. When she looked up again, he had taken his slacks off and hung his clothes on the chair by her desk like he'd done that first night.

Ivy couldn't help the fact that her eyes gravitated to the hard length of him underneath his boxers and felt a fist of regret settle in her stomach even as her body throbbed for him.

He climbed onto the bed next to her, got under the covers with her when she held them up for him. When their skin touched, she couldn't help but burrow back into his chest as if she could absorb his warmth. She felt him come up hard against her, but she didn't mind considering she was about as turned on as he was. He wrapped his arm around her waist, nestling the other under her pillow.

She couldn't help the stupid grin that spread over her face as she lay facing away from him, couldn't help but feel a small shiver of excitement at what tomorrow would bring. She leaned over her nightstand and turned off the lamp, plunging them into darkness. "Night," she whispered.

He didn't reply, and Ivy could tell by his deep, even breathing that he was drifting off to sleep. Huh, she'd have thought he was the tossing and turning type.

Obviously not.

The thought that she didn't know that much about him took her completely by surprise, sent a small jolt of alarm coursing through her, but she pushed it aside and closed her eyes, nestled into his chest and sighed, content to slow her breathing to match his, despite her doubts.

Chapter 11

Ivy laughed at the story that David was telling her and chose to gently put her wine glass back down on the tablecloth so that she didn't choke, or worse, spit it all over him. "So, what did you do?" she asked, enjoying the way his eyes lit up with humor, replacing the serious glint she so often saw sitting there.

"I was twelve!" he laughed. "Of course, I ran away as fast as my legs would carry me and never told anyone about it. Ever."

"Not even your parents?"

He sobered instantly, grinning at her despite the fact she had noticed the exact moment that his eyes shuttered. "No," he replied, "the opportunity never really presented itself. And they would have been pissed."

She smiled at him and, noticing the faraway look in his eyes, chose to change the topic because he didn't seem comfortable talking about his family. She wondered, briefly, why that was. She knew that he'd had a privileged upbringing, knew from when they'd spoken about their backgrounds that his father was an investment banker too. She knew that money didn't always equate to happiness, but still couldn't deny the fact that she was curious. She was interested in the people who had shaped him.

"How did that pitch you were telling me about go?" she asked, consciously turning the conversation back towards his comfort zone—work. "Did you win the deal?"

He smiled and leaned back in his chair slightly so that he could look at her. "We did. It'll be an interesting time," he said. "We don't have much experience in renewables, so it'll add measurable diversification to our quals."

She nodded, happy for him. She knew he'd been distracted by the looming presentation, knew he'd been stressed about appearing an expert in a field he knew very little about. She knew he'd flown to Texas to give the pitch because it was the only night that they'd spent apart since they'd started dating. She remembered the day the presentation had been on because she'd struggled to sleep without him there and had ended up calling him in his hotel room. She'd missed him and the fact that she couldn't sleep because of it had embarrassed her so much that she hadn't told him about it at the time. She didn't want to appear needy or dependent. Especially, she reminded herself, considering they'd only been dating for a few weeks.

She still couldn't believe it had all happened so recently; it felt like she had known him longer, felt like she had dated him longer too. She felt that she could tell him anything and, well, now that she thought about it, she did tell him everything. She told him way more than he told her.

Since they'd officially started dating, they'd spent almost every evening together. David would come over to her apartment after work and spend the night, or sometimes, he'd pick her up and take her back to his house for dinner and then drop her back home the next day because she had three weeks of medical leave. As it turned out, Fitch and Mathers didn't think that having a lawyer on staff who looked like they'd been beaten to a pulp was good for business, so she'd been forced to take the time. She couldn't even work from home because of the sensitive information she handled. Not that she minded that much. She had read more fiction in the two weeks she'd had off than she had in the entire time since her undergrad.

And she'd had a distraction in David.

She extended her leg under the table, flexing her knee while consciously masking the grimace that rose to her face from the pain of the simple motion.

"How are you doing?" David asked, his eyes concerned when he noticed the look on her face and the fact that she'd moved her leg. He touched her thigh gently under the table, sending little jolts of awareness from her leg to her very center.

It was the first time they'd had gone out since her accident and they'd picked a casual, neighborhood Italian restaurant down the street from David's house so that Ivy didn't feel self-conscious about hobbling around, even if she no longer needed the crutch to walk. The bruising on her face, although not entirely gone, had faded to the point that she could cover it with makeup and brave being seen in public again.

"I'm okay, actually," she said, smiling. She felt perfectly content sitting there with him. "It's just weird, you know. Because I'll forget that it's hurt and then move unconsciously and set the whole thing off again."

He nodded and reached a hand over the table to rest on hers. The feeling of his large palm covering hers still brought a flush of awareness to her cheeks, still made her belly tighten with anticipation. It was as if the entire restaurant fell away, as if the world around them dimmed and all that she was aware of was him, was the feeling of his skin on hers.

She knew what he could do to her body and every time that he touched her, even if it was in the most casual way, she wanted him all over again. She looked up from their joined hands and met his eyes, saw her own need reflected in them, and felt her heart trip in her chest. "I'm ready for the check if you are," she said in a breathy whisper.

He grinned and sent her a wolfish look that made her breath catch in her throat. He signaled to the waiter, hurriedly signed the check when it arrived and then helped her to her feet.

He led her from the restaurant slowly, his arm crooked to take her bodyweight so that she could walk without looking completely absurd.

"I'm sorry," she chuckled when they came to stand on the sidewalk and the valet went off to get the Porsche, leaving them alone together. "I don't think it'll be like this much longer. It feels better every da—"

"Ivy," he said, cutting her off with a small smile. "Stop apologizing. You were mugged for Christ's sake. You have a torn ACL. Just let me help you."

She chuckled, aware of the fact that she felt self-conscious about being dependent on him for something as simple as walking. "It's just…" she struggled to find the right way to phrase what she was thinking. "It's just that this isn't exactly how I imagined our first few weeks of dating."

He intertwined his fingers with hers so that their palms met in the center. "You mean you didn't imagine us having fantastic, creative sex, two weeks of time home alone together, and infinite sleepovers?" he asked. When she blushed, he cupped her cheek and turned her face so that she was looking into his clear, blue eyes. "This is exactly how I would have wanted it in any fantasy." He paused, tilted his head, and smiled. "Well, minus the injury, of course."

She shook her head, but a small part of her brain told her that he was right. It had been fun and…insanely intimate. The time that they'd been forced to spend home alone together because of her physical state had really just meant that they'd learned as much as they could about one another in a very short period of time. They hadn't had the distraction of going out, or socializing; they'd been at home alone in their pajamas getting to know one another and, at least for her, in her worst possible physical state.

She wondered if that was why it felt, at least to her, like she'd known him for so much longer than she really had.

When the car pulled up to the curb, David held the door open for her so that she could awkwardly drop into the bucket seat and then shimmy into the Porsche so that she didn't strain her knee.

David closed her in and tipped the valet before climbing into the driver's seat beside her.

The distance to his house from the restaurant couldn't have been more than two miles, but with the Saturday night neighborhood traffic, they seemed to inch forward from stoplight to stoplight.

David turned his indicator on and smiled as Ivy leaned forward to change the radio station. He loved how easygoing she was, loved how comfortable he was around her, how…himself he was. He never felt like there was any pretense between them. He felt like he didn't have to be on all the time like he did at work or at events or around his parents.

When she turned the radio station to AC/DC radio, he looked at her with raised eyebrows. "I think you're just going to have to marry me."

She chuckled good-naturedly, but David felt a small burst of panic when he realized that the idea didn't seem that bizarre to him. The thought surprised him because, well, he actually didn't understand the whole marriage thing. He wasn't a religious man. So, the way he saw it, the marriage license was just a piece of paper from the government affirming his commitment to someone. Which made no sense at all in the modern world. But Ivy—she was different. He could go the whole nine yards with her.

He looked over at her as she watched the houses pass in the night, her eyes dreamy as she looked out of her window. He loved the way her hair tumbled down to her waist in a thick blanket of mahogany; it made him want to bury his hands in it. He looked back to the road, aware of the fact that he was already hard just thinking about her.

When he sighed, she turned to look at him, her wide eyes green and catlike in the dark car. "You tired?" she asked, casually placing her hand on his upper thigh.

The gesture was one she had fallen into the habit of doing when they were in the car together, one that he usually would have smiled at and not made anything of. Tonight, the simple movement made his whole body awaken, made his pants feel impossibly tight.

"Not really. You?" he asked, trying to ignore the fact that her hand was only an inch or two from finding out exactly how awake he was.

"Not at all," she said, moving her hand so that it gently rubbed against him.

Fuck. He squinted. "I'm going to get us in an accident."

She giggled and moved her hand again. "I have more faith in you than that."

He shifted in the seat of the car, exhaled on a long breath when she started rubbing him slowly. "Christ," he managed as blood filled his ears.

The world around them seemed to slow as the soft night lights filtered in through the windows of the car. To David, nothing seemed real except them in the car, shrouded in darkness. He could feel exactly where her hand touched him, sending small shocks of pleasure through his system. Somewhere in the back of his mind, he was viscerally aware of the smell of leather and the musk of excitement that seemed to envelop them in the car.

When he pulled into his driveway, Ivy opened her door and gently eased herself out of the bucket seat.

He took a full minute to calm himself enough to the point where he could walk past his erection and then followed suit. He walked to her, shook his head when he noticed the laugh in her eyes, and, because he could, swept her off her feet and started up the stairs that lead to his front door.

"David!" she said. "You can't carry me up all of these!"

"Challenge accepted," he replied, making her chuckle.

She kept still as he reached the top of the staircase, and he felt her brace against him as he gently lowered her onto her uninjured knee so that she could take her weight without hurting herself. He unlocked the door, his other hand still holding hers, and then stepped aside so that she could go in first.

For some reason, he couldn't help but remember the first time that she'd come over, the first time that she'd seen the Spanish tile on his steps and asked about it. He smiled at the memory. He was pretty sure the fact that she'd noticed had been what had done it for him initially. He had never told her that the tiles had basically been the entire reason he bought the house. He didn't tell her that he'd walked in for the showing not feeling much of a connection, and left knowing that he'd pay anything to have the house.

For someone as rational as David, the fact that he'd had a completely irrational reaction to the hand-painted tiles with their miniature pastoral scenes had been a sign of sorts, a good feeling that the house was right. His grandmother would have called it an omen. He just considered it luck.

"I'm just going to go and clean up," she said and hobbled past him to the stairs, her slender legs perfectly molded by the tight jeans she wore.

He nodded. "I'll pour us some wine."

He watched her make slow progress up the stairs, waited until she disappeared into the bedroom before moving towards the kitchen, a genuine smile on his face.

He poured them each a generous glass of wine and sat on the sofa, waiting for her. When she didn't come down again, he moved to the stairs and called, "Ivy?" When she didn't reply, he walked up the stairs slowly. Dread filled his chest as he approached the bedroom door and he had to consciously push it aside. "Ivy?" he said again as he opened the door.

He saw her sitting on the bed staring at her cellphone in her hands, her face pale with shock, paler even in contrast against her dark hair. She wasn't crying but he still felt his heart sink in his chest. "I'm so sorry," he said and moved to sit down next to her so that he could wrap his arms around her.

She didn't need to tell him what had happened because, well, the truth was that they'd both been waiting for it the last few days. They'd both been ignoring it completely until it happened and they couldn't pretend anymore.

He felt her tremble in his arms, felt her body begin to shake with grief. Because he didn't know what else to do, he held on to her as she crumbled, sat still with her without saying anything as she cried. He didn't know what to say. He had never lost a parent. His mother's parents had died when he'd been too small to remember and Daniel, his grandfather, had died when he'd been a young man, old enough to process the loss. Hell, David realized, he was completely unequipped to comfort her, he realized.

So, he didn't offer her hollow words of comfort or camaraderie. Instead, he picked her up and walked over to one of the oversized chairs in the corner of the bedroom, cradled her in his lap as he would have a child.

He let her cry until her tears ran dry and her sobs quieted down to small breathy gasps. Eventually, she sat up and wiped her eyes, her hand bringing away black mascara stains. "I'm sorry," she said. She brushed her hand over his shirt where her makeup had stained it.

He caught her hands in his. "Stop."

When she looked at him silently with so much sadness in her eyes, he sighed and kissed her forehead. "It's alright to grieve, Ivy," he said.

She sighed once and nestled her head back on his chest. "Do you know what my first thought was?" she asked quietly.

Because he knew that she had to say it, he shook his head. "Tell me, baby."

"I thought, 'Thank God he's finally gone'."

He nudged her so that she looked up at him. "That's normal." He sighed when she closed her eyes but carried on with, "He was the person that you loved most in the world and you've seen him suffer for three years. You're allowed to feel relief."

She nodded and nestled back against his chest. When she didn't say anything more, he wrapped his arms around her and leaned back in the chair, content to sit there quietly until she was ready.

Chapter 12

She burrowed deeper into the covers until her back came up against his chest, sighed deeply in her sleep, and then stilled.

David felt his entire body constrict with something he couldn't identify. Maybe it was panic. Maybe it was love. He wasn't sure, but he knew that he felt both when he looked at her, knew that the intensity of neither had diminished in the three months that they'd been dating.

He looked down at her again, touched the cheek that had been black and blue before; smooth, creamy skin had replaced the mottled bruising, and Ivy had almost fully recovered. The knee still hurt her occasionally, but the doctor had recommended she undergo at least five months of physical therapy before committing to surgery. Ivy had agreed and was in month three of five; so far, the improvement was promising, and David was relieved the need for surgery seemed to be dissipating.

He glanced at the clock on his bedside table, saw that it was nearly seven, and shifted so he could turn the alarm off before it blared her awake. When he turned back to gently wake her up, her eyes were already fluttering open from his movement. He kissed her gently on the cheek. "Good morning."

She smiled, still half asleep, and rolled into him so that they were chest to chest, her head resting on his arm. David felt his pulse tick rapidly in his throat, welcomed all of the feelings that flooded his chest.

"Good morning." She yawned once, closed her eyes as they adjusted to the bright light filtering in through his

167

bedroom window. "What time is it? I didn't hear the alarm go off."

"It's seven," he replied, stroking her arm with his fingertips. "I woke up just before it went off."

She shivered in pleasure as his fingers trailed lightly over her skin, smiled, and opened her eyes when he brushed another kiss on her forehead. Despite the growing ball of lust in his stomach, he knew that he had to get going soon or he'd be late for work. Again.

Not that he didn't enjoy their mornings, but he did have a job to keep.

"What's so funny?" she asked, smiling because he was smiling.

"I was just thinking that it's a miracle I've kept my job these last three months. What with coming in late, leaving early, skipping events, not working weekends, and Gordon making my life miserable at every opportunity."

Where he had been trying to make her laugh, Ivy frowned. "You're genuinely joking, right?" she asked, sitting up beside him suddenly. "You know that I would never begrudge you working long hours, don't you?" She looked at him seriously. "I knew going in what you did for a living...I would never ask you to jeopardize that to spend time with me."

He smiled. "I know," he replied and gave her a quick kiss before standing. "But that doesn't mean I want to be in an office with thirty grumpy dudes when my beautiful girlfriend is home alone."

She blushed, sat back against the headboard of his big bed. He felt his stomach and his groin tighten at the same time as he took in the image she made, her long, brunette hair spilling over the tight white tee shirt she wore and onto the white linen duvet she'd tugged up under her arms.

Turning towards his closet, he briefly flicked through his laundered shirts and pulled out a plain white Hugo Boss shirt because he knew he had a clean pair of black slacks.

"I've got a meeting at four," he said as he stepped out of the closet and unbuttoned the shirt before slipping it over his shoulders. "It might last two hours but I'm pretty sure everyone will leave after it. So, I'll be home around seven or seven-thirty."

She nodded as she watched him change unashamedly, her big, green eyes wide now. David buttoned up his shirt slowly, enjoying the fact that he wasn't the only one so easily distracted. He looked into her eyes, grinned when she blushed, and promptly lost every thought in his head when she pushed the covers back and moved over the bed towards where he stood, wearing only a tiny pair of black, lace underwear and the white shirt.

She stopped at the foot of the bed, knelt there, her legs tucked up and underneath her as she looked at him. "I'm going to be back around eight," she said, carrying on the conversation as if she hadn't just stopped every neuron in his brain from firing. "I have to stop by my apartment and switch out some clothes and grab a few things, do some laundry…"

"Why don't you just do laundry here?" he asked, frowning down at her, though still not ignorant of her small nipples pressed against the white shirt.

"I want to switch out my clothes so I may as well just do the laundry while I'm home. Besides, I promised Damien I'd check-in," she said.

She stood and moved towards the bathroom. David's mouth went dry as he watched her pad away, her long, slender legs pale and impossibly smooth, her waist-length hair trailing behind her in a mass of thick waves.

"I can pick up food on my way over if you want. Just text me what you feel like."

He frowned after her as she closed the door, slid into his slacks while she used the bathroom. He sat on the end of the bed to tie his shoelaces and wondered when they had gone from dating to living together.

Not that he minded. In fact, he found it silly that she carted her stuff back and forth from her apartment to his house every few days. It was a waste of time. More than that, he hated when she wasn't in his house when he got home, taking up his space, cooking in his kitchen, or curled up on his sofa watching a movie or reading a book.

He loved having her there.

He glanced at the bathroom door, wondered what she'd say to the idea he was currently playing with. Would she freak out? He wasn't sure. The idea of her there permanently didn't scare him, hell, it was exciting...felt right somehow. But he knew that Ivy also liked her independence, liked knowing that she could afford a place of her own easily, especially now that she didn't have to worry about paying for her dad. Hell, she could've moved into a place of her own if she wanted, but he also knew that she liked living with Damien.

"What are you thinking about?"

David hadn't noticed that she'd come out of the bathroom, but when he glanced up and saw her standing there, her arms crossed over her chest as she smiled down at him, he knew that he wanted to ask her. "I was wondering if you'd freak out if I asked you to move in with me."

He watched her face register surprise, watched her eyes widen as the full weight of what he was asking settled on her mind. She didn't say anything, just stared at him, speechless.

"I'm not pressuring you," he said, not trying to hide the small smile that spread across his face when he saw her surprise change to a look of slight panic. "I'm telling you that it's what I want, but that I'm prepared to wait until you're ready. No pressure."

"We've...we've only been dating three months," she said finally. "Don't you think it's too soon? I mean...how could we possibly know whether this is going to work?" she asked, her hands fluttering nervously in front of her.

He chuckled and stood to his full height, moved over to her and bent down to take her mouth when she glanced up at him, panicked. The kiss was gentle and slow, but it tore through him mercilessly. When she wrapped her arms around his neck and angled her head so that she could deepen it, he sighed and brought his hands to her waist, pulling her as close to him as possible.

He didn't mind that she was less sure of them than he was, didn't expect her to come crawling to his every whim. He was over ten years older than her. He had lived long enough to know that he'd never feel for anyone else what he felt for her. And he was okay with waiting until she was ready too. When he broke the kiss, she rested her cheek against his chest and sighed.

"I'm in love with you." He hadn't planned on telling her quite yet and especially not as he was hurrying to get ready for work, but the words just spilled out of him. He felt her tense in his arms, looked down at her and then let her go so he could turn her face towards his. When she met his eyes, he added, "I want you to know that I wouldn't have asked you to move in without knowing it's what I want…because I love you; I have for a while now."

She smiled despite the uncertainty in her eyes. "I've been in love with you for a while too," she said. "I just thought it was…infatuation. That it would die down."

He felt his grin spread, pulled her close again, and brushed his lips over hers. She smiled against his mouth before returning the kiss, this time with an urgency that left him breathless.

"You're going to be late again," she said when they eventually broke apart, her voice breathy.

He glanced at the clock, gave her one last kiss, and shook his head as he moved towards the door. "I'll see you tonight," he said from the doorway as he turned to look back at her. "Think about it."

She nodded.

171

He jogged down the stairs, grabbed his keys, phone, and wallet from the table by the door and was in his car in under two minutes. As he started the car, he thought about whether or not she'd say yes. Not that he could do anything to influence her decision; he'd asked, and now that she knew what he wanted, it was up to her to make the choice.

Still, he was aware of the fact that he was grinning like an idiot as he pulled out of his garage, but he didn't care. For the first time in his life, he'd told a woman that he was in love with her, that he wanted her to move in with him. More than that, he realized, he was happy for the first time in a long time.

Scratch that, he was the happiest he'd ever been.

She watched the Porsche pull out of the driveway, rested her fingers on the windowsill as she watched him drive away. How was it possible that she was sad to see a man leave for work? *Oh, girl.*

She shook her head, trying to dispel her unease. He'd asked her to move in with him, she realized. Like live together and everything that came with it. She realized that he hadn't waited for an answer, but knew that he probably figured he'd made his point.

Now, the decision was hers.

She wondered why that scared her, why her heart started racing at the thought of moving in and sharing space with David? It wasn't like she'd been in a relationship like this before, or had learned from some horrible mistake in her past. Maybe that was it? Maybe she was unfamiliar with the territory and needed time to mull it over?

She walked over to the closet, pulled out the only two clean dresses she had left, and, after holding them side-by-side, picked the black one. It was a midnight black, square-cut dress that hugged her curves and had simple, clean lines. It fell just below knee level, and Ivy knew that it looked just as good with her sturdy work heels as it did with her spiked, black going-out ones.

She slipped it over her head as she made her way to the bathroom to put on her make-up for work.

As she applied her base, she thought about moving in again. It would be a lot easier, that was for sure. As it was, she and Damien were splitting the use of the car, which meant that on some days she either couldn't make it to see David, or he'd end up picking her up and dropping her at work the next day, or, if she actually needed a car, he'd let her take the Jeep or the Porsche—a habit which she wasn't entirely comfortable with yet. And when she did make it back to her apartment, it was only to see Damien, do laundry, and repack her clothes.

She sighed, leaned closer to the mirror to put her mascara on. It made sense, she realized. She wanted to move in, wanted to live with him. So, why was she hesitating? It was just such a big decision. It could be a life-altering one. If it didn't work out, she was the one who'd have to find another apartment, maybe even another roommate.

When her phone pinged on the sink next to her, she picked it up, smiled when she read the text and her heart flipped over in her chest.

Stop overthinking it and take your time. I'm not going anywhere. Love you X

She hesitated for only a moment as she thought about what to say.

I'm going to make sure that Damien can manage without me paying rent...I think I'm ready too! 😊

173

She stared at her phone, waited while the little typing bubbles flashed across the screen.

Great! Let me know what he says? I'm very happy.

Because she knew that he would be texting and driving, which was probably his worst bad habit, she replied with a simple X and then slipped her phone into the pocket of her dress as she hunted for her shoes and hurried out the door before she too was late for work.

After a grueling workday, Ivy let herself into the apartment, glanced towards the kitchen when Damien came padding out, his jeans torn at the knee, his tank top showing off his ridiculously bony shoulders.

"Oh my God, she lives!" he said exaggeratedly, a look of mock relief on his face.

"Hi, Best-Friend-in-the-World," she said and wrapped him in a hug. When he chuckled and patted her back, she added, "How have you been since…a whole two days ago?"

"Ha. Ha. Ha," he replied, unoffended. "But, to answer your question—good. Everything is hunky-dory."

She moved into the lounge, dragged her bag, which was full of laundry, to the sofa, and dumped it unceremoniously onto the floor, spilling her clothes, bras and panties included.

"Laundry day?"

She nodded, only just managing to sit in the tight black dress that she'd worn to work that day so that she could separate the laundry. She wondered how to broach the subject of moving out, wondered how he'd take it. "How is Louie doing?" she asked when he padded back towards the kitchen.

"He's good!" he shouted back. "Told his parents back in Missouri that he's gay and, well, they aren't too happy. But other than that, he's good."

She frowned as she glanced towards the kitchen. When Damien came out, carrying two glasses of wine, she chuckled and took the one he held out to her. "I'm sorry," she said. "I had no idea they didn't know."

Damien laughed. "Oh, they knew. I mean, come on! Louie may as well have 'I like boys' painted on his forehead."

She smiled because it was true. "That doesn't mean he's not hurting, and I'm sorry about that," she said, rephrasing her thoughts. "Louie doesn't deserve it."

"No, he doesn't," he said, still smiling. "But I think they'll come around. He's an only child so the stakes are higher for them."

She nodded, took a sip of wine, and then set it down on the carpet as she stood with the first load in her hands. She walked through to the kitchen, where incidentally, their laundry and dryer were located. "You two seem serious," she said, raising her voice as she stuffed the first load in and turned the machine on.

"We are. Like the whole bang shoot. I'm going to marry this guy, Ivy."

Ivy poked her head out of the kitchen, stared at Damien across the room. "What did you say?"

"You heard me," he replied, a huge grin in his blue eyes.

"Oh, shit! You're serious!" She tried and failed to keep the shock and excitement out of her voice. She clapped her hands together and moved over to where he'd sat on the floor by her laundry so that she could wrap him in a hug. "When did this happen?"

"I don't know," he said, honestly. "It was kinda out of the blue, you know. I just woke up one day and looked at him and...that was it."

"And he feels the same way?"

"Yeah, he does," Damien replied, a goofy look in his eyes. "We want to wait until his parents calm down enough to at least attend the wedding, but…that's the plan."

Ivy felt the tears prickle her eyes and didn't try to stop them. "Shit. This is *huge*."

He nodded, reached across the laundry pile to take her hand. "Will you be my best woman?"

She hiccupped as the tears flowed freely, nodded because she couldn't reply just then.

Damien laughed and hugged her. "It's the end of an era, baby," he said, simply. "We went from college besties to decade-long roomies, and now…now we're moving on with our others." He looked at her. "Do you think our kids will like each other?"

She laughed then, a weird strangled sound through her tear-choked throat. "They better, or else we'll sort them out."

He chuckled and squeezed her hand. "I love you always."

"Ditto." Noticing his faraway look, she tapped his hand to bring his attention back to her. "This is the perfect segway into what I have to say," she began.

"You're moving out."

He said it as a statement, not as a question. She looked at him, surprised.

"Come on!" he laughed. "You've been in love with David since like day one. I'm honestly just surprised it took you two this long."

"Really? You don't mind?" she asked, watching for the Damien-tells that she had learned over their impossibly long friendship.

He raised his eyebrows. "I'm sad that I'm losing you to another man," he joked. "but considering you're losing me to another man too…"

She shook her head, her grin wide. "It does seem fair when you put it like that."

He nodded. "Louie's lease actually ends in two weeks so he can take over your half of the rent then. If that's okay?"

"Perfect," she said. "It'll give me time to pack the things I want and throw the rest."

"I get Sally," he said, referring to their trusted brown sofa, with the hideous upholstery and the colorful throw pillows her grandmother had made. He rubbed his hand along her to prove his attachment.

Although she'd be lying if she said that she didn't have a little soft spot for the sofa, she smiled, knowing that Sally would be horribly out of place in David's house. "You better look after her. She's the only girl we've ever fought over."

He laughed and leaned over to wrap her in a hug. "I promise."

The door opened just then, and Louie stepped inside. "Hey, hey, get your hands off my man, lady," he joked and walked over to where they sat.

He plopped down on the floor next to them. If he noticed Ivy's tear-streaked face, he didn't say anything. "How are you?" he asked, looking directly at her, his hazel eyes friendly.

She smiled. "Fantastic." She stood and moved towards the kitchen. "Although I think some congratulations are in order."

"You told her?" she heard Louie ask Damien. "Is that why she's crying?" he whispered, only just loud enough for her to hear.

She laughed when Damien began to explain, opened their liquor cabinet, searched for a bottle of champagne and, finding none, text David asking him if he could stop by and bring a bottle. She realized that if he had time to come over, she wouldn't have to uber home either. She smiled when she realized that she'd called his house 'home', felt a small shiver of nervous excitement when she realized that she'd felt weirdly comfortable doing so.

She gave them another minute before returning. "David's going to bring a bottle of champagne over and then drive me home afterward," she said. "I'll take a small load with me tonight and then slowly have everything out in the next week or so as I have time and," she looked at Damien, "the car. I can buy another one maybe Saturday, but need to switch off until then."

He nodded. "You own half of it, so I'll find the Blue Book value and pay you half of that?"

Ivy hadn't even considered taking money for the car, and she had her mouth open to say so when Damien held up a hand. "We have always split things fairly and just because you're going to marry an investment banker doesn't mean I can't foot my half of the bill."

"You're getting married?" Louie asked, a bright, happy smile on his face.

"No," Ivy replied, looking at Damien. "And okay, I won't argue." She sat down again. "I have no idea how David and I are going to figure out the rent thing. We haven't even talked about it," she said, honestly. "We only talked about moving in together for like five minutes this morning."

Damien and Louie shrugged, the gesture a mirror-image of one another.

"You'll figure it out," Damien said.

She nodded. "I guess so."

Chapter 13

David watched from the door as Ivy pulled another pair of heels from her suitcase and placed them in the neat row she'd formed in the walk-in closet. He wondered how it was possible that she had so many. This pair was a fire-hydrant red with spiked heels and thin straps, and he couldn't help but picture her wearing them. Only them.

He grinned as she frowned and started re-positioning them all toes out, rather than heels-out as they had been before. He would never have guessed that she'd be more OCD than him, but strangely, she was. A lot more. At least when it came to her clothes.

He crossed his arms, smiling to himself, content to watch her figure out the closet space. But after a few minutes, when she started tying the shoelaces of all her sneakers, he walked in and then smiled when she glanced up at him, a worried look in her eyes. "If you rearrange those shoes one more time, I'm going to throw them out," he teased and gave her a hand so that he could pull her up from her cross-legged position on the floor.

He felt himself harden when she came to stand chest-to-chest with him, grinned down at her when she chuckled and stood on her toes so that she could brush her lips over his. The kiss, even as casual as she had intended it, made his breath tighten in his chest.

She sighed. "I'm sorry. I just feel...weird. Like I'm taking up your space, you know?" She looked at him once and then leaned her cheek on his chest with a resigned sigh. "It feels weird." She pointed at the neat row of shoes as an example. "I already take up more space than you do!"

179

He felt his heart knock against his chest at her proximity, at the feel of her impossibly soft breasts pressed against his chest. Because he loved the feeling of her, he closed his arms around her and rested his chin on her head in a gesture that he knew she found funny. "You do have a lot of clothes," he said, looking into his—no, their—now-overflowing closet.

"I know. I don't know what to do."

He rubbed an open palm down her back, which was bare through the strappy, black top she was wearing, chuckled when she sighed and leaned into the massage, arching her back against his hand as a kitten would have done.

"I'm happy," he said, drawing her gaze up to his face, her head tilted back so that she could meet his eyes. "I don't care if you have a shit ton of clothes or shoes, Ivy. I'm the happiest I've ever been having you here...in *our* home. And if we need more closet space, we'll add a second closet or store some clothes in the other bedrooms." He nuzzled the soft, sensitive spot beneath her ear. "Point being, space is not a problem."

She smiled and wrapped her arms around him. "I'm really happy too." She took a small step back. "Which brings up a concern that I have..."

"Oh?" He felt his heart sink a little at her tone and at the serious look that had instantly replaced her smile.

"How are we going to figure out the rent thing? I know that you're going to say that you don't need the money, but I can't live here for free. It wouldn't settle well." She said the words in a rush, all the while twisting her hands in front of her.

David thought about it for a second, because the question had taken him by surprise. The truth was that the idea that she would pay for anything hadn't occurred to him. He'd literally never stopped to consider the fact that she'd want to. No, he realized, looking at her, that she'd need to.

He wondered how to approach the situation delicately and then settled on an honest compromise. "Having to figure it out now would be more of a hassle than just paying it myself—"

"I have to pay something!" she interjected, cutting him off instantly.

He held up a hand. "Let me propose a compromise." When she nodded, he said, "You have student debt from all three programs, right?"

She nodded wearily, her narrowed eyes skeptical.

"Why don't I keep paying off the mortgage while you finish paying off those? It'll take what? Three years to pay them off?"

"About," she replied.

He could see that she wasn't happy about his compromise, so he changed his rationale. "Ivy, we're living together because we both plan to be in this for the long haul. Do you agree?"

She nodded but added a good eye roll at his tone. He found it funny that she knew exactly what he was doing. "So, one day soon, when we get married and start a family, wouldn't you prefer that we do so with a joint bank account and no debt?"

She narrowed her eyes at him.

He chuckled. "If I didn't think it'd freak you out, I'd join our bank accounts tomorrow," he said honestly. He had never really thought or worried about her being with him for his money as he might have any other woman. He had learned early on that she just wasn't motivated by more money than she needed.

She sighed and he sensed that she was caving just a little. "I know," he continued, "that it's important to you that you pay your way. But the truth is I'd be paying the exact same bills if you didn't live here and, at this point in our lives, paying off your debt would help us more."

When she rolled her shoulders, taking a minute to let the decision settle before nodding, he grinned. He took a step towards her, wrapped his arms around her. He breathed her in, felt his stomach roll with lust when her lily scent entered his system. He knew it was the shampoo that she used, had seen her put it in the bathroom just yesterday. Lily of the Valley. That's what it was called.

When she tilted her head back to smile up at him, he kissed her, nipped her lip gently before sinking deeper into the kiss. She sighed and ran her hands up his chest to his shoulders where she gently kneaded, her touch sending a small shiver of need down his back. "How about a ten-minute break from unpacking?" she asked in a breathy whisper as she trailed her hands down his abs, her voice growing heavier with lust.

"Ten minutes?" he teased. "I was thinking closer to thirty." He scooped her easily off her feet, making sure not to hit her head on the closet door as he carried her to the bed.

He lay her gently down before positioning his body weight off her and to the side, a habit that he'd fallen into when they'd been trying to have sex without hurting her injured knee. He looked into her emerald eyes and smiled, took a moment to just enjoy seeing her there, her thick, hair spilling in stark contrast over the white bedcovers. When she ran her hands underneath his shirt, gently raking her nails down the ridges of his abs, he tensed and let the pleasure fill him.

"Take this off," she said, giving the shirt a gentle tug.

He reached down and pulled the bottom of the shirt up and over his head, threw it to the side when it came loose. She trailed her fingers, feather-light, over his skin, leaving a line of goosebumps where she went. When she moved to undo his belt buckle, he caught her hands in his, waited for her to meet his eyes. "Your turn."

She grinned then, reached a hand behind her neck to undo the bow that held the top together. When she gave it a single tug, the whole ensemble unraveled to pool at her waist, leaving her generous breasts bare.

He felt his stomach tighten as he bent to nuzzle her gently, taking one small nipple in his mouth. When she moaned and fell back against the bed, taking him with her, he moved to the other, running his hand up and down her thigh softly as he teased her. He trailed open-mouthed kisses down her flat stomach when she lay back, marveling at how soft her skin felt on his lips—as soft as rose petals. When he reached the waistband of her denim shorts, he nipped her hip bone, slid a hand underneath her so that he could pull them off once he had unfastened the button.

She helped him with the last bit of fabric, kicked her feet so that the shorts landed in a lonely pile on the hardwood floor of the bedroom. He moved a single finger down her upper thigh, whisper-light, as he took in the tiny, lace thong that she was wearing, rubbed his hand along her leg as he bent his head and used his tongue on the sheer lace. It didn't matter that there was a barrier between them; he could taste her, hot and wet through the thin layer of fabric.

When she bucked her hips, her breath coming shorter and faster, he hooked his finger in her underwear and pulled them down, letting her kick them off as she had the shorts. The way she arched her hips drove him wild, made him want to bury himself in her and let her ride him to the point of exhaustion. Instead, he moved up so that he could watch her eyes cloud as he touched her gently, felt his own body tighten when he dipped a single finger inside of her and she trembled and pulsed around him eagerly, welcoming.

He felt his heart race in his chest, felt the same impossible urgency to take her then, but forced himself to wait. He wanted to give her everything, wanted her to feel the need, the same lust that he did, and wanted her to know she felt it all for him—just as he did for her.

He looked at her as her eyes darkened with unrestrained need, watched her as her body responded to his touch. He loved the shape of her, curves perfectly sculpted over a slender frame. When she tensed in anticipation, he crushed his mouth to hers, swallowed her ragged breath, excited by what he could do to her. What they could do to each other.

"David," she whispered. "Please. I'm so close."

"I know, baby," he replied, his own voice husky. Raw. He spread her legs with his hand, felt a frenzied need to consume her when she opened her legs further, inviting him to take her. Instead, he moved down her waist, found her center with his tongue again, and lost himself there.

She raked her hands through his thick hair and gripped, holding him in place when she felt her body rise another inch closer. She could feel the blood rushing in her ears, and every time his tongue touched her, she felt her heart race with increasing urgency, felt her body tighten impossibly.

She moaned, the sound loud to her own ears as he increased his pace; she bucked her hips, begging him to take more when she felt the edge of the first rise. She didn't think her body had ever been so tight as he ran his hands up her thighs and under her so that he could lift her hips more. When he changed the angle, his tongue dipping instead of stroking, she cried out, felt herself snap. The orgasm tore through her in a brief flash of pure ecstasy. Her body pulsed gently in the aftershock, trembled and tightened as David kissed her inner thighs.

She felt liquid, warm and loose as he brought his face back to hers, a self-accomplished grin in place. She smiled, turned her naked body towards him so that her breasts touched his chest, and smiled when his grin died. "I want you inside me," she whispered, grinning when his eyes glazed over at the simple truth in her words.

She unbuckled his belt for him, watched as he hurriedly stripped and threw his jeans, boxers and all, onto the floor beside her own shorts. She took a moment to look at him, all of him.

He was gorgeous, she thought, as she did every time she saw him naked. She wondered if the feeling would ever get old, if she'd ever see him like this and not think about how beautiful he was. Bronzed skin, tight, muscular torso, and long, rangy legs. One thing was for certain, she thought, when he noticed the look in her eyes and grinned, David Van den Berg did not look like he worked a desk job.

She moved closer, rubbing her naked body over his so that she could kiss him, her tongue tasting both him and her as she took the kiss deeper.

When he moved over her, she broke the kiss, closed her hand over him, and saw his eyes darken as she guided him inside her. He inched in slowly as if he was afraid of hurting her, and Ivy arched her hips so she could take him the rest of the way. She could feel her lust for him sharp in her center, a gnawing need that seemed to intensify every time he touched her.

He exhaled sharply, and she smiled, aware of his thinly veiled control. His hands were clenched in the sheets on either side of her and he paused for a moment, stilled inside her. She could feel how close he was to losing himself in her, and she ran her hands over shoulders bunched with tense, corded muscle.

Because she loved seeing him, usually so composed and in control, so close to his breaking point, she moved her hips forward slightly, wrapped her legs around his waist. Her body tightened when he started moving inside of her, slowly at first, each thrust pulling her tighter, closer to the precipice.

In the back of her mind, she could hear her breathing coming in short, ragged gasps, but she didn't care. She closed her eyes as the pleasure took her under, wrapped her arms around his broad back as he nipped her neck with his teeth, and tasted her skin with soft lips. Her body felt so heavy, but so alive at the same time, like a boulder careening off a cliff with little thought of the impending crash.

But she did crash.

She felt her body explode with as much impact as she could endure, felt herself pulse around him as he covered her mouth with his, swallowing her cry as, with one last thrust, he followed her over the edge.

She could have stayed there, in that exact position, forever. Or at least that's what Ivy told herself as she burrowed further back into David's chest, content when he tightened his arm around her and nuzzled her neck, his breath sending a chill down her spine.

She gazed out of the wide, bedroom windows, caught glimpses of the tall trees in the back yard through the sparkling glass. She noticed how the sun filtered in through the window at an angle that avoided direct sunlight and felt a moment's appreciation for whoever had built the house. They had cared, she realized.

"I could spend every Saturday afternoon exactly like this," he said and kissed the side of her face before pulling his hand out from around her so that he could stroke her arm.

She smiled at the thought, realizing that it would be quite a perfect way to spend eternity. "Aside from the unpacking," she added, grinning when he just chuckled.

She spotted her last suitcase of clothes by the door, felt a resigned urgency to unpack it, so that she could be done. "Speaking of which..." she started to say.

"You want to get it over and done with today?"

"Yeah. Otherwise, my OCD is going to tick all night," she replied, sitting up in the bed. She took the covers with her, wrapped them around her waist as she leaned against the headboard of the big bed.

"Is there anything else I can do to help?" he asked, as he rested his head on his palm and studied her with sincere blue eyes.

She shook her head. "It's only the one bag of clothes, and there's not much you could do that would make unpacking them more efficient."

He chuckled. "Alright. How about I run to the store and pick up some dinner? And wine? We can celebrate your first official night here."

She felt her heart twitch in her chest and couldn't quite hide the smile of pleasure that bloomed on her face. She wasn't quite sure why it had taken her a week to realize it, but she was living with a man for the first time in her adult life. That constituted a big occasion. "Dinner and wine sound amazing." She leaned forward and kissed him on the lips. "I promise I'll be done by the time that you're home."

"Don't rush," he countered. "We have time."

As he put his clothes back on, she took a minute to burrow into the covers for a moment longer. It felt so good with the blankets pulled up to her chin while the air-conditioned room swirled around her, her body loose and relaxed. When he gave her one last kiss and made for the door, Ivy sighed. As comfortable as she was, she knew that the sooner she finished the chore, the sooner she could relax and enjoy the rest of the weekend.

Their weekdays seemed to go by too quickly, the hours that they were apart stretching between their professions. Time together during the workweek wasn't easy to navigate, especially because David traveled a lot for work, but Ivy fully anticipated making up for their busy schedules on every day that they had off from now on.

With that thought preoccupying her, she stretched one last time and rose from the bed with a sigh. She cast one last look at the thick sheets, reminded herself that she could revisit them in just a few hours, and changed back into her denim shorts and the black, strappy top before slipping her white Nike's on. Dragging the bag towards the closet, she unzipped it and plopped down on the floor to start rummaging through.

She didn't throw anything away; mostly because she constantly updated her closet by buying new outfits and donating what she no longer wore, or, at least in her case, didn't wear enough given all her other clothes. She hung and folded, making sure that everything was color-coordinated in the space that David had given her in the huge walk-in closet. A long rail for all her hangable dresses and tops, ten built-in drawers for all her foldables, one drawer for accessories, and the mat lining the wall on the bottom right for all her shoes. Now that she thought about it, he had pretty much given her the entire right side of the closet. More than, considering the drawers were on his side of the walk-in.

She smiled to herself, felt her heart skip along in her chest. She was happy, she realized. Really happy. Probably the happiest she had been since her father had been diagnosed. The thought took her by surprise; although she often felt the hole that her father's death had left behind, she felt guiltier about how relieved she'd felt, how…at peace. She was relieved he wasn't hurting anymore, relieved he wasn't slowly watching his body die as his mind stayed sharp, even, she realized, selfishly relieved that she didn't have to watch him suffer anymore. It had been too much, even for her, and she was glad he was finally at rest.

Or simply gone.

When the doorbell rang, distracting her from her task, Ivy frowned. As far as she knew, David wasn't expecting anyone, and, she glanced at her watch, he had only been gone twenty minutes. It usually took him thirty to forty because he had to drive to Whole Foods, which was a good two miles down the road, just inconvenient enough that he had to take the car.

She stood and made for the door, jogged down the stairs when it rang a second time. She opened the door slowly, poked her head out, smiling, her hand still on the doorknob, her body in the doorway.

An older couple stood on the front step, their twin expressions of thinly veiled curiosity blatant. Ivy blinked once before composing herself and opening the door wider so that she could greet them with a quiet, "Hello."

The woman smiled politely, nodded her head once in a gesture that Ivy found slightly condescending, or maybe just cold, and replied, "Hello."

Ivy looked at the man. He stood shorter than David, but not by much. He was handsome and strong for his age, with bright blue eyes and a smile that half-grinned at the corners. She had made the connection a second too late. "You're David's parents?" she said, feeling the full weight of the situation press down on her suddenly. *Shit.*

The woman nodded again.

The man chuckled, clearly amused by her predicament, his kind eyes laughing good-humoredly. "We are," he said eventually when his wife didn't offer anything further.

Ivy stepped back. "Please come inside. David didn't tell me that you were coming," she said, clearly unprepared and, she realized, inappropriately dressed in her tiny denim shorts and backless top.

"We decided to drop by before we attend a dinner party this evening," his father said. "So, he isn't expecting us."

"Oh," Ivy managed lamely, unsure exactly what she was supposed to say…or do. She led them to the lounge, waited for them to sit down before adding, "David just ran to the store. He should be back any minute now." She clasped her hands together nervously, eager to escape the situation. "Can I offer you a drink? Some wine? Beer? Water?"

"I'll take a beer," Mr. Van den Berg said, a mischievous twinkle in his eye. "But, before you do," he hesitated, "could we get your name?"

Ivy flushed with embarrassment. "I apologize. How rude of me not to introduce myself. I'm Ivy Watts," she said, not offering any more. If David hadn't told them that they were dating, or that she was moving in, he probably had a good reason.

Mr. Van den Berg nodded, remained quiet for a second as if waiting for her to add more detail. Like, what she was doing in their son's house on a Saturday afternoon, maybe?

She didn't.

After a moment, he added, "I'm Michael. And this is David's mother, Camilla. It's very nice to meet you, Ivy."

"It's nice to meet you too," she replied with a genuine smile before turning to Camilla Van den Berg. "Can I get you anything?"

"Some water would be perfect, thank you," she replied firmly, her cold, clear eyes staring directly into Ivy's as she assessed her, her face a perfect mask of composure.

Ivy nodded and forced the embarrassed flush she felt rise to her cheeks back down. "I'll be right back."

She made a beeline for the kitchen, took a moment to lean against the cold refrigerator, enjoying the electric chill that traveled the length of her spine. The shock of the cold metal gave her the kick she needed, and she hurriedly grabbed a cold beer out of the fridge and popped the top. She looked at the beer in her hand for a second and felt an irrational, niggling panic creep into her chest. Did she get a glass? Did she pour the beer into the glass? What about the water—did she add ice? Oh, God, she thought to herself, this was so much easier when her roommate's parents had known her for ten years and she wasn't having sex with their son.

She wished that Damien was here now; he'd know what to do. Or better, she wished that David would hurry up and come home. She looked at the time again; he'd probably only be another few minutes, but even that seemed like an eternity given the current situation.

She opted for the beer bottle with a glass on the side and added ice to the water. She stared at the drinks for as long as she could and when she couldn't procrastinate any longer, picked up all three and made her way back to the lounge.

She noticed, as she walked back in, that the Van den Berg's had chosen opposite sides of the same sofa, their bodies completely separated on the large piece of furniture. No touching. No conversation between one another as Michael scrolled through his phone and Camilla gazed out of the tall windows at the Hollywood Hills.

Ivy walked around and placed their drinks on the table, then cleared her throat awkwardly as Michael Van den Berg moved forward to grab his beer. He took the bottle, not bothering with the glass, and Ivy filed the information away for another time.

"Thank you, Ivy," he said.

Camilla nodded, gave her a small smile too. "Thank you."

Ivy noticed that she didn't touch the water.

"How was your drive?" she asked as she sat down opposite them. "David mentioned that you live in Santa Barbara?" She realized after the words were out, that their place of residence was about the only thing he'd told her about them. She knew that they weren't close, that he'd had a high-pressure childhood, but other than that, she didn't know one thing about the couple who sat opposite her. In fact, it was weird how little David talked about them.

She had told him everything about her upbringing, everything about her own family and yet…he hadn't even told her his parents' names. How had she missed that, she wondered? She was usually so astute, yet David had managed to keep his family from her the entire time they'd been dating. She hadn't exactly asked him either, she realized. She had been so enraptured with him and the newness of their relationship that she had overlooked the most important people in his life. The thought made her shift guiltily in the chair.

Michael nodded. "It was perfect. Missed all the traffic!"

Ivy smiled, appreciating the fact that he was at least trying to go-along with her lame attempt at small talk. "That's always something to be happy about." She tapped her fingers lightly on her knee, then jerked upright, relieved when she heard the front door open.

"Babe, I'm home!" David called, obviously expecting her to be upstairs.

Ivy flushed with embarrassment and stood just as he came through, his arms laden with Whole Foods grocery bags. He looked in and saw her standing there, saw his parents sitting in the lounge, and added, "Let me just put these down."

Ivy noticed that his voice had changed, that he'd instantly drawn back into himself. "Excuse me," she said as he disappeared into the kitchen, "I'm just going to help him put those away."

She hurriedly followed him, entering the kitchen just as he put the bags on the counter and turned to face her. He looked…weary, she decided. His blue eyes had frosted over, giving nothing away and only the smallest tightness in his forehead indicated that he was a little stressed by the situation he'd walked in to. His eyes cleared slightly when he saw her. He smiled and took her hand. "I'm sorry," he said. "They didn't tell me they were coming."

"Yeah, your dad said as much," she replied, keeping her voice low. "What's the plan?"

He cocked his head. "The plan?"

"Yeah, like, how are we going to justify the fact that I was randomly in your house alone? None of my stuff is down here, so we can go with anything. We just have to corroborate."

He looked confused for a moment, and then when he realized what she was suggesting, she noticed a brief flash of hurt in his eyes. She touched his face. "I don't care what you say. I just…I just figured that there was a reason you hadn't told them yet."

If she was honest with herself, she had also thought that maybe he'd been avoiding telling his parents the 'how we met story'. She knew that she had. The few people who had asked had gotten the very unromantic and unsatisfactory reply of, 'at a friend's party', which was the closest to the truth that she could get without telling her friends and acquaintances that she'd been an escort for over a year—and was dating one of her ex-clients.

He took her hand and kissed her palm. "Yeah, there is. I don't have that kind of relationship with my parents. It has nothing to do with the fact that I'm dating you or any reason related to that," he said. "I love you. I'm happy, proud even, that you're mine."

She smiled when he wrapped his arms around her, breathed in his scent as she came up against his chest. She would have gladly stayed there, in his arms, forever. But, aware of the fact that they'd been whispering in the kitchen for a solid five minutes, she said, "We should get back in there."

"Yeah." He sighed and led the way.

Michael stood when he saw them coming, shook David's hand, a wide grin on his face. David pointedly ignored the smirk and just shook his head, although she could tell he was trying not to grin back. There was a joke there, she realized. Something that only they shared, or maybe that only men shared. She didn't know.

Camilla Van den Berg frowned at him but gave him her cheek so that he could issue her a quick kiss on either side.

Ivy shifted uncomfortably at the formal greeting. It was weird to see such a businesslike interaction between parents and their only child. If she and David ever had kids, they'd be the hugging, teasing, laughing kind of family, she decided, and snuck a glance at David. Yeah, she could do it with him. Not that she was in a hurry, but the thought, the confidence with which the realization hit her, made her feel calmer, centered somehow under the slight edge of panic.

She was about to assess the thought further when David turned to her, his blue eyes calm but alert. He stretched out a hand and she walked to him despite the lead in her feet.

"I see that you've met my girlfriend, Ivy," he announced.

As both pairs of eyes turned to her, one pair curious and assessing, the other completely guarded, Ivy knew where David had inherited his ability to close himself off. David might look exactly like his father, but it was Camilla Van den Berg who gave nothing away, including what she thought about the situation she had just found her son in.

Michael saw his grown son, holding the hand of a woman he clearly loved and, he realized with a punch of regret, hadn't even told them about. He wondered if this was the same woman David had mentioned at the party all those months ago. Judging by the way that they were looking at each other, he concluded that it was, but still felt hurt that he and Camilla had been left out of their son's happiness. Why was it, he wondered, that his only child didn't mention that he'd found a steady girlfriend? A girlfriend who was steady enough to stay home and wait for him while he went to the store? Had he fucked up so badly as a parent? He tried to think of the last time that he and David had spoken. Had it really been when he'd last visited them in Santa Barbara over three months ago? That didn't seem right, but try as he might, he couldn't recall a more recent conversation with his son.

Because his thoughts bothered him, he pushed them aside, plastering his well-practiced grin in place. "I'm just wondering why you were so content on keeping such a gem a secret," he laughed, trying to forge some form of apology. For some reason, Ivy Watts blushed furiously, and Michael quickly changed the subject when he saw David subtly squeeze her hand. "So, Ivy," he began, wanting to ease the blush that had spread across her cheeks, "what do you do?"

He didn't want to be pushy. He wanted to make conversation, wanted to find out more about the gorgeous woman who had enraptured his son. But as soon as the question was out of his mouth, he wished he could take it back. Ivy was too pretty to have a career, surely. Every girl that he'd met who looked like Ivy did things that he, as a sixty-five-year-old, semi-retired investment banker, didn't understand. Like, pose on Instagram, or host parties for their friends while somehow still making enough money to live on.

His son's girlfriend was beautiful, not David's usual type. Michael knew that he usually went for leggy blondes with perfect figures, pristinely styled hair, and tepid personalities, but Ivy was unlike anyone David had ever brought to a social engagement before. She was tall, and still had a perfect figure, but her skin was the color of fresh cream, her hair was pure brown and clearly natural in the way in tumbled down her back, and her eyes were so large and cat-like that he felt like he couldn't maintain eye-contact for being distracted by them.

She looked like one of the Instagram models he saw posing on the beach by the Rosewood Hotel in Santa Barbara, not a career woman, which is why he held his breath the moment the question hung in the air between them.

"I'm a patent attorney," she said quietly and gently tucked a strand of hair behind her ear.

Michael felt his eyebrows shoot up and had to consciously lower them. He had not been expecting that. He glanced at Camilla with a small smile. His wife wasn't even trying to hide her surprise, he realized with an inner sigh. Her eyes were as big as saucers, her mouth usually so perfectly settled, was slightly open in blatant disbelief.

"That is very impressive," he replied. "Which firm?"

"Fitch and Mathers."

He nodded. "They're very prestigious," he replied, approving. "Andy Mathers is a dear friend of mine. We went to college together."

The truth was that Andy and he had been rivals of some caliber until they had left school and realized that it would behoove both of their careers to know one another, but nobody, including Ivy, had to know that tidbit.

Ivy smiled. "The firm is great. I'm very happy there." She chuckled prettily. "Although I'm not quite at a level where I'm interacting with Mr. Mathers himself, especially because I don't ever really have a need to travel to the New York office"

He saw his son touch her back in a gesture of comfort, saw the way that Ivy leaned into his hand, drawing on the support, and felt a small ball of happiness lodge in his chest. He'd never seen David touch another woman in public, never met an actual girlfriend of his. Oh, he brought a catalog of girls to the social functions that his mother told him required a plus one, but he never interacted with them as he did with Ivy. Never even pretended to be interested in them, no matter how pretty or educated they were. And he definitely did not look at any of them with such unguarded affection in his eyes. In fact, he would go as far as to say that, aside from his grandmother, David didn't show love to a single other person, including him and Camilla.

Before now.

Michael followed David's lead and sat back down on the sofa, very aware of the fact that Camilla was uncommonly quiet. She would usually be half-way out the door by now, having paid her familial duty. But instead, she sat quietly, her legs perfectly together and crossed at the ankles, her back ramrod straight as she listened to the conversation.

David leaned back on the couch that he'd sat on, pulling Ivy back with him so that they were nestled together.

"How's semi-retirement going, Dad?" David asked him, reverting to the small-talk that was so common between them. Too common, Michael realized.

He shrugged, chuckled at David's knowing grin and held up his hands in surrender. "I'm down to forty hours a week and don't touch my computer on the weekend at all," he said, laughing. "Your mother is starting to complain that I need to find a hobby, something to do with all the free time I have."

He turned to Camilla expectantly, trying to draw her into the conversation. He'd never had to make an effort to get her to talk before, and somewhere in the back of his mind, he was worried about her, about why she seemed so detached. Or at least more detached than usual.

She took the cue, smiled calmly and said, "It is unusual, after having him for only an hour or two a day for most of our married life, to now have him working from home and done by four o'clock. I don't know what to do with him," she teased, good-naturedly.

She turned to him, and although her eyes were smiling, Michael could see the tension between her eyebrows. He reached across the sofa and patted her hand, aware of the fact that he had to stretch to close the distance between them, aware of the unfamiliar feeling of her hand underneath his. There was a time, he remembered, when they couldn't take their hands off one another, when they'd acted much like David and Ivy were now. "I've been thinking about taking her to Europe," he said easily, choosing to change the topic of conversation. "It's been a good ten years since we went away together."

Camilla frowned at him, hearing his plans for the first time. He grinned, enjoying the feeling of unsettling the perfectly-primed Camilla Van den Berg.

"That would be nice," she said, taking him completely off guard. He had expected some push back, some argument about the social engagements they'd miss, or the charity events they'd promise they'd be at.

"I think that sounds amazing," David seconded from his seat across the room.

Ivy nodded, a small smile in place. "Where will you go?" she asked, kindly, not realizing that he hadn't thought that far ahead.

"I'm not sure," he replied honestly. "I guess that'll be up to Camilla." He looked at his wife, saw that she was watching him, her eyes drawn and cautious.

She noticed that everyone was waiting for her to reply, shook her head. "I'll need more time than that to make up my mind." She laughed a little. "Maybe the French Riviera."

He felt a small kick in his stomach when she looked up and he saw something in her eyes that he hadn't realized had been missing. Camilla was excited. Not the type of excitement that she got when she was planning a party or talking to one of her friends about a project, the type of excitement that was always accompanied by the pressure of expectation, and the stress of follow-through. The excitement that he saw in her eyes now was the type that he'd seen in her eyes when they'd found out that, after a long, painful year of trying, she was pregnant. The type of excitement she used to have all the time when they were young and planning to do something utterly foolish together. When had that disappeared, he wondered?

He shifted on the sofa, then cleared his throat. "Maybe we could add the Hotel de Paris in Monte-Carlo? You used to talk about going there all the time…"

She nodded, her eyes far away. "I forgot about that."

"You'll have to tell us how it is," David added, sensing that the mood in the room had changed. "Maybe I can take Ivy next year. She's never been to Europe."

Michael glanced at Ivy. She smiled and tilted her head to look up at David. "You've never been to Camp Wakamehu, so we're even."

They chuckled at what was clearly an inside joke, a shared secret about what he could only imagine was the difference in their upbringing. "Well, before you go to Europe, you should come visit us in Santa Barbara," he said, fully intending on blackmailing his son into coming to stay. He wanted to know more about Ivy Watts, wanted to get to know her better because clearly, David was head over heels. "You can introduce Ivy to your grandmother. We'll make it a family occasion."

He noticed that Ivy had paled a little, and she glanced at David. "Ivy's met Amanda already," he said simply.

He rubbed his hand up and down her arm, clearly trying to relax her and Michael wondered what he'd walked into.

"My father was at Hanley Hospice for a few years," she said as if sensing the unasked question. "He passed about three months ago, a few weeks after David and I started dating."

"I'm sorry," Camilla said, expertly covering his embarrassed silence. "That must have been very difficult."

Once the embarrassment faded, Michael felt surprise; David and Ivy had been dating for three months and his son hadn't even told them let alone planned to introduce them.

"My own parents died in an accident when David was just a baby," Camilla said, smiling sadly. "It was about the loneliest I've ever been in my life. Michael was working his way up in the world, and David was too young to understand so…it was…hard."

Michael sat up straighter on the sofa. He'd never heard his wife so much as mention her dead parents, let alone their accident. He thought back to what year that had been and, much to his surprise, he couldn't remember. She was right; he had been busy.

He felt the guilt settle in his stomach, felt the knowledge of his absence spread. He had a wife who'd gone cold on him years ago and a son who hadn't told him that he had a serious girlfriend and, well, he couldn't blame either of them. Worse, he didn't know why he was only realizing it now. Maybe it was because, for the first time since his son had been born, he'd only now realized by the addition of Ivy Watts that he didn't know David at all.

When he'd been a young father, he hadn't gotten home early enough to see David before he was put to bed, and he'd been out of the house first thing in the morning so he could be the first in the office.

"I'm glad that he's not suffering anymore," Ivy was saying. "Glad that he's at peace, but it's a strange thing to know that your aging grandparents are your only remaining family."

"No. They're not," David said and kissed her temple. "You know that."

She smiled at him, touched her cheek when a single tear escaped, and then laughed at herself. "How did we get on to such a morbid topic?"

David chuckled and said, "Maybe we'll bring Ivy's grandparents up and make a day of it? That way they can meet Gran too?"

Because Michael knew his son was trying to ease Ivy's embarrassment, he nodded, looked to Camilla for confirmation. "That sounds perfect."

Camilla nodded. "Let us know which weekend suits you? We can make plans anytime."

Michael stared at her, shocked by the invitation; his wife never suggested a gathering unless she fully anticipated following through. In fact, she had told him just yesterday that he couldn't go on a weekend fishing trip with two of his oldest friends because they were booked through to the December holidays. Huh, he realized with a small kick of satisfaction. She must actually like Ivy. Either that or she was planning something that he hadn't thought of yet so that she could learn more about the girl.

"Thanks, Mom," David said, clearly just as surprised as Michael.

When he looked at Ivy for confirmation, Michael thought it a day for the record books. His son, the overly serious, calculated, almost-standoffish investment banker, was in love with a gorgeous patent attorney he couldn't stop staring at, and who clearly felt the same way about him.

He took Camilla's cue when she glanced at her watch, sighed as he stood, and steeled himself for the evening ahead. Strangely enough, for the first time in his life, he would have rather been in a pair of sweatpants at home, talking to his wife, son, and his son's new girlfriend.

You're getting old, Michael. He thought the knowledge would scare him, thought the spread of age would feel like cancer to him, a long, slow death of sorts. But now, looking at David so happy, he felt like he'd done enough, felt like he'd lived a full life, made enough money that his son would never have to worry about it. He would, though, Michael knew. David would keep climbing because he had been raised to. He'd be more successful and wealthier than Michael himself.

He just hoped that David learned from his and Camilla's mistakes, kept a tight grip on Ivy as they moved up in the world. The thought made him look at his wife, made him wonder if there was something between them still, something that they could unbury and revitalize.

Chapter 14

David winced when he heard Gordon shout his name from the far side of the office, his bellowing voice reverberating in the airtight room. He looked up as the short, plump man walked with brisk, inelegant steps towards his office, sighed at the cat-like grin on Gordon's face. What could he possibly have to be happy about?

Just yesterday one of their long-term clients had moved away from the firm, choosing to place his trust, and considerable portfolio of businesses, in their direct competitor's hands rather than allow the Black Finch team to advise him on his acquisitions and sales. It had only been a single client and he knew that it wouldn't make a dent in the firm's transactions, but it still hurt. And, unlike Gordon, who hadn't lost any sleep over it, David considered it a personal failure.

Sitting back in his chair, he waited for Gordon to push his office door all the way open without knocking or even sparing a wave through the big, glass windows.

"You're never going to believe this!" Gordon said, his face red from the brisk two-hundred-yard walk, his voice puffing slightly. He closed the door behind him, having issued his statement just loud enough for their associates and analysts to have heard before he shut them out.

David cringed, thankful that none of the other partners or other executive staff worked on their floor. He remained silent, waited patiently as Gordon plopped his significant bulk in the chair across from his desk. He raised one eyebrow when Gordon just sneered at him.

"Bruce and Deborah Standard are moving to Los Angeles," he said suddenly, unable to contain himself.

David deliberately refrained from showing his reaction to the news; instead, he nodded slowly and leaned back in his chair a little further. As long as Gordon didn't know that his heart was racing away from him, or that his palms were suddenly sweating, he didn't care. He could keep his face as blank as if he'd just been told what Gordon had eaten for lunch.

"I heard from Jerimiah Abelman in the New York office this morning," he continued, even though David hadn't asked. "Apparently, both offices are going to announce the transition at the end of the week."

"It makes sense." David saw some logic in the decision. "New York is one hundred percent in-line, perfectly greased. Los Angeles on the other hand…"

"I resent the insinuation," Gordon retaliated instantly, his brow furrowing and, somehow, adding volume to his already-plump face. "We run a tight ship here. This office has thrived for thirty-three years."

"Yes." David sighed, refusing to take the bait. Gordon was a chronic underperformer and a big talker, which was something that made David exceptionally weary of him. "But we've sailed off a lot of the New York connections, Gordon. There's no denying it. More than that, we only have Tom Delton and four other managing directors in the LA office. We're growing and it's about time somebody stepped in to oversee the spread."

David glanced at his computer screen as an email notification popped up, briefly noticed that it was from his secretary, and ignored it so that he could finish the conversation currently unraveling in his office.

"Anyway, I just thought that you might like to know." Gordon leaned back in his chair, his belly pulling his dress shirt out from the waistband of his slacks.

God, he's a smug bastard.

"I can imagine that some…reorganization might take place once he's here," Gordon continued, clearly trying to rile him. "You know, it's not every day that the CEO moves across the country to keep an eye on things."

David nodded. He was aware of the implication, but he didn't care. The numbers coming out of the Los Angeles office alone stood as evidence that they were managing. More than that, David knew that he was competent, significantly more so than Gordon at least.

He tried to ignore the fact that the end-of-year promotions were only six months away; if an investment banking firm wanted to rid themselves of a VP or MD they simply didn't promote them until they got the point and jumped ship. But, even considering that, David didn't think anyone would be getting fired. Tom did a fantastic job as COO and, at least in David's opinion, the firm and all of their senior staff were unreproachable. Even Gordon had a considerable Rolodex, which was probably the only reason that he hadn't been fired purely for being insufferable.

That left a flaw in his own logic that even he couldn't ignore. So, why? Why would Bruce Standard, a native New Yorker and self-made millionaire several times over, uproot his middle-aged wife to come and live in California at the tail-end of his career? Corporate restructuring aside, it didn't make much sense, even if he'd never admit that to Gordon. "Any idea when he's arriving?" he asked, hoping that Gordon could at least be of some use.

"Word on the street is as early as three weeks." He stood and stretched, glanced out the glass windows of David's office. "By the way," he said, turning back suddenly. "I mentioned to a friend that you were, ah, quite serious with a certain Ivy Diana Watts."

David felt his heart drop through his stomach to his feet. He looked up at Gordon's face, knew that his eyes glinted dangerously, but didn't try to contain the anger. "Oh?"

Gordon at least had the grace to flush a little, but to his credit, he maintained eye contact, even as a light band of sweat beaded on his forehead. "Just…be careful. Apparently, she's been…how do I put this delicately?" He raised a hand to rub exaggeratedly at his jawline. "Seen around a bit. You should be…more careful." He sighed and gave a dramatic shake of his head. "I'd just hate for Bruce Standard to find out."

David felt the rage lash through him instantly, and for only a moment, he imagined plowing his fist into Gordon's soft, weak chin. Instead, he stood slowly, making sure he held Gordon's gaze the entire time. "There isn't anything I don't know about Ivy," he said firmly. "And, considering I'm going to marry her, I suggest that you be a little more…*discreet* about what you say."

Gordon took a step back when he saw the raw fury in David's eyes. "Congratulations," he mumbled. "I didn't know that you were engag-"

"I haven't asked her yet. Irrespective, that shouldn't make a difference when it comes to how you treat a woman," he said. He paused for a fraction of a second. "Get out. *Of. My. Office.*"

Gordon bobbed awkwardly as he fumbled with the door handle before yanking it open. Flustered, he glanced back at David and added, "Never would have taken you for the type to date a whore."

David saw red.

He took one step around his desk, fully intending to slam Gordon's face through the glass wall of his office, but the smaller man whisked away, closing the door with a frenzied bang as he half-ran back to the protection of his office.

David kept walking, clenched his fists as he fought the urge to track the weasel down and throw him from the rooftop. Instead, he reached the door, touched the handle, and then turned back to his desk, his long stride eating up the space in two quick steps. *Fucking asshole*, he thought as he tried to sweep the self-satisfied whine of Gordon's voice out of his head.

He walked back around his desk, sat down slowly. When he steepled his fingers and placed his elbows on the desk, he glanced outside and noticed two of the analysts looking at him, their eyes showing the same unease. *Oh, Christ.* Had they heard?

He tried to tell himself that it didn't matter, that he loved Ivy for who she was, knowing full well how they'd met and how she'd supported herself before. And, truthfully, it didn't matter to him. It didn't make a difference to how he felt about her. But it did scare him. Men had been ousted for a lot less in the industry. His entire job as an MD was making connections, bringing people and businesses with money, oftentimes old, conservative money, into the firm, and preferably, keeping them there.

Sighing, he glanced at his computer, tried unsuccessfully to staunch the rising flood of panic. What would he do? He'd meant what he'd told Gordon. He loved Ivy, fully intended on proposing when he thought that she was ready and, above all else, didn't want to see her hurt.

But, he realized, it was her reputation too. He reached for his cellphone so that he could call her, but just as quickly put it down. It was only two o'clock. There was no point in ruining her day too. He'd talk to her when he got home; that way, they'd both be prepared to deal with it when it came up to bite them in the ass.

Because if David knew one thing about Gordon, it was that he couldn't keep his mouth shut. One way or another, everyone, including Bruce Standard, would soon know exactly how he and Ivy had met and, best-case scenario, at least they'd be prepared to deal with it together.

Ivy glanced up from her perch on the sofa when David walked in through the front door. She felt her heart give a small kick and smiled up at him as he placed his gym bag on the floor and came towards her. She saw the strain around his eyes, wondered if something had happened at work that he was worried about, or if he'd just had a long day. She would have asked, except she knew that he'd just push her concern aside, tell her that he didn't want to bring his work home to her.

When he collapsed onto the sofa next to her, she moved her legs out from under herself and crawled over so that she could snuggle up against him. "Long day?" She kept her voice casual.

He wrapped an arm around her and kissed her temple, squeezed her arm gently to acknowledge her. "It was…interesting," he said, his voice cautious.

He didn't look at her. But it was more than the fact that he didn't meet her eye, more than the tone of his voice, cold and far away, that concerned her. It was the way that even with her body aligned next to his, he seemed absent, as if he was trying hard to be there, but just couldn't bring himself away from whatever had happened.

She felt a small, gnawing worm of worry crawl into her stomach and settle there. "Do you want to talk about it?" She had come to know his moods better since they'd been living together, and she had come to understand that David was not a cold person. He was impossibly kind and generous and the icy, detached façade that he so often wore was a barrier of sorts, a way to protect himself from feeling too much.

He didn't answer her right away, and she felt his eyes harden, ice blue against whatever he was thinking about. Ivy sighed and touched his face, gently kissed his lips when he turned to look at her. She hated that he still didn't share these, the most important things to him, with her. Even as she ran her hands up his chest, she felt the tight set of his muscles, the tension in his shoulders. She sank into the kiss when he sighed and relaxed against her, used her tongue to tease his mouth. She wondered how, even so distracted, he could make her stomach flop around endlessly inside of her.

She moved over him, straddled him so that their centers came up against each other. She smiled against his mouth when she felt him, long and hard, against her.

He trailed small, hurried kisses up her throat, nipped her lip playfully as one big palm reached up to cover her breast, his fingers teasing her nipple through the fabric of her cotton shirt, just enough that her breath hitched against the onslaught of pleasure.

"I missed you today." She purred the words as his hands worked wonders over her skin, touching, squeezing, grazing, caressing. She ran her hand down his torso and, pulling out his dress shirt from his slacks, ran her palm up against the hot skin of his bare chest. She felt his abs tighten when she touched him, felt his pleasure flame her own need.

She touched him everywhere, taking her time as she explored him. When he gripped her hair in one hand, she smiled and slowly, looking into eyes glazed with lust, unbuttoned his shirt and pulled it off his shoulders. She felt her own wet heat through the slacks that she hadn't taken off from work, felt her body pulse in anticipation when her hands reached for the waistband of his. She wanted him like she had never wanted anything before. She wanted him to fill her, wanted him to lose himself in her, wanted everything he was willing to give her.

She unzipped him, ran her hand over his boxers, over him, felt her body tighten in pleasure when he groaned and let his head fall back. Any other time she would have pleasured him, felt her need rise as they brought each other closer and closer to the edge. But now, as she looked at him, she felt her body respond with an urgency that demanded satiation. She wanted him right then, more than anything.

"David." Her voice came out hoarse.

He looked at her, taking a second to focus on her face.

"I want you. Now."

He grinned, a dangerous gleam in his hard, blue eyes and Ivy slid off his lap, stood up, and slowly removed her slacks. She refrained from checking which underwear she'd put on before work that morning; he didn't care, though she usually would have. Instead, she slid them off and left them there on the floor.

He stood beside her, kicked his shoes off before hurriedly going for his pants. Ivy met his eyes, grinning when he hobbled a little trying to get his right foot out of the cuff.

Because she could, she moved to him, watched his eyes darken with awareness as she drew nearer, blacken as she closed her hand over him. He let out one long, shuddering breath as she stroked, gripped her upper arms with big hands, and closed his eyes against the sensation as she quickened the pace.

For a moment, he let her have her way, let her torture him until he was as hard as steel in her hand. She watched him as he stood, fingers gripping her arms, eyes closed, jaw clenched, and felt her own need spread. He opened his eyes, saw her watching him, a wicked gleam in her gaze and, slowly released his grip on her arms.

Ivy thought he was going to take her right there in the living room, and squeaked unexpectedly when, instead, he bent down and picked her up, carried her over to the stairs and began to climb. "David," she began, feeling self-conscious. Vulnerable. "I can walk up."

"I know," he said simply, not stopping until he'd carried her easily up the rest of the stairs and into their bedroom.

He put her gently on the bed, walked over to the big windows, and drew the blinds shut before coming back to her. He positioned his body against hers and Ivy felt a single tremor run the length of her spine when he began a slow exploration of her body. This wasn't how she imagined it, she realized, as a small ball of fear unfurled in her chest.

It was so much more. And for one small moment, she felt panic, sharp and desperate, clawing at her throat.

"I don't just want to fuck you, Ivy," he whispered, his eyes meeting hers. "I want to make love to you. I want to love you. Only you."

Her body responded to the husky need in his voice, even as her heart thumped in her throat. She knew that she loved him already, that she was in love with him. But something about the simple way her chest expanded every time he said it made her want to snatch the feeling and bottle it away somewhere. Somewhere she could keep it safe. Somewhere nothing could touch it.

"I love you," she said, unable to find the words.

He smiled at her as he lowered his body down on top of her, gently brushing her lips with his own as he eased inside her and sank to the hilt with one, long stroke.

She closed her eyes, welcomed the sensation of him. When he started moving slowly inside her, she moaned and gave in to the heat that was pulsing along her skin, through her veins. When he quickened, matched his need to hers, she arched her hips and welcomed the pace, felt her body pull impossibly tight with each thrust of his hips.

"Baby? Look at me."

She shifted her gaze, vaguely aware of the fact that her vision had blurred around the edges; she focused on his face, looked into eyes heavy with lust and heat and love. Her body, taut near the first rise, ached for release, poised somewhere between pain and pleasure. Ivy savored the feeling even as she wrapped her legs around him and took him deeper, rotated her hips in the smallest encouragement.

He groaned and buried his face in the hollow between her neck and shoulder, supported himself on his elbows as he drove them right to the edge. When the orgasm finally tore through her, she gasped and dropped her hands from around his neck to the bed, gripping the covers as she pulsed around him. Her skin felt electric, alive, and everywhere that his skin touched hers felt raw and exposed, a bundle of nerves against a live wire. David sped towards his own release, his breath coming in small pants until, with one last shuddering thrust, he came, his thick muscles bunching and contracting for a single moment before he collapsed on top of her.

For one stunned moment, Ivy lay still underneath his full body weight, enjoying the comforting pressure even though she had to take small, controlled breaths to fill her lungs. She ran her fingers over his back, delighted when the hair on his arms rose at her touch. "Well," she laughed, "that wasn't such a bad way to greet each other at the end of the workday."

His chuckle was muffled by the pillow, but then he rolled off her, propped his head up on one palm, and ran a hand up her side. "Not bad?"

Before she could reply, he sighed, and her mind instantly snapped back to whatever it was that he needed to tell her, ruining the warm afterglow that she'd been enjoying only a moment before.

They hadn't been together long, but six months was long enough that she knew when something was bothering him. "Are you going to keep it bottled up until I torture it out of you?" she asked. She smiled to take any sting out of her words. "What is it, David?"

She touched a finger to the single crease on his forehead. "I can see the secret between us and it's sitting right here."

He frowned even as his fingers continued to stroke her, up and down, sending little jolts of pleasure through her. He was quiet for a moment longer, then said, "Gordon, you know, the asshole from work? The one from the party all those months ago?"

She nodded even as she felt her stomach bunch. Had Gordon made Partner before David? She felt her stomach drop. That would devastate him, she realized. He had worked so hard and, although he'd never admit it, he cared so much. Too much. To him, it wouldn't just be a personal failure, it would be one that he'd have to brandish to his parents, worse, to his family's social circles.

"He...he mentioned today that he knew about the escorting thing, said some pretty fucked-up shit and implied that he'd let it slip to Bruce Standard, who, as it turns out, is moving to LA." He looked at her then. "I'm sorry, baby. I didn't even want to tell you, but knowing him, it's going to get out sooner than later, and I don't want you to be taken by surprise."

She felt a long, cold tendril of fear spread through her, tried to smile even though her vision was blurred with unexpected tears. Gordon could use this against David, she realized. Even if he hadn't made Partner yet, he might be able to sabotage David's chances with information like that.

She pushed off the bed, took to pacing back and forth across the room, forgetting her nakedness for a moment. She felt the fury, cold and hard, push through the fear and sadness. God, how had she thought that it would never come back to bite her? How had she been so ignorant? So naïve?

"Ivy, it's not a big deal." David stood as he said the words, reached for her and smiled when she walked straight to him, nestled against his chest.

"Don't lie to me," she replied, quietly. "You know that this could be really bad for you."

To his credit, he didn't flinch, didn't deny the words that came so bitterly from her. Instead, he rubbed a rough palm down her naked back, tried to soothe her, she knew, even as his own mind had to be spinning. "There's nothing we can do about it," he started saying.

"Yes," she argued, taking a step back from him so that she could meet his eyes. "There is."

"No." His eyes glazed over with anger. "I know you," he said. "You think some vindictive asshole is going to end the best thing that's ever happened to me?"

"You would be wiser for it, David." She smiled sadly. "You *know* that I'm right."

"I don't care. It doesn't matter to me." He raked a hand through his hair, frustrated by the situation. "I only told you so that we could prepare," he said, raising his voice. "I didn't even think about breaking up with you, Ivy. And quite frankly, it hurts that you think so little of me."

He looked at her then, and she felt the guilt spread through her. She wouldn't have judged him, would have understood, even if she'd have been devastated. She held up a hand, took a few moments for herself when her throat clogged. "I'm sorry. It's just...we've been through this before, and I...I guess I don't know what I'd do if our situations were reversed."

"I left the first time because you scared the shit out of me. I left because I fell in love with you after forty-eight hours of knowing you and that was fucking frightening for someone who'd never even loved a puppy before!"

She took a step back, alarmed by the anger in his voice. He *never* raised his voice. Usually, she could tell when he was angry by how quiet and withdrawn he behaved, so seeing him with his fists clenched at his sides, his face red with rage brought on a flush of regret.

"Stop holding that over my head, Ivy," he said, quietly this time.

"You're right." Her admission surprised her, but she knew that it was true. "I'm petrified by you and it's easier to just expect that it won't work out, that you'll leave me eventually." She looked up, met his eyes again. "I'm sorry."

If he was surprised, he didn't show it. He sighed. "I'm sorry too. I just...God, you frustrate me sometimes."

She smiled at that, knew that it was true. "So, if you're not going to be logical about it, what now?"

Sighing, he dropped into a seated position on the bed before looking back up at her. "We're going to sit tight, and when it does come out, because it will, we're going to be one-hundred percent honest."

"Do you think that's a good idea?"

Although he didn't say yes, she saw him nod, even though he was looking at the carpet. "Honesty is always better. We'll downplay it a bit but essentially tell people the truth."

"It is the twenty-first century for Christ's sake," she said. "It's not like most of the men at your firm haven't hired escorts before, or worse, paid pennies for prostitutes who have no option except to sell themselves!"

"Hey, hey," he said, holding up his hands in mock surrender. "I'm on your side, remember?"

She groaned, tapped her palm to her forehead. "I know. Let's just hope that we can play it off as a funny meet-cute and let it naturally die down from there."

"I agree."

Because she needed to distract herself, she took a step back and bent over to pick up her clothes before moving through to the shower. When he followed her through, she added, "I just hope word stays far away from my work."

David nodded, watched her as she turned on the shower, and waited for it to go hot. "If it doesn't, maybe we can have my father speak to Andy Mathers. He could probably work something out quickly and quietly."

She nodded, felt a little relief when she remembered Michael Van den Berg had been in Andy Mather's college class. Maybe the fact that they were friends would make a difference when the time came. *Maybe.*

Because she needed to wash the day off her skin, and because she didn't want to be alone, she half turned to face him and held out a hand. "Shower with me?"

"I thought you'd never ask," he replied, and grinning, stepped into the shower with her.

Chapter 15

Amanda didn't consider herself old fashioned despite the fact that she was eighty-four; and, if anyone had cared enough to ask, she'd have had substantial evidence to support the fact that she was about as hip as someone who'd lived for over eight decades could be. She loved her clothes, like to wear fashionable items that, on a younger person, would have been called 'bohemian'. She ate everything, including sushi, which, when she was a child, would have been considered uncivilized.

The only thing that belied her age was the fact that she used it to her advantage as often as humanly possible, but that was only because she'd found that old people could generally get away with anything if they just owned their years instead of shying away from them.

So, when she rang her grandson's doorbell, having not announced her intention to pay a visit, she didn't think much of it except as to her own inconvenience if he and Ivy hadn't been home. But she knew they were because she'd already seen both his Porsche and Jeep side-by-side in the driveway.

She straightened her loose-fitting blouse, which had been fluttering in the quiet breeze, straightened her spine when she heard David's footsteps, and smiled like the Cheshire cat when he opened the door.

Oh, he was surprised to see her, she realized with a small chuckle. Maybe it was because it was eight o'clock on a Wednesday night? Maybe it was because he hadn't called her in over a week and had suddenly remembered, after seeing her standing on his front steps, that she was still alive.

"Gran," he said, his smile wide.

Lord, but he looked like his grandfather. Every time she saw him, her heart caught in her chest, stuck there for a minute as memories of her youth, of love and life and loss flooded back to her.

"I thought that I'd stop by and check-in on you, seeing as though you didn't call me this week," she said, not bothering to hide the truth. She was old. The single phone call that her grandson paid to her every week was something she looked forward to. "I haven't even seen you in months, David. And, worse, you've kept Ivy from me for *weeks*."

She stepped into the house, aware of the fact that his eyes darted up the stairs, searching for his girl. She smiled, felt a little kick of joy at the simplicity of it all. Her grandson had gone from frigid workaholic to normal forty-year-old male in the short time that he had been dating Ivy and, to Amanda, nothing in the world could have made her happier.

Oh, she'd been surprised when they'd showed up at her house together, holding each other's hands and sending secret glances when they thought she wasn't looking. Hell, she'd sent a prayer to Mother Nature right then and there, thanking her for ingraining an iota of normalcy in her grandson.

"I'm sorry, Gran," he said, looking sheepish as he took her hand. "I've had a lot going on. I've been traveling a bit with work and then...just busy." Again, he glanced up the stairs. "In fact, why don't you have a seat and I'll go and hunt up Ivy? She was just saying yesterday that she wanted to see you soon."

She nodded, pleased that he wasn't going to make excuses. That was her grandson. Honest to the last. "Yes," she said, "off you go."

She chuckled when he kissed her on the cheek, then moved over to the sofa to wait for him.

It was only two minutes later that she heard them coming down the stairs, chuckling quietly over some shared joke. Again, her heart did a little flip and turned over in her chest. She turned to face them and smiled when Ivy grinned and walked straight into her offered hug.

Amanda rubbed her back affectionately, ignoring the tears pooling in her eyes that threatened to spill over. "How did this happen?" she asked. "I still can't believe it most days."

She remembered giving David's number to Ivy, remembered the distracted way the girl had glanced at the piece of paper, and lost any hope that she'd reach out. But now, only six months later and they were clearly as in love with each other as she had ever been with Daniel.

She looked at Ivy, the understanding passing between them easily, then she clapped her hands together. "Oh, never mind. I'm just so happy!" She saw David grin and smiled.

"We're sorry that we haven't come over," Ivy said. "We've been…"

"Holed up," David finished. He draped his arm over her shoulders. "Holed up at home. Together."

When he kissed Ivy, smiled down at her when she flushed in embarrassment, Amanda's heart gave a small tug. Finally. Smitten. Her grandson was smitten.

Her eyes were definitely old, but she still saw the way that Ivy's misted over, the way she leaned into David's chest in acknowledgment. "I don't think either of us was expecting things to move so quickly," Ivy said simply and swiped at her face with a nervous chuckle when Amanda laughed. "It was petrifying. Still is to be quite honest."

Amanda felt a single tear run down her cheek. "This is the happiest I've been in a long time," she said, honestly. "Shame on you for not visiting me this month! I'm old! I could have died! Tsk tsk!"

"You're a long way from dying, Grandma," David said and rolled his eyes mockingly. "Besides," he kissed the top of Ivy's head, wrapped his arms around her from behind, "you have to stick around for the wedding and the grandbabies and the great-grandbabies."

Amanda noticed that Ivy blinked at that, wondered if they'd talked about getting married already, or if David's statement had taken her by surprise. And why not? She'd accepted Daniel's proposal after two months of courting and they were married forty-two years.

"Anyway," Ivy said, and Amanda noticed that she was a little flushed. "Can you stay for dinner, Amanda?"

She nodded, felt another tear slip over, and hastily wiped it away. "I would love to." She didn't mention that she'd eaten already; she'd just eat again so that she had an excuse to spend more time with them.

Ivy turned to David. "Why don't you take your Grandma out to the balcony and I'll grab some drinks," she said. "We can enjoy the evening outside." She turned to Amanda. "Wine okay?"

"Yes, that would be lovely."

Ivy walked away, and Amanda knew it was to give her time with her grandson. Time which Amanda did not take for granted. She followed him out onto the deck, smiled when the balmy evening warmth enveloped her. She looked out at the view, marveled at the gorgeous homes nestled cozily in the hills, squinted to see if she could see downtown Los Angeles in the distance.

She rested her hands on the metal railing and peeked down into David's back yard, enjoying the feeling of her knees going weak with vertigo. There were ways, she knew, that an old lady could recapture the wild abandon of youth. For her, heights was one of those ways.

"I am sorry," David was saying as he pulled out her chair and guided her away from the balcony towards it, "for being absent." He paused while she sat down, moved around the table to take his seat. "We, ah, had a rough start of it...and now that things are calming down, it's been nice to just...get lost in one another."

She noticed that he flushed a bit, noticed that the direction his thoughts had taken seemed to be sitting between them, but refrained from interrupting. He needed to get it out, so she remained quiet.

"Gran..." he started. Paused. He took a minute to gather his thoughts, and Amanda didn't rush him. Eventually, he added, "You know that I've never been capable of...anything close to this," he said, waving his hand in the general direction of the house. "I've never even wanted a dog because it's too much work and emotional commitment." He laughed then, and Amanda noticed it was an amused laugh, not a bitter one.

"So, loving her scares the shit out of you," she said. "So, what?"

He nodded, smiled at her candor. "I, ah, left." He saw her raised eyebrow, and chuckled, "Realized my mistake soon enough," he teased.

"Well, thank God she took you back," Amanda said seriously. Why was it, she wondered, that the idea of them having missed each other scared her? Probably because they looked so goddamn perfect together; both full of absent touches and longing glances, as if they needed the contact to keep breathing.

"I'm going to ask her to marry me."

She felt her heart give one hard shove before settling in her chest. The admission from her too-serious grandson surprised her, but she wasn't about to object. "I got the general impression," she said, "when you mentioned children. I am *very* happy for you."

She reached across the table so that she could pat his hand, smiled when David grinned back at her with Daniel's eyes.

"I still can't believe you tried to set us up," he said. "How on earth could you have known that we'd work?"

She leaned back, grinning. She'd have liked to have said that time had given her the ability to cut through the bullshit, to see where people belonged in life. But that would have been a heap of crap. She only saw the things that the young people took for granted or didn't understand. Those things that the young were moving too fast to see.

"I didn't," she confessed. "Honestly, there were days that I'd given up on you entirely. I thought you'd just be happy being single your entire life. Making money and working your way up." She realized that she hadn't answered the entire question and added, "But Ivy was the first young woman I'd met who I ever even thought about setting you up with." Her next thought surprised her, but she added it anyway. "You know, I don't know if I even thought about it working; to me, it just made sense."

David laughed. "I'd mostly given up on myself too. She…" He shook his head. "She took me completely by surprise."

She wondered how to phrase the last thing that needed to be said; that he needed to take care to nurture what he'd found now that he had it. As always, she opted for the brutal truth instead. "It's not only your fault," she said, "that you turned out as scared of…feeling as you did."

When he opened his mouth to protest, she steamrolled him, talked over him. "The people who molded you added the curves, David; they filled you with things that you had to overcome, that you still have to overcome." She held up a hand when he would have made excuses for his parents. "I love my son with every beat of my heart, David. But Michael was a shit father. Too busy with his work to notice his wife growing cold and his son freezing out."

David nodded. "He was a good provider."

"Money is fine and dandy, but it doesn't compensate for love. You'd do well to remember that."

Where she had expected an argument, he surprised her by running a hand through his hair as he looked towards the inside of the house where Ivy was buying them time from the kitchen. "She hasn't mentioned marriage or kids," he said, a small smile turning his mouth up at the corners. "I'm trying to mention it as often as possible so that she gets used to the idea."

"But?"

"She's so much younger than I am. I...want her to be sure."

"And?"

He shrugged, looked over the balcony. "I'm afraid it won't work out. And, trust me, I know it's irrational, but what if it all ends? What we no longer love each other?" He looked at her then, his eyes wide with fear. "What if we end up like my parents after all?"

"That's bullshit." She felt anger, ripe and warm, bloom in her breast, saw his eyes widen in surprise. "The fact that you're even thinking about it, even aware of the burden, tells me that you'll be just fine." She sighed. "You know, I'm hard on Michael because I raised him and his behavior pains me, but your grandfather was a hard man too. Wasn't much for physical affection, especially towards a son. But he still goddamn showed up, which Michael was never good at."

"You can't be too hard on Dad," David said, gently. "He's done well by the family."

She nodded, conceding his point, yet still unwilling to make excuses for Michael. Her son didn't know what it was like to sneak up the dark stairs in the middle of the night to hug a little boy who'd been sent to bed alone after playing the perfect six-year-old to a group of strangers. Amanda did though.

She realized the moment that Ivy returned, not because she heard her, or saw her, but because David's eyes lit up, stared past her to Ivy.

"Sorry that took so long," she said.

Amanda reached forward to help as Ivy placed three glasses and a wine carafe on the table. "We were just talking about you," she teased.

223

"Oh, I hope only good things," Ivy said with a small chuckle. "Let me just go get some water and then you can fill me in on where I can do better."

Amanda laughed, aware of the fact that she was being given her own back. She liked that about Ivy, liked that there was no veneer, no false politeness, or trite smiles. The fact that she wore her heart on her sleeve might make her vulnerable, but she knew from having watched her cope with her dying father over the years that Ivy had a backbone that would compensate for it if and when she needed to be strong.

As she watched them together, Amanda marveled at them. How wonderful life was that, at the end of a fruitful and full existence, she would be blessed with this: seeing the man that she loved most in the world, her only grandson, so happy, so full of love, and with his whole life ahead of him. The thought, where it might have made her sad before, excited her, made her look forward to sitting on the sidelines and living vicariously through the new generation.

She laughed as David and Ivy told her about Michael and Camilla's unexpected visit, had tears coming out of her eyes when Ivy described the outfit she had been wearing. Oh, she'd have loved to have seen Camilla's face.

She reached for the pitcher of water just as Ivy reached for it too. Amanda noticed their hands against each other, so similar yet so different, before Ivy pulled hers back and offered to pour the water for her. One so young, so smooth and bare. The other so wrinkled, gnarled, and, she realized with a small kick, sporting a single piece of jewelry that hadn't been removed in nearly fifty years.

"Grandma, how is Ike?" David asked, catching Amanda off-guard.

"Mnn?" She looked up at him, distracted, and her mind took a few seconds to reply to his question.

"My grandma has a, eh, gentleman friend," he explained to Ivy, deliberately stalling while Amanda recovered her faculties. "Ike."

"Oh, he's doing just fine. Brought me flowers just yesterday."

"Oh, I remember you mentioning him," Ivy said, smiling.

Amanda met wide, cat-like eyes, bright with intelligence. She crossed her legs, rocked her hanging ankle back and forth as she gazed out at the millions of lights below. "He is a very nice man," she replied, fondly.

She thought about Ike Matenzo for a moment, thought about how much she liked his crooked grin and wicked sense of humor. "He makes me smile, which I tell you takes a lot of effort when you get to my age."

She chuckled when David rolled his eyes good-naturedly.

"You wait," Amanda laughed, "when all your friends talk about their aches, pains, medications, and who's died this week, you'll need something to make you laugh. We're at the age when we're using funerals as an excuse to socialize."

He reached across the table and touched her hand. "I'm really happy for you."

"I know."

It wasn't that she didn't want to talk about Ike, or that she wasn't aware of how lucky she was, but tonight, with them, she didn't want to talk about herself. She wanted to talk about them, about how they were doing, what their upcoming plans were, and more, what their plans for the future were. Although, she realized, maybe she'd wait on the plans and let David work it out. From the way that Ivy looked at him, he wouldn't have to put in as much legwork as he might imagine.

"Speaking of socializing," Ivy began, from her place next to David, "I'd really like you to get to know my grandparents." She paused briefly. "I think you might have met them at Hanley Hospice once or twice over the years, but if you're available any time soon, I'd like to get us all together. Maybe have lunch?"

Amanda heard David groan and both she and Ivy looked at him in surprise. He held up his hands. "Camilla already offered to have everyone over some time," he said in explanation.

Amanda chuckled and met Ivy's confused eyes. "If Camilla Van den Berg mentions hosting a 'get-together', just let her do it."

"It's a...tradition," David said, floundering for the right words to describe his mother's need to put on a show.

"It's a goddamn obsession," Amanda countered, drawing a chuckle from Ivy. "If she said she wants to do it and you go ahead and arrange it yourself, she'll make your life miserable for years to come."

"It's true," David affirmed with a small nod. Hosting is like Camilla's...thing.

"Okay, okay." Ivy grinned. "The last thing I want to do is offend anyone, but, when she does get around to hosting, I'd appreciate it if you could come and meet my grandparents."

"It's a date," Amanda replied, knowing full well that, Ivy's grandparent's aside, she wouldn't skip the opportunity to see David and Ivy again. She might joke about it, might brush her age aside often, but the truth was she could die at any moment. Although she personally didn't intend to meet her maker anytime soon, she wanted to take the time to see her grandson's new love blossom and grow.

Oh, she had selfish motives too. Being around them made her feel twenty years younger, as if her body could sense the static in the air and feed off the youthful excitement. And that, she decided, was a hell of a lot better than getting your kicks from vertigo.

He watched as she went through her nightly ritual; the same ritual that she'd had for all the years that they'd been married. He used to love watching her go through the process, loved the smells that flooded his senses when she'd finally climb into the bed beside him glowing from all the special creams and butters, and what-nots that she'd massaged into her skin.

Michael realized with a small kick that somewhere along the way, they'd stopped going to bed at the same time altogether. Instead, he'd stay up late and unwind from a long day of work while she opted to get a full eight hours before getting up at the crack of dawn to go jogging with whichever friend she had who could keep up with her insanely committed routine.

"I've finally put the guest list together for the party for the kids," Camilla said, drawing him away from his thoughts. He looked up then, met her eyes in the mirror of her vanity. "It'll be an occasion."

He knew that his brow furrowed, and he tried his hardest to relax his face when Camilla's eyebrows raised slowly, purposefully.

He wasn't like her and David; he couldn't turn his emotions off at the drop of a hat. He had tried often enough, but it just wasn't in his nature. Even now, when he would have given anything to be able to smile and nod his head, he knew that his expression was closer to a grimace.

"What is it?" she asked with a purposefully restrained sigh.

Michael sighed and opted to distract himself by shoving the oversized throw pillows that his wife loved behind his back so that he could sit up fully in the bed.

"Michael?" she asked, not giving him the chance to think of a lie.

He didn't care about the money that he knew she'd spend on the event, was already prepared for the expense from the way she'd referenced it as an 'occasion'. He didn't care about the time it'd take out of his day, or the pain he'd have to live through for the days leading up to it. He was, after all, used to accommodating his wife's event calendar.

"I just…I really would have liked to meet just her family the first time, you know? No other guests, no show, no pretenses. Just…family. Hers. *Ours*."

He watched as she stood from the little ottoman that she used with her dressing table, felt his mouth go dry when her long, silk gown fell to her feet. She was still beautiful, he thought, with clear eyes, long limbs, and soft, smooth skin.

"Why?" She came to lie on the bed, opted to lie on her stomach so that she could prop herself up on her elbows as she looked at him in silence, waiting for his reply.

He took a moment to gather his thoughts, knew that she wouldn't push him, that she would give him time to articulate. Finally, he said, "I know that I wasn't around much." He noticed that she didn't protest, didn't give him false gratification where it didn't belong. It hurt, he realized as he looked into her clear, blue eyes, to have the person you loved most in the world be so honest about your greatest failures. "I know that I was too busy with work and…money," he forced himself to say. "I know that I let things between us go, that I didn't pay attention where I should have."

"I never begrudged you working hard, Michael."

"I know." Because he wanted to feel the soft skin where her wrist touched her palm, he picked up her hand, rubbed his thumb there. "But, I lost touch; with you, with David, God, sometimes I think I lost touch with reality."

She nodded. "I understand."

He glanced at her in surprise, never having expected her response to be one of empathy.

"You don't think I miss my only child feeling comfortable enough to give me a goddamn hug?" She sighed and withdrew her hand from him so that she could rub her temple. "I just...I don't know when it started, or how it progressed to this extent without me noticing."

Michael noticed that her eyes had misted over and felt his own burn. He hadn't seen her cry...in years. "Seeing them together...David and Ivy. The way they touch all the time, sneak looks when they think nobody is watching..."

"Made you think about how we weren't so different once upon a time?"

She smiled, not her polite, practiced smile, her smile that reached her eyes and made them dance with color. "It did," she said with a small nod. "But it also made me wonder when David and I lost the familiarity, the mother-son connection we used to have."

Michael nodded. He could remember a time when David had been small that she and their son had been thick as thieves, their heads always together looking at worms, or giggling as they splashed in the waves on the days they'd frequent the beach. He remembered seeing them and feeling left out...an unwelcome third...then he'd leave for work and forget all about feeling anything at all.

He folded his hands over the linen comforter when he wanted to reach out and touch her face. "Do you think we can remedy it?" he asked.

"I think we can at least try," she replied. Still on her stomach, she raised slippered feet in the air unconsciously, smiled up at him when her robe pooled around her thighs, leaving her smooth calves bare.

Michael had the strangest urge to touch her but...he was afraid. It had been so long since they'd had any intimacy in their marriage, so long since he'd made an effort to bridge the gap between them. Sure, they'd slept in the same bed their entire adult lives, and, as far as he knew, neither one of them had sought pleasure elsewhere, but it was...hard, scary even, this fear of rejection he felt rising in his chest.

"So, just family the first time," she said. "I think that'll be nice. For David and for Ivy."

"And for us," he added and reached tentatively forward to touch her cheek.

She didn't pull away as he thought she might, instead she rested her cheek against his palm. "I'd like that."

He cleared his throat. "I'm really sorry, Milla," he said, using the pet name that he'd lost over the years. "For not always being there for you."

This time she opened her mouth to protest, but Michael held up a hand and spoke over her. "I need to say this…"

She nodded, her eyes soft and sad.

"I would like to say that I was just preoccupied, but the truth is that once we reached the stage where we couldn't communicate, it became hard for me to want to try. I was so scared…that there wouldn't be anything between us once I tried to resuscitate it. So scared that I didn't even try."

When the first tear slipped over her long lashes and started a slow trek down her cheek, he wiped it away with his thumb. "I was afraid that you'd leave me, afraid that you'd take David and just go." He sighed. "The money…even when I knew we had issues, the money always seemed to make things better. A new piece of jewelry, a vacation for you and David, a new car. And, for me, money was easy to always get more of…"

She sat up at that, leaned back on her knees as easily as she had when they'd been twenty. He saw the look of shock in her eyes, felt guilty for having put it there. "I'm sorry." He smiled sadly.

"You're a fool, Michael."

The words were said so simply that he couldn't formulate a reply, instead he just stared at her.

"The only reason I ever loved the things that you gave me, was because it meant that you'd thought about it." She touched her heart. "Thought about me. I've never loved another man in my entire life, thought about others, sure, when you'd been away for a month and I hadn't been touched in longer."

He glanced up, horrified.

"Don't worry, nothing ever happened, which," she added, "is my point." She looked away, gazed out the balcony doors at the starry night. "Even at my loneliest, I never thought about moving on. I just...missed you."

"You seemed so unreachable."

"It was either toughen up or crumble, and I had a child to raise. Crumbling wasn't an option for me."

He felt his stomach twist with guilt, even as his body responded to the small swell of her breasts through the sheer silk of her nightdress. "Forgive me?" he asked.

She smiled and, with a small chuckle, shook her head. "Only if you take me to Europe."

He knew that she was teasing him, but took the opportunity to reach into the drawer of his bedside table. He pulled the folder out with a flourish. "I thought you might say that."

"You didn't!" she said, failing—for the first time that he could remember—to hide her shock.

"French Riviera for two weeks. Hotel de Paris in Monte Carlo. Followed by a week in Barcelona and a week in Barolo. Figure we'd do the wine tour since we've kept the region afloat all these years. The works."

"When did you do this?" she asked, opening the folder and glancing at the front page, which happened to be the flight confirmation.

"The night I told David I'd take you," he said. "I just...hadn't found the right time, or the courage, to tell you."

She smiled and, to his surprise, put the folder on the nightstand. He felt his body tighten when she moved over the bed towards him, felt his mind go blank when she touched her soft lips to his.

"Thank you," she said.

He sighed, reached up to bring her face back to his. "It's my pleasure," he replied before taking her mouth.

As they touched each other, explored the changes that had taken place while their lives had moved forward separately, he couldn't help but feel that the pieces of their marriage could be salvaged, joined back together to make something beautiful again. Different perhaps than it once had been, but beautiful all the same.

Chapter 16

She looked at the flowers on the table in the foyer and clipped a single red rose shorter so that it didn't detract from the gorgeous protea that served as the centerpiece of the arrangement. Once she had reinserted the rose, Camilla took three steps back from the entire display and considered it from the front door. She wanted to see it from the perspective of someone who had just walked into the house.

Perfect.

The arrangement was both deliberate and wild, with ruby red roses and fronds of maiden's hair fern—both of which she grew in her own garden—offset by the huge protea that she had bought at the State Street Farmer's Market just that morning. The deep reds and hunter greens complimented the dark Spanish tile of the foyer floor and also inadvertently showcased the crystal chandelier that hung ten feet above the display.

She knew in the back of her mind that the floral arrangement would go largely unnoticed by her family because, well, she always had flowers in the house. But she didn't care. The process of setting up for a party, of making sure that every aspect of her house, from the flowers to the polished tile, was perfect, made her feel good about herself. Made her feel...useful.

Inviting people into her home had always excited Camilla. Hosting made her feel proud of her husband and the work he'd put in over the years, proud of the choices they'd made as a couple, and proud of the things they'd accomplished as a result.

She didn't care that her friends thought she was high-maintenance or over the top. A *perfectionist*. She was all those things and, if she were honest with herself, she liked it. She liked who she was.

Besides, she thought, the people who had an opinion didn't know what she and Michael had gone through to be able to live the way they pleased now. They didn't care that Michael had put in twelve to fifteen-hour days for over thirty years. They didn't care that she had raised a child alone because of it. And that, Camilla reminded herself, was why you could never take people's judgments to heart. They didn't know what you had been through; they didn't care about the nights you'd cried yourself to sleep with loneliness.

She hummed to herself as she cleaned up the table the flower arrangement was on, picked up her shears and the flower scraps, and moved towards the kitchen so she could throw them in the composting bin.

She cast a quick look at her watch and, seeing that she had two hours before everyone arrived, moved quickly.

Where had the time gone? She was supposed to have started prepping dinner nearly forty minutes ago; she wanted everything to be ready so that by the time everyone arrived, all she had to do was pop it in the oven and check on it every thirty minutes.

She would have had any other party catered, but because Michael had wanted to make it family only, she had chosen to cook a big Sunday roast herself. She was, like most things in her life that she applied herself to, a fantastic cook. It wasn't a secret that she used recipes and never digressed from them. The way that she saw it was that anyone successful enough to publish an entire book about chicken, or baking, or soups, must know what the hell they were talking about. Who was she to change things up?

"Milla?" she heard Michael call through the house.

She pulled the prime rib roast from the fridge and stuck her head through the door to shout, "In the kitchen!" down the long hallway.

By the time he walked in, she had already sliced ten cloves of garlic and washed and cleaned the onions her recipe book told her to put in the oven with the roast.

She felt her stomach flutter uncomfortably when he moved closer to her, glanced up at him when he asked, "Can I help with anything?"

She tried not to frown when she met his sky-blue eyes, tried to smile despite the situation she'd found herself in. He never helped her plan or set up for a party. She planned, sent out invites, hired the caterers, and, if need be, the bartenders and staff. She organized everything and told him when and where to be so that he could help host their guests. That was the way that they'd always done things.

"Ah…" What did she say?

"I don't want to get in your way," he added instantly, obviously sensing her hesitation. "I just…wanted to hang out."

She stopped seasoning the meat on the counter in front of her, the salt grinder still in her hand, and looked up so that she could stare at him. They hadn't 'hung out' since before they had been married.

When he met her eyes and grinned, she felt the blush warm her cheeks instantly and forced her mind from the night before. She still didn't quite believe how…uncontrolled they'd been. How passionate. The memory had her body tightening inadvertently, which naturally forced a ruby-red blush into her cheeks.

Because he was waiting for her to say something, and because she really didn't want him to go, she said, "You could wash and chop all those vegetables that I have there." She pointed to the side of the sink, where a huge pile of produce sat on the glistening granite counter.

He nodded and moved past her to wash his hands.

She heard the water running behind her, felt another blush rise to her cheeks when she remembered the shower that they'd taken together afterward. She cleared her throat

235

quietly, trying to dispel some of the awareness she felt lodged there, and rubbed the salt and pepper into the lamb, before placing it in the huge pan she usually reserved for the holidays.

She went about her task with a militant precision, but only because having Michael so close was distracting her. Even now, she could hear his uneven chopping, an irregular clomp, clomp, clomp. It wasn't his laborious chopping that was bothering her. It was the fact that he was so close that she could smell the aftershave on his skin and the pure male smell of it was warming her blood even though she was making a solid effort to ignore it.

"I hope everyone gets along," she said, trying more to distract herself than voice a genuine concern. If Ivy's family were anything like Ivy was, she didn't think that there'd be a problem; at least not one that would be bigger than her own tenuous relationship with her mother-in-law. For some reason, she and Amanda had never seen eye-to-eye.

"Don't worry, Milla," he said, and she could tell, by the change in the tone of his voice, that he had turned to look at her.

"I'm not worried," she corrected, refusing to meet his eyes. "I'm...nervous. We've never been introduced to a girlfriend of his before, let alone her family." She turned to look at him then because talking about the occasion was making her nervous. "This is a big deal. For David. For us. I just...I want it to be perfect."

He nodded and, wiping his hands on a nearby kitchen towel, walked to her. She felt her breath catch in her throat when he wrapped his arms around her waist and looked into her eyes. "It'll be fine. He's going to love her no matter what we tell him so...all we have to do is love her too."

"She's hard not to love," Camilla said. "I mean for God's sake, Michael, she's a drop-dead gorgeous patent attorney. And she's *normal*. She laughs and teases and," she sniffled as tears filled her eyes, "she makes our unapproachable little boy smile. Genuinely smile."

She laughed against his mouth and sighed when he took the kiss deeper. Because she wanted to be distracted, but because she didn't have time to be, she broke the kiss first and said, "Can we pick this up after everyone leaves tonight? I'm *really* behind schedule."

He grinned down at her and gave her one last quick kiss before taking a step back. "I just can't believe that he finally found someone," he said with a wide grin as he moved back towards the sink. "I'd honestly just given up hope. Stopped wondering about it if I'm completely honest."

Camilla nodded and moved the huge pan so that she could work beside him. "I did too. There were a few girls that I was hopeful about over the years, but God, Michael they were all so...blonde. So...insufferable."

He chuckled. "I would never have thought that you'd like Ivy," he said honestly. "She doesn't fit your ideal or, at least, is nothing like the other girls you've set him up with over the years."

She felt a small ball of shame curl in her chest, let it sit there for a moment before she deliberately discarded it. "Honestly? I just worried that he'd never have anyone, that he'd end up alone and...those girls that I tried to set him up with..."

"Would have suited the lifestyle," he finished for her.

She nodded, despite the embarrassment that she felt. "I wanted him to find someone so badly that I forced girls on him who wanted the social standing, who understood how his world works. I never really thought about love...or passion. I just didn't want him to be lonely..."

Michael nudged her gently with his shoulder. "You were a good mom, Milla." When she shook her head, he added, "No. It's true. We both have a lot to make up for but you...you always looked out for him even if he never saw it."

"I tried my best," she said sadly. "I know he thinks that I'm...cold," she forced the word out, past the shame that had lodged like cement in her chest. "But...it was just easier to be...distant."

"I wish you had told me," he said quietly. "I wish you had told me how lonely you were."

She sighed and nudged him gently with her hip. "I wanted to. But you already had so much going on and...then you'd get home at ten at night after a long day of work and what was I supposed to say? I was a stay at home wife whose only job was to raise a single child and host parties...I felt like I didn't have a leg to stand on. I felt like a...failure. There was no reason that I shouldn't have been happy. I had—have," she corrected, "everything."

"He wrapped an arm around her shoulders and hugged her to his side. "I promise I'm going to give my retirement to you, Milla. You and David and Ivy, if she stays."

She sighed and, although she couldn't voice it, felt her heart swell with emotion. She hadn't realized how long she had waited to be seen by him again, to be hugged and kissed and...wanted. God, she had missed being wanted. Missed him. "I love you," she said instead of voicing her thoughts and stood on her toes to kiss him on the cheek.

"I love you too."

Ivy wasn't entirely sure that the party was a good idea. Yes, she wanted her grandparents to meet David's and, yes, she wanted to get to know his family too; but wasn't a party this soon in a relationship a bit premature?

She thought so.

She hadn't wanted to tell David that she wasn't exactly looking forward to the event, hadn't wanted to seem ungrateful, but when her stomach gave another uncomfortable heave, she turned to look at him behind the wheel of the Porsche.

Her heart gave a little kick in her chest at the picture he made; his blonde hair, although cut short, was thick, and now that she knew what it was like to grip her fingers in it, they itched to do just that. His broad shoulders looked a little oversized in the small car, and the linen button-down that he wore did nothing to hide the fact that he had a perfect, muscular physique. When he sensed her gaze and turned sharp blue eyes on her, her breath caught in her throat and she smiled.

"What's wrong?" he asked gently. When she made to shake her head, he placed his hand on her thigh bringing her gaze back to his face. "I can feel you panicking from here."

She chuckled nervously. How did she say, 'I don't think I'm ready to socialize with your parents,' exactly? Especially when Amanda and her own grandparents were all making the two-hour drive as well. And Camilla had planned the entire day already.

Because she didn't have the heart to tell him how scared she was, she smiled. "I guess I'm just nervous." She paused, focused on the feeling of his big hand resting on her thigh, holding her down. "I've…I've never been taken home to the family," she said, eventually.

He chuckled. "I've never taken a girl home to the family." He squeezed her leg and when she met his eyes again, added, "We don't have to do this if you're not ready. Just tell me. We'll say that I have food poisoning, or that I fell and broke my ankle."

She laughed. "You don't think they'll find it suspicious considering it's an hour before we're supposed to be there?"

She shook her head when he chuckled. When he looked at her again, waiting for her to reply, the realization that he'd one-hundred-percent lie to his family because she was scared of meeting them hit her full force. She swallowed past the lump in her throat. All she seemed to be able to remember was the picture of his huge frame sitting uncomfortably on the barstool in her apartments as he'd

239

entertained her grandparents. She placed her hand palm-down on top of his. "No," she decided. "I don't think it's ever going to get easier so we ma—"

"May as well get it out of the way," he finished for her. "That's exactly what I was thinking."

She smiled and looked out of the window as they drove in companionable silence on the 101. The ocean glimmered turquoise and cyan, iridescent underneath the wide expanse of golden sky. It was so beautiful, she thought as she spotted a group of surfers bobbing over the swell.

"How long have your parents lived in Santa Barbara?" she asked. She was thinking what a beautiful retirement it must be, to be surrounded by the ocean, sunshine, and smiles all day long.

"About five years now, I think," he replied.

"Do you miss them being closer?" she asked, curious.

He laughed and shook his head. "Honestly, I think I see them more often now. Something about the distance makes it necessary to plan, you know?"

She nodded and her stomach gave another uncomfortable twist as he turned the Porsche onto State Street. Ivy chose to distract herself by looking out the window again. She loved the layout of State Street, with the perfectly planned hacienda-style retail centers below neat, terraced apartments. She had no idea why people called this part of town, with its red tile roofing and whitewashed walls, the 'Funk Zone'; it reminded her more of a 'Suburban Hub' or 'Center for Procreation', a place where people with two point five children came together for Sunday brunch.

She turned, surprised when David pulled into a small parallel parking spot and stopped the car. She knew that his parents lived in the hills, not near the beach, or even remotely close to where they were now.

"I want you to meet someone," he said, turning blue eyes on her. "We're really early and my mom wouldn't appreciate us ruining her schedule by arriving before she's got everything in order." She looked at him, knew that the expression on her face was uncertain, but couldn't quite mask it.

"Come on," he said and got out of the car before she could say anything else.

She sighed and opened the door. She hadn't been prepared to meet anyone else and a not-so-small part of her mind wondered why he wouldn't have just told her.

Stepping onto the sidewalk, she couldn't help but smile as the balmy air wrapped around her skin. California beach weather was unbeatable, she thought to herself as she walked around the car to where David stood. Because he offered her his hand, she took it and smiled when his huge palm covered hers. How was it that holding hands with him made her feel like a teenage girl again? Made her feel young and inexperienced and completely out of her depth?

When he walked a few feet, straight up to an interior design store, and opened the door for her, her eyebrows shot up inadvertently. They were meeting this person in an interior design store?

When a small bell announced their entry and a crystal-clear voice called, "I'll be right out!" Ivy frowned. Why was it, she wondered, that she could tell that the voice belonged to an attractive woman? Was it the tone? The pitch?

She looked at David, eyebrows raised, and he chuckled. "Don't look so skeptical," he said and wrapped an arm around her shoulders before leaning down to brush his lips over hers.

She smiled just as the faceless voice said, "Holy shit!"

Ivy blushed scarlet and turned to face the woman. She wasn't surprised to see a five-three blonde with perfectly bronzed skin and a cute pixie cut looking at them as if they'd just morphed into a single dog in front of her. She was surprised to see that the woman had a huge pregnant belly that extended far in front of her.

They took a split second to assess each other before the woman broke into a huge grin and waddled over to her, wrapping her in a friendly hug that was only made awkward by the fact that she could barely reach around her own belly.

The woman patted her back and, when she broke the hug, looked at David with a wide grin on her face. She looked like an ad for Good Housekeeping, Ivy decided. Her pregnant state did not detract from the fact that she was supermodel pretty with wide, blue eyes and full, pouty lips.

Ivy blinked when David grinned and leaned down to give her a kiss on the lips. It wasn't that she was jealous; there was something about the woman's energy that exuded genuine kindness and affection, not desire. Ivy was just shocked by the easy affection that David showed the woman. She had never seen him interact so openly with anyone, not even his parents.

She remained quiet as they grinned at each other.

Finally, David said, "Ivy, this is Meg." He looked at her. "My best friend since third grade, interior designer extraordinaire, and soon to be the mother of twin boys."

Ivy blinked once before the pieces fell into place. "Did you do the interior of David's house?" she asked.

Meg nodded proudly. "It was no small feat either. David is…impossible to understand."

David grinned and added, "Says the person who's known me best for the longest."

Ivy smiled. "I love it," she said, honestly. Meg tilted her head and looked at her until Ivy had to consciously refrain from blushing.

"Is James here?" David asked.

Meg shook her head. "You should have given us a heads-up that you were coming. I know that he's dying to meet Ivy too."

Ivy blinked. David had told them about her.

Meg laughed at her expression. "Girl, we have been waiting years for this," she said and indicated the space

242

between her and David. "And look at you," she said with a big sigh. "Not what we expected, that's for sure." When Ivy raised her eyebrows, Meg laughed and added, "Much better than what we expected."

When tears rose in Meg's eyes, David chuckled and Ivy looked at him, horrified. They had made a pregnant woman cry. What had they done?

"You're going to have to excuse me," Meg said and swiped at her eyes. "I'd lie and say that it's pregnancy hormones, but the truth is, I've just wanted this for so long."

"Meg and her husband, James, have been nagging me to settle down for...ten years?" he said, offering Ivy explanation.

She nodded and said, "About that long," with a small chuckle. She gave her eyes one last wipe and then asked, "What are you guys doing here? Are you staying for the whole weekend?"

David shook his head. "No. We're having lunch with my parents and Ivy's family and then heading back tonight." He looked at her. "We both have a bit of work to catch up on and I don't think subjecting her to my mother overnight is fair."

Meg laughed. "The fact that you're introducing her to your mother at all just makes me...endlessly happy."

"Oh, she's met Camilla," David corrected her. "Mom is throwing a family luncheon so that she and Dad can meet Ivy's grandparents."

Ivy noticed that Meg's eyes had gone wide and barely refrained from asking her what she found so surprising.

"Your mom is throwing a family-only luncheon so that they can meet Ivy's grandparents?" she asked as if she hadn't quite heard right the first time, or worse, didn't believe him.

He nodded and Ivy saw his ear-to-ear grin.

"Holy. Shit."

"I know," David countered.

When Ivy just looked from David to Meg confused, David took her hand again and Meg reiterated. "Holy. Shit." She laughed and raked a hand through her spiked hair. "I mean I'm your best friend and I know that you're in love just by looking at you, but...Camilla noticed?"

Ivy felt the world slow around her, felt her heart flutter in her chest just once, and refused to look up at David, choosing instead to focus on Meg again. "Fuck me," the small woman was saying. She looked at Ivy. "Welcome to the fold. Officially."

When she leaned in for another hug, Ivy chuckled and patted her back awkwardly. She wasn't entirely sure what the big deal was, but no matter how she tried to ignore them, Meg's words, 'I know that you're in love just by looking at you' reverberated in her mind. She knew that David loved her, knew that she loved him, but there was something so novel to her about the fact that people could tell just by looking at them together.

"How are you feeling about all this?" Meg asked, looking from her to David. "Both of you," she reiterated, taking Ivy's hand.

Ivy met David's blue eyes and felt her heart settle in her chest when she saw her own fears reflected there. "Scared by how impossible it all is?" she asked him.

He nodded. "Petrified."

Meg dropped Ivy's hand and clapped her own together. "Oh, perfect!"

Both Ivy and David chuckled. "Ivy, I have to give you the rundown before you go to the Van den Berg's for lunch," Meg said.

Ivy nodded at the exact same time that David groaned. She smiled and squeezed his hand. "I'd appreciate any help I can get."

"I don't care," he said, looking at her. "I don't care what my parents think. They like you already and, well, they have to love you, because I love you."

Ivy thought she might have actually felt her mouth drop open and she turned to look at Meg, incredulous.

Meg laughed and waved a flippant hand in David's direction. "Men, no matter how much we love them, will always be inferior beings, Ivy."

Ivy giggled. Even David chuckled. "Okay, fine," he said. "But I'm nervous enough as it is, so I'm going to go and grab a cup of coffee while you two gossip."

When Ivy nodded, he smiled and took her mouth for a quick kiss that stole her breath. "Want anything?"

When she shook her head, Meg added, "A large Mocha Frappuccino. Two sugars, please."

Ivy watched him walk out with one last smile and then turned to face Meg with a deep sigh. "Okay," she said, "tell me what I need to know."

Chapter 17

She hadn't thought about what she'd say when the time came, and if she were honest with herself, would admit that she'd deliberately pushed the thought of Gordon and his threats out of her mind. Because more than she knew anything, Ivy knew that mulling over it as she waited for the potential outburst would drive her crazier than just pretending that everything was fine.

So, as fall hit Los Angeles, although the temperature hovered at a sweltering point that made the back of her work dresses stick to the seat of David's Porsche, Ivy ignored the constant niggling in the back of her mind and deliberately focused on cramming her life with as many distractions as possible.

She put in her ten hours at the office every day, started frequenting the gym—which had never been a relaxing habit for her—and then once she got home, spent her last hours of energy with David, curled up on the big, grey sofa in the lounge, or cooking dinner together.

Sometimes they'd abandon cooking altogether and stroll, hand-in-hand, down to the small, Italian restaurant a mile away from the house. For all intents and purposes, their life together was perfect.

But underneath it all, she saw the strain around his eyes, knew that the pressure of having Gordon, and now Bruce Standard, in the Black Finch office was wearing him down. She knew that it wasn't a performance issue, knew that David could hold his own and would almost certainly surpass expectations.

She also knew that if she hadn't come into his life when she had and specifically the way that she had, the partner promotion would have been a no-brainer. Instead, the pressure of having Gordon's previous threat constantly hanging over his head, and the fear that everything he'd built for himself would come crashing down around him were wearing him down. Although he came home happy with a forced smile on his lips, Ivy saw the weight of their predicament getting heavier every day and she hated herself for it.

She tried her best to alleviate the stress without haggling him into talking about the minutiae because, if she had learned one thing about David Van den Berg in the last eight months, it was that sharing didn't come easily to him. He could easily pick up the bills when they went out with Damien and Louie or a few of their work colleagues, offer to drive his grandma to the grocery store on weekends, and listen to Ivy as she spilled her heart out to him when something went wrong. But he never let anybody, herself included, return the favor.

He was generous and kind, but more than that, he was self-critical and proud, sometimes to a fault. It didn't bother her because she knew that he valued his strength, knew that it was important to him that his public veneer, his perceived persona, never cracked. But sometimes...sometimes she just wanted him to snap, to throw things in a rage, or shout when he was pissed off, or express sadness when he needed to.

So, when he pushed open the door to the house late on a Tuesday evening after being away for work the entire previous week, and bent over the sofa to give her an absent-minded kiss, Ivy felt her resolve to leave him alone tearing at the seams. "David," she said, forcing him to look down at her as she sat cross-legged on the sofa.

She tilted her head back so that she could meet his eyes, deliberately ignoring the fact that seeing him again after only five days apart made her mouth water, made her pulse jump erratically under her skin. God, she wanted to run her hands under his shirt, grip them in his hair as he crushed his mouth to hers.

"Yes," he returned, in the same tone that she'd used on him, his eyebrows raised questioningly.

She saw the moment that his eyes shuttered, felt the wall that he built around himself as if it were a physical barrier separating them.

She sighed and, tabling the need to touch him, stood so that she could face him before he moved away from her. "Is everything okay?" she asked, unconsciously wringing her hands in front of herself. When he didn't reply immediately, she added, "I feel like I can't reach you. Like you're shutting away whatever's bothering you."

He groaned in frustration and raked both hands through his hair, turned and paced in the direction of the door before turning back towards her suddenly.

"Everything is fine," he started. But when she rolled her eyes, he sighed and added, "I don't want to add my stress on top of everything else you have going on. I just got home." He sighed and reached for her, rubbed his hands up and down her arms. "I haven't seen you all week. Can't we just relax?"

She heard the exasperation in his voice, and where usually she would have backed off, now, she stiffened her spine, closed her fists at her side in a gesture that she would have marked as defiant if she'd realized she'd done it. "I can handle it!" she said, angry that he thought she couldn't. "What's the point in being in a relationship if it's entirely one-sided, David?"

He dropped his hands from her arms and just stared at her, his blue eyes wide with surprise. "One-sided?" he asked quietly.

She nodded.

"Ivy…I rely on you for *everything*. Just because I don't want you to stress about things that I'm worried about, doesn't mean that our relationship is one-sided."

"Yes," she returned, irritated, "by definition, it does."

He looked at her in silence, clearly calculating how to approach her current mood, and Ivy, knowing exactly what he was thinking, felt her blood run hot beneath the surface of her skin. He was managing her emotions.

"If you can't talk to me about everyday things you have going on, about your bad days, and your shit moods, then what's the point?"

He sighed. "You can't even handle your own stress, Ivy." He said the words calmly, quietly, as if reasoning with a small child who was having a temper tantrum.

"I resent that." She felt her anger lash just below the surface, had to mentally calm herself even as he raked his hands through his hair for the second time, clearly frustrated.

"Well, what do you expect me to say?" he asked. "You're barely sleeping, I've seen you cry more than once in the last two weeks alone, and you what? Want more to take on?"

"I cry because it's therapeutic, David. I get freaked out, or stressed, maybe I cry and then talk about my feelings! But you know what? I resolve a lot more of my issues than you do! You're so closed off! So…cold."

He groaned loudly and put his hands on the waistband of his slacks. "Why are you making such a big deal out of this tonight?" He threw his hands in the air, exasperated. "I just got home."

"Because," she said calmly, "I can see that you're stressed and I want to know how I can help, figure out what I can do to make you feel better, or here's a crazy idea: just be an ear to listen so you can get it off your chest! Why is that so hard for you to comprehend?"

"Because you're the first person who's ever had a problem with the way I deal with things!"

"Because I love you Goddamnit! I care about the fact that you're holding it all together and I want to share the burden."

He looked at her face then, met eyes that she knew were filling with tears, and hated the fact that the first one slipped through her lashes before she could swipe it away. God, she hated crying, especially when she was trying to make a point about how resilient she was.

The irony was not lost on her.

Because she saw the look of pure confusion on his face and because she could acknowledge her foul mood had escalated what should've been a pointed conversation into a fight, she took a step towards him, closed the space between their bodies and wrapped her arms around him before resting her head on his chest. She sighed when she felt the heavy thump of his heart under her ear. Despite the fact that she was mad, she was happy to be close to him after a long week alone. She had missed him, missed the contact. God, she'd even missed his smell.

When he circled her waist with his arms, rested his chin on her head, she said, "I don't want to fight. I just want you to know you can tell me anything. You should tell me everything." She tilted her head back to look at him. "That's the point."

"I don't think it'll make a difference, Ivy. I can deal with everything and talking about it just makes me think about it more."

"It would make a difference to me," she said," if you'd at least try to include me when you've got something on your mind."

He sighed, resigned to placate her, and she knew that she'd take it. She'd take being appeased if it meant that he learned to rely on her—learned that she could be relied on. She was strong for Christ's sake, she thought as he gave her one last squeeze before taking a step back.

"So?" she asked.

"Now?" he countered, with an incredulous laugh.

"I'll give you ten minutes to grab a glass of wine and take off your shoes, and then yes, I want to hear about it now."

Because she knew that he was going to argue, and because she didn't want to re-start the fight when she had the higher ground, she sent him a saccharine smile and turned her back on him before plopping back down on the sofa.

She heard him groan behind her back, tried and failed to hide her grin, which accompanied his self-suffering sigh, and chuckled to herself when she heard him walk to the kitchen, resigned to at least be drinking when he talked to her.

It wasn't anything unusual. That's why David hadn't wanted to talk about it. It was simply a combination of the stress from his usual workload, combined with the constant energy it took to avoid Gordon's leering.

More than that, David didn't want to talk to Ivy about it because he didn't want her to feel responsible for the stress he was under. He didn't want her to know that a genuine fear of her past catching up to them sat in his throat all day when he was at work or in the office. Because it shouldn't have made a difference. He knew that intrinsically, but still, it petrified him that his flawless reputation might be marred by their relationship.

She petrified him.

Ivy, with her kindness and her need to support him, made the entire situation worse. How did he tell her that her past could mean absolutely nothing, or it could ruin his career? That was something a man shouldn't share with his girlfriend. That was the type of thing he should bottle up and never *ever* discuss.

He sighed as he poured himself a glass of wine, wondered if he should just lie to her and say that something went wrong at work. He dismissed the idea instantly. Not because he didn't think it'd be a good idea, but because he knew that she'd be able to tell that he wasn't being entirely honest.

He picked up his glass, realized he didn't know if she had one too, and shouted, "Babe! Do you want a glass too?"

"I have one!" she called back.

He reentered the room, sat on the sofa next to her, and leaned back, putting his feet on the coffee table as he did. When she moved from the other side of the sofa so she could lie on him, her head in his lap, David smiled and felt the first knot of tension from the week uncoil. He roped a single arm over her and rubbed her upper arm where it was bare.

"So?" he asked when she remained quiet. "What do you want to know?"

She sighed as if he were quite stupid and he couldn't help but grin down at her when their eyes met.

"I just want to know if you're okay," she said and placed her hand on his to stop his from stroking up and down her arm. "I know that the stuff with Gordon is freaking you out and that you're trying to keep it together. I know that you're insanely busy and probably don't need more to deal with…"

He felt his eyebrow raise, still unused to living with someone who could read him so easily.

"It is bothering me," he said, honestly. "Sometimes I can feel his eyes burning into me from across the office and my skin crawls." He paused for a second as he tried to gather his thoughts. "I've just…I've never had to worry about what people think about me before," he said. "I've never even had to worry about being judged before. It's why I don't talk about politics or anything emotionally charged at work. People are weirdly judgmental about stuff like that…"

"I understand," she said simply.

David took a sip of his wine and used his free hand to brush her hair out of her face. "I know you do. It's everyone else I'm concerned about."

She smiled at him, turned her head further back so that she was almost looking at him upside down from her position. He felt his breath catch in his throat when he met her eyes, saw his emotion reflected back at him in hers.

"I wish this part could all just be over, you know? Even five years from now, people won't care about how we met." She chuckled. "Time is weird that way."

David smiled down at her, nodded more to himself than to her. "It's only a matter of time before he says something, and I'd bet money on the fact that he's going to do it before the holidays."

He felt his heart sink with the realization, forced a smile when Ivy said, "You mean before the end-of-year promotions."

He nodded because she wasn't wrong.

"I think we should warn your family, David." When he looked down at her, his face frozen in shock, she sat up, touched her hand to his cheek in a gesture that somehow centered him, made him feel calm. "Your dad has stakes too. He's been an industry leader for over thirty years. Your mom…God, her social standing is everything to her. They should know."

He groaned and closed his eyes, unwilling to voice the only thought circling his mind—how on earth would he make his parents see his side of things, *their* side of things?

When she chuckled, he opened one eye and looked at her, felt his heart patter hurriedly when she sent him a slanted look. "Fine," he said. "But I'm inviting grandma too." When she laughed, he added, "I need to stock my defenses."

"Deal."

"Now the only question is when? When do we tell them?"

"I was thinking more along the lines of how?" Ivy countered with a chuckle, her face transforming as the realization of the absurdity of their situation struck her. "How do we tell your parents that we met when you, ah, hired me?"

"A party," he said, the beginnings of an idea taking place.

"David," Ivy looked at him, incredulous. "A party is not the right setting to break this kind of news."

"No, you're right," he said, grinning. "But it is the perfect setting to celebrate, say, a life event? Something big enough that the 'how we met' story pales in comparison."

"I think I'm catching on," she said with a small laugh.

David felt his stomach knot nervously and tried to push it aside. He looked at her, wondered if she knew what he was implying or if she had something else in mind entirely. Either way, he wanted her. He already knew that. God, he realized, he wanted her as he'd never wanted anything else before. He *needed* her. And not like he needed to work, or needed to exercise—he needed her like he needed to breathe. He needed her because he knew what his life was like without her and he never wanted to go back there again.

"Wait one second," he said before hopping off the sofa.

As he trotted up the stairs to their bedroom, he chose to ignore the panic that was working its way up his throat, chose to push aside all thoughts of failure and rejection. He wanted her, would wait for her if she wasn't ready.

He opened the closet and walked in, past the drawers and shoes to the railings at the back where he kept his suit jackets hanging. He brushed past the first five until he came to the charcoal suit that he only used for weddings and funerals, fished around in the left breast pocket until he found what he was looking for.

He turned, the grin on his face instantly fading to a look of pure panic when he saw Ivy standing in the doorway looking at him. He hadn't heard her follow him up the stairs. That was the only thought running through his head as the black, velvet box burned a hole in his hand.

She didn't say anything. She didn't move, or, he noticed, smile. Instead, she stared at him, her jaw slack with shock, her lips forming a perfect O.

David cleared his throat and walked towards her, felt his heart clench in his chest when she took a single step back.

"I was going to wait," he said, "plan things out. Make it special."

"David," she whispered, her voice shaky.

"Don't panic," he chuckled, feeling strangely centered by the fear in her eyes. He didn't know why but the idea that she was as scared as he was settled something inside of him. So, he closed the distance between them and when she didn't move away, he cradled her face in his palm and brushed his lips over hers. "Ivy Diana Watts," he said, meeting emerald eyes that were wide with surprise. "I love you. I am in love with you," he clarified.

She sighed and nestled her face in his collarbone. "I love you too, David."

Instead of kneeling in the closet that they shared, he took a single step back from her and opened the box. He heard her let out a small gasp and flinched, afraid that she didn't like it. But when he looked into her eyes, they were misted over.

He lifted the ring out of its velvet pouch, studied the single, square-cut emerald set in yellow gold, nestled with two glinting diamonds on either side. "I was hoping this would be an amazing surprise at just the right moment," he began. "But I want you to know that I've had the ring for weeks, that I want to marry you, that I wa—"

"Yes."

He looked at her, saw everything that he'd ever need from her reflected clearly in her eyes. "I'm going to ask anyway," he said. "Will you marry me?"

She chuckled and, flinging her arms around his neck, crushed her mouth to his.

David felt the blood leave his body in one swift punch.

She said yes.

Holy shit, she said yes.

Because her tongue was quickly leaving him incapable of coherent thought, he put her down on her feet and took her hand in his, giving him the distance that he needed. He looked into her eyes as he slipped the ring with an emerald as green as her eyes onto her finger before brushing his lips over hers.

"It's not exactly how I planned it," he said.

"But it's perfect," she countered immediately. "It's us, David." She laughed.

"What? You mean nothing's gone as planned since we met?" he teased.

"Exactly," she chuckled, looking at the ring briefly before walking into his arms again. "It's been so much better."

As he held her in his arms, surrounded by their clothes hanging in the walk-in closet that they shared, he smiled and knew that she was right. It was perfect. Perfect for them.

He just hoped to hell that everyone else saw it that way.

Chapter 18

Amanda hadn't been told what the occasion was, nor she realized, did it particularly matter. Being invited to a party by her grandson and Ivy was reason enough to go, and, she knew, it was guarantee enough that she'd have a good time too.

She looked at her reflection in the mirror of the dressing-table that her own mother had given her and marveled at how time could simply slip away, leaving only a map of wrinkles as a parting gift.

She sighed and smeared on another layer of base; she had learned after sixty-five that only one layer didn't quite hide the mish-mash of spots and veins that were all linked by her web of wrinkles. She didn't consider applying a lot of makeup to her weathered face to be vanity. She considered it a necessity, a sure sign that, despite her age, she hadn't let herself go. Yet.

Her Daniel would have laughed at her, she realized a bit forlornly as she powdered her nose. He would have asked whom she was getting all dolled up for because, according to him, his eyesight couldn't discern the difference. But Daniel was gone. Long gone. And where her memory of him left a small, dull ache, her appreciation for the years and years that they had lived together washed away the throbbing like fresh blood pumping and healing an old wound.

She applied her mascara in record time despite the small tremble in her hands, blinked at herself in the mirror to prove that all of her lashes were still there. And still real. Now that, she would concede, was vanity.

When her bedroom door opened and Ike stuck his head in, she met his eyes in the mirror as she flicked her blush brush high over her cheekbones. "I'm almost done, Ike. I'll be out in a minute," she said loudly so that his hearing aid would pick up her words even though he had learned to lip read for the details most people mumbled over.

"How about a drink before we go?" he asked, his head still peeking around the door.

She smiled, nodded. "That sounds lovely, dear. If you pour me a brandy, I'll love you forever."

"At the rate you're going, we'll still be drinking our brandies when forever rolls around."

She chuckled as he left the room. Amanda listened as he walked slowly, step by step, down the short flight of twelve stairs to her small foyer and sighed when his clomping leveled out.

Why was it, she wondered, that when you got old you constantly braced for injury or death. She smiled to herself. Maybe it was nature's way of preparing you; as if making you think about all the dozens of ways you could die would make your eventual last breath less traumatic, less...final.

Because she noticed that she had fallen down the rabbit hole and because she didn't like how claustrophobic her thoughts were, she pushed them aside and pulled her favorite lipstick from the top righthand drawer. She glanced at the familiar label, smiled at the name 'Tantric Dreams' that was pressed into the enamel tube. She hadn't really liked the shade of lipstick when she'd first tried it on. It was a dark almost-plum color that she had thought was too young, too avant-garde for her. But now, almost ten years after she'd been convinced to buy a tube by the name of the color, she was loathe to wear, let alone try anything else.

With one final smack of her lips, she rose from the chair, deliberately ignoring the pain in her knees and the wobble in her step. She gave a twirl, a slow twirl, and sent her lilac dress whirling around her shins. *Not bad, Amanda.*

Not bad at all. At least that's what she chose to tell herself and she grabbed a matching shawl before making her way down the stairs.

"I can't believe you drink this crap when I make such good cocktails," Ike said when she came up beside him and he passed her the brandy on ice. He smiled to take any sting out of his words, winced exaggeratedly when she took a sip, and smacked her lips together.

"Well, if I ever saw such a beautiful woman, it was in my sleep," he said, taking her in.

Amanda laughed and welcomed the blush that rose to her cheeks. She hadn't lived eighty years to be coy now. In her opinion, there was nothing wrong with showing a man that his words had given you pleasure. Especially when you were both eighty and words were about the only pleasure you were up for.

They sat together on her old, leather couch, sipped their drinks slowly because, having lived for eight decades, they had somehow fallen into the trap of being ready far too early. For everything.

"What is this shindig for?" Ike asked, filling their companionable silence with his deep voice.

"I have absolutely no idea," she replied. "But I'm hoping that David proposes to Ivy soon, so I'll be at all foreseeable events in the future."

He laughed and raised his glass in cheers of agreement.

"Oh, Ike, she's...impossibly perfect for him. I just can't believe it, you know? That my perfectionist grandson found a woman who drives him crazy *and* is gorgeous *and* smart."

"Quite the hat-trick."

"He's always been impossibly perfect," she said sadly, recalling the hundreds of social events that had shaped him from a little boy with scraped knees to a man with no time for any activities that could possibly lead to scraped knees. "But this girl brings out the..." she searched for the word with her hands, "light in him. The mojo."

Ike nodded. "I always think about that when I look back on life. The things that I wouldn't have taken so, seriously, the things I wouldn't have worried about so much."

"God!" Amanda laughed. "Think of the time we could salvage if we just eradicated time spent worrying!"

Ike chuckled. "Years."

"Absolutely," she seconded. "They don't say that life is wasted on the young for nothing."

Ike smiled and nodded before taking a sip of his drink, his hand trembling noticeably even to Amanda's old eyes. "You want me to drive?" she asked, standing eventually so that she could put her glass down on the kitchen counter.

Ike shook his head and followed suit. "Driving is about the only thing I have another year or two left of," he laughed. "Don't deprive me of that!"

She smiled because she knew he was trying to play it off as a joke. She felt her heart sigh a little because she knew that the next time the government sent him a notice to renew his license, he wouldn't pass the test. For good reason too, she thought, but nonetheless, she could still hurt for him.

Chapter 19

"You. Did. *What?*"

Ivy chuckled when Damien made a grab for her hand and, once he saw the ring, gave an exaggerated sigh and fanned his face theatrically.

"Good Lord," Louie countered as he too took a turn to inspect her ring. "That is a gorgeous piece of jewelry." He turned to look at David, who stood just outside of their circle, his hands in the pockets of his slacks. "You done good."

David chuckled and rubbed the back of his neck. "Ah, thanks."

"Is this why you're throwing the party?" Damien asked. "To announce the engagement?"

When David nodded, Ivy chuckled. "We figured it would be easier if we just gathered all our favorite people together and got it over and done with," she said, placing a hand on her stomach to try and calm the nerves that had settled there.

She refrained from mentioning that they were also planning on telling David's family, including his eighty-five-year-old grandma, how they met. That was news better left to the actual family conversation that they would be having in, oh, less than thirty minutes.

"Well, we are so glad that we're included among your favorite people," Damien teased. "Honestly, girl. I haven't seen you in like…"

"Five days," Ivy corrected with a giggle, pleased by the momentary distraction. "We had brunch last Sunday."

He sighed exaggeratedly and rolled his eyes. "Brunch once a week is not enough considering we lived together for nearly a decade."

When she noticed that David had come up behind her, she leaned her back into his chest, welcoming the feeling of his solid chest against her. She turned to look up at him, smiled when Louie added, "You two are adorable."

"*We* will be better about seeing you," David added, deliberately placating Damien. "You guys are family."

Ivy smiled, then felt her heart stutter to a halt in her chest when the doorbell rang. The full force of what they were about to do hit her, and she froze on the spot.

She took one deep breath to calm herself and sighed, relieved when David kissed the side of her neck. "Let me get this one."

"Hi!" Camilla said and stepped into his arms.

David, still holding the door, gave her an awkward one-armed squeeze, surprised by the friendliness of the gesture. No air-kisses?

He looked up into his father's eyes, noticed his own ice blues grinning back at him, and frowned skeptically as he unwrapped his arm from his mother and extended it so that he could shake his father's hand.

"Thanks for coming," he said politely, trying to calm his unease. "You both look amazing," he added, noticing their twin tans from their month abroad.

"We had the most amazing time, David," Camilla said, clasping her hands as she spoke. "We just can't wait to tell you about it."

"Come in," he said with a nod and waited for his father to step inside. "We invited you and Gran early because Ivy and I wanted to talk to family before the other guests arrived."

He noticed his father's raised eyebrows and the way his mother's face settled into a perfect mask and tried to smile to relieve some of the tension.

"Is everything okay?" Camilla asked, her voice calm and unemotional, a stark, cold comparison to just moments before.

He noticed that his father touched his mother's back in a gesture of comfort that David had never seen before, noticed that she turned and leaned into him slightly in an acknowledgment even more foreign to him. What had happened on their trip abroad, he wondered?

"Everything is fine. We just have some news."

"Oh my God! Is Ivy pregnant?" Camilla asked, her façade crumbling completely in a huge smile.

David couldn't help but chuckle despite the lead in his stomach, partly because of the absurdity of the situation, and partly because his mother was in for a whole other shock. "No," he replied, "although it is heartening to know that if and when she ever is, you'll be happy."

He hadn't meant the words to sound like a judgment, but they came out quick and cold, exactly like Camilla Van den Berg had taught him to deliver criticism.

He saw her wince, saw a brief flicker of disappointment in his father's eyes, and turned away, embarrassed by his bitterness. "I'm sorry, Mo—"

"No," Camilla said, holding up her hand to silence him. "I deserved that." She looked at Michael, who nodded and smiled sadly at David.

"We want to try harder," Michael said, quietly. "We weren't very good parents. We were so distracted by life and…doing well, but we want to be…better."

David looked down at his hand when his mother placed hers on top of his and said, "If and when we do have grandchildren, we want to be there. In every way."

David nodded, feeling uncomfortable and awkward in the face of his parents' apology. He took a step back so that they could come into the house fully, cleared his throat. "I appreciate that," he said, trying to sound genuine. "Luckily for us, we won't need to think about that for a few more years."

He hated the flatness of his own voice, hated the disbelief that rang in his ears, but knew that there were a million reasons that he felt disenchanted.

Michael cleared his voice as he stepped past David and walked towards the lounge. "Ivy," he said, walking straight up to her and wrapping her in a hug.

David felt his heart soften at the simple gesture, felt his anger melt a little at the way that first his father, and then mother, embraced the woman he was going to spend his life with. He watched from the sidelines as Ivy introduced her best friends to his parents, couldn't help but marvel as even Camilla softened under Damien's casual teasing. They were an odd bunch, he thought. Completely mismatched, but completely content to be so.

"How about a drink while we wait for Amanda and Ike?" Ivy said, distracting him from his reverie.

"Sure," David said and moved towards the bar. "What can I get everyone?"

While Damien and Louie chose Manhattans at Ivy's insistence, his parents went for their usual, and David poured for them as they sat on the sofa next to each other. A Sauvignon Blanc for his mother and a Whisky Soda for his father. At least that much hadn't changed overnight.

He noticed how close they were, noticed that their bodies touched from shoulder to ankle, and couldn't help but feel a small tug of hope. Maybe they had figured it out in Europe? He wondered if their newfound romance would last but pushed the thought aside, ashamed of himself. His parents, despite their differences, deserved to be happy too.

As he carried their drinks over, he caught Ivy's eye and felt his grin spread. His parents had yet to notice the ring that she wore and Damien and Louie, clearly found it hilarious; although they sat on opposite sides of the room, David noticed the grins and winks they kept sending each other.

When she came to stand beside him, David took Ivy's hand and smiled down at her, aware of the fact that she was probably feeling as sick in the stomach as he was. He wasn't quite sure how they had decided that telling his family would be a good idea, but she had insisted that they needed to be prepared, and not ambushed, by the information.

So, here they were.

When the doorbell rang again, David released her hand and made for the door, saying, "That will be Gran and Ike."

"It's nothing serious, is it?" he heard his mother ask Ivy as he opened the door for his grandmother.

Amanda beamed up at him, her smile wavering when she noticed the expressionless set of David's face. He tried to smile, but the gesture fell flat.

"Hi, Gran," he said. "Ike." He reached past her to shake the older man's hand, then ushered them inside and towards the lounge when Amanda tried to ask him what was wrong.

"We'll explain in a minute."

It seemed like it took them ages to get everyone a drink and seated in the lounge, but, finally, six pairs of expectant eyes blinked at her and David.

Ivy felt her palms start sweating instantly and had to consciously refrain from wiping them down the front of her dress. Her stomach danced nervously in her throat, and she clenched her fists at her side, digging her nails into her palm in an attempt to calm herself down.

Suddenly, this didn't seem like a good idea.

"Oh, for Christ's sake!" Amanda said, breaking the silence. "Spit it out, you two!"

David chuckled nervously and reached for her hand, unfurling the fist that she'd made and enveloping her hand in his. The moment their palms touched, she felt her heart steady and her mind calm, as if she could draw off his strength as they stood side-by-side.

"Ivy and I have something to tell you," he started.

"What's happened?" Michael asked, frowning as he glanced from David to her.

"You'll understand soon. But first, we want to tell you the story of how we met," David said simply. When everyone frowned in confusion, he added, "It's going to be important to understand what's going on."

Ivy gripped David's hand as he told his family the truth, kept her eyes cast down when he gave them the details about her past and tried not to blush when the room fell into a deafening silence.

By the time he had explained about Gordon, she was ready to run away, grab the keys to the Porsche, get onto the 101 and keep driving.

They were going to hate her.

They were going to blame her for ruining David's career. Worse, she'd be the reason that the family tore apart because she knew, beyond a doubt, that David didn't care, that he'd chosen her over his family, over his career.

"I…," Camilla started before faltering. "I certainly wasn't expecting that."

Ivy flinched at the tone that her soon-to-be mother-in-law had used, forced herself to look up at Camilla as her stomach clenched in a tight knot.

To her surprise, Camilla was looking at Michael, and Ivy saw the exact moment that he nodded to her and took her hand in his. When Camilla turned back to face her, she was shocked to see curiosity in the woman's eyes, not the judgment she had been expecting. The first sliver of hope slid into her stomach, a warm rush against the icy unease solidifying there.

"We're agreed that he's equally complicit in this," Camilla said, nodding in David's direction. "As far as we're concerned, you were in an impossible situation, Ivy."

"And even if you weren't," Amanda chimed in from her position on the sofa, "it's the twenty-first goddamn century! A woman can do what she pleases with her own body."

"Here, here," Ike seconded. "In our day you would've been burned at the stake," he joked and winked. "Both of you."

Ivy laughed and felt the relief slide through her like a wave. She felt her pulse thrumming in her throat and found that she couldn't speak just yet. So, she didn't try to stop the first few tears that slipped over her perfectly done lashes, nor did she care if she had to spend time redoing her makeup.

"I totally would have bet money that this ended differently," Damien chirped in from his seat on the barstool a few feet away. "I was preparing to defend your honor."

Louie giggled and slapped him half-heartedly on the arm. "Stop interrupting."

"We'd be foolish to ignore how happy David has been since he met you, Ivy," Michael said and touched Camilla's hand again in a gesture that seemed to take the residual stiffness out of Camilla's shoulders.

When David wrapped an arm around her and pulled her close, she sank back into his chest and let the feeling of his heart beating heavily against her back settle her racing pulse. She gripped the arm that was wrapped around her and managed to say, "I'm really happy that I found him too."

"So, what is your plan with this idiot…Gordon, you said?" Michael asked just as Camilla let out a quick gasp and leaped off the sofa.

She grabbed Ivy's hand, inadvertently yanking her out of David's arms, before demanding, "What's this?"

"We were getting there," David said with a small chuckle.

"Oh, I knew it!" Amanda exclaimed and, pushing herself to her feet with a little more effort than Camilla had, came forward to peer at Ivy's hand, which was still in Camilla's vise-like grip. She took a long, slow look at the ring. "Gorgeous."

As the girls gushed over the jewelry, Ivy felt David leave her side and watched as he walked towards his father. "I was hoping to tell you before I asked, but the opportunity never really presented itself," David was saying.

Although she didn't hear Michael's reply over Camilla and Amanda's excited chatter, she noticed the way Michael grinned and pulled David in for a hug.

"You have to have a spring wedding!" Camilla was saying when Ivy finally managed to bring her attention back to the women still oohing and aahing over her ring. "Santa Barbara is beautiful in the Spring."

"Who says they are getting married in Santa Barbara?" Amanda asked haughtily, her eyebrows raised at Camilla.

"Oh," Camilla said simply as if the idea that they wouldn't get married in Santa Barbara had just occurred to her. "I suppose that's true." She looked at Ivy then. "Honestly, I'll be happy with whatever you two decide, but you have to let me help in some way."

Ivy laughed. "Of course. Once we set a date *and* location, you'll be the first to know. I promise."

Camilla nodded, seemingly satisfied. She cast one last teary-eyed look at the ring before dropping Ivy's hand and walking to David.

"You're going to do just fine, Ivy," Amanda added. "But make sure she doesn't bully you."

"I will," Ivy laughed.

When the doorbell rang, she felt her stomach lurch uncomfortably. She had been so wrapped up in telling the family their history and news that she'd basically forgotten that they were having a party.

She glanced at David and judged, by how his blue eyes had frosted over, that he was feeling the same way.

Before she could catch his eye, Michael slapped a hand on David's back. For the first time, she saw why Michael had been such a successful businessman. She saw the determination in the angry set of his jaw, the steel glint in his blue eyes, and heard it in the way that his voice dropped an octave, causing everyone, including David, to turn and look to him. "What's your plan?"

David looked at her, nodded. "Honesty."

Ivy saw the doubt creep over Michael's features and noticed the moment that he looked up and, seeing Camilla's quick shake of her head, clenched his jaw shut and shuttered his gaze.

Even though she and David had talked extensively about what the right course of action should be, she couldn't help but feel disheartened by Michael's instant skepticism. What if things went wrong? What if her past was exposed? What if David's career ended because of her?

Ivy would never forgive herself if she ruined the one thing that he had worked his entire life for. She looked at him, heard him saying, "Ivy and I have that figured out, but...we can't tell you just yet."

"Why?" This from Camilla.

"We don't want to make a scene if we can avoid it," Ivy said, contributing to the conversation. "So, we're hoping to throw him off a little." She paused, looked every one of them in the eye before adding, "We just wanted you all to know so that you could be prepared if things go wrong tonight. My family, well my best friends, know." She looked at Damien and Louie pointedly. They grinned. "But I didn't feel a need to tell my grandparents."

"And if things do go wrong? What then?" Michael asked again, his eyes still set in the same determined glint.

"We'll figure it out." Ivy took David's hand in her own again. "Together."

Michael opened his mouth as if he would argue, and Ivy saw Camilla place her hand on his arm. He looked at her, sighed, and nodded. "Alright. Fine. Do it your way."

"But if you need anything," Camilla added, "you just ask."

Ivy felt David relax at her side and gave his hand one last squeeze before dropping it.

When the doorbell rang again, everyone froze and glanced at them. Ivy tried to settle her heart by forcing a watery smile to her face, but the attempt fell flat as her heart sped in her chest.

"I'll get it," Damien said and took a few steps towards the door before turning around to look at them all. "Oh, for Christ's sake people, pull yourselves together! You look like you're waiting for your turn at the guillotine."

Ivy felt the room deflate as everyone tried to return to business as usual. Camilla and Michael picked up their drinks and started showing David their vacation pictures. Amanda sat back down on the sofa next to Ike. Louie chuckled and shook his head at the scene.

Chapter 20

He had never been to David Van den Berg's house. Correction, he thought, he had never been *invited* to David Van den Berg's house. He wasn't entirely sure why the thought made him mad, wasn't entirely sure why he felt the blood beneath his skin run hot. He wasn't quite sure why he was invited tonight. Hell, Gordon wasn't entirely sure why David pissed him off in general.

It wasn't because David was from family money or had connections to boost his career in the industry. After all, he was too. No, he thought, it wasn't money or family.

It might be the fact that where he was short, plump, and balding, David was tall, athletic, and had a full head of hair. Looks, and what some would label charisma, were the only things separating him and David from being promoted at the same time, of experiencing the same advantages after years of slaving away and selling their youth for a fat paycheck.

It was only fair, he thought with a healthy dose of bitterness, given that he had no control over how he looked once he exited the womb, that Gordon hated David on the principles of nature. He shrugged off a swell of rage as it seeped into his throat and forced himself to swallow it as Phillip came up to him to chit chat.

While he largely ignored the ramblings of the associate, Gordon glanced around the spacious living area. He noted the tasteful interior, felt his lip curl at the expansive nighttime view of the Hollywood Hills, the blinking lights ranging from amber to vermillion.

When he spotted the whore laughing with Bruce Standard, his blood pressure spiked. He saw the way she

273

sidled up to him, took note of the way she touched his arm casually and looked down on him, her cat-like eyes sparkling with some small shared joke.

He stared, incredulous, when Standard's wife walked up to them, a small smile on her face, and leaned into the hug that Ivy offered. Was she so oblivious that she couldn't see the Jezebel rubbing up against her husband? Maybe, he mulled, Deborah Standard was a whore too. He had found that women in general only performed well when they were being paid to pretend.

"Everything okay, Gordon?"

He turned to stare at Phillip, aware of the fact that he hadn't heard a word of what the associate had said. Not that he cared, but, he sighed, appearances were not insignificant in the industry and he knew that certain games had to be played. "All good," he replied. I think I need another drink."

He moved away from Phillip without another word of explanation or apology, and picked his way through the crowd to the bar, shouting, "Van den Berg!" as he drew nearer to David.

When their eyes met, Gordon forced himself to maintain the icy stare, forced himself to smile despite the hot blush he felt creeping up his neck. "There you are!" he said as he came to stand beside him.

"Gordon," David said and gave him a curt nod. "I'm glad you could make it."

"Well," Gordon shrugged, his mind reeling with how to rile his colleague up further, "I heard that a lot of people were going to be here and just couldn't contain myself."

He glanced around the room, pretending to be impressed. "Quite a few important people here," he said suggestively and felt a sharp slice of pleasure when David's eyes shuttered.

Enjoying his power play, he leaned casually against the bar, looked David up and down with what he knew was thinly veiled contempt. "I see that Ivy is quite the…sensation among the guests." He saw the clenched fists at David's side, felt the muscles in his legs shorten just in case the thin temper he faced finally snapped.

"I swear t—"

"You must be Gordon Smith?"

He turned around with a slight frown on his face, met a second pair of David's eyes, and blinked at the resemblance. He knew Michael Van den Berg by reputation, knew that even his own parents knew Michael Van den Berg by reputation. He was a legend, a man who even after years of retirement could still pull anyone's strings. A master puppeteer.

"Mr. Van den Berg," Gordon said, flushing slightly as he extended a hand. He couldn't forget that riling David would most certainly hurt his reputation with Michael. He took a brief moment to think about which was more important to him and, having decided, added, "I was just telling David what a great party this is."

Van den Berg nodded, a polite smile on his face. "I hear from David that you have quite the Rolodex. Perhaps we should talk sometime."

Gordon glanced at David, noticed the cold, calm face, and felt a small flush of embarrassment creep under his skin. The only reason that Michael Van den Berg would know him would be if David had talked about him and, try as he might, Gordon had no idea why David would recommend him.

As if the universe had heard his thoughts, Michael added, "Selby Waters, unfortunately, has strong anti-nepotism policies, so David plans on the long run at Black Finch, but…" he shrugged.

Gordon leaned forward, willing the man to finish his sentence.

Michael blinked a few times, rolled his shoulders.

Gordon noticed the steel in David's eyes and felt a small ball of hope and glee settle in his chest. Could he be poached by Selby Waters over Michael Van den Berg's son? Even if he were retired, Michael had been CEO of the firm for fifteen years. Gordon knew that if he was offering, he could guarantee him a job.

"I would love to meet sometime," he added, trying to prompt the connection.

Michael nodded. "Perfect. I'll arrange a meeting next week."

Gordon watched, shocked, as Michael Van den Berg nodded to his son before ending the conversation with a brief, "Gordon. David."

He watched the man walk away, felt the tap tap tap of his heart against his ribs as if his very blood were aware of the opportunity that he'd just been given.

"Well, it looks as if my father has singled you out," David said coldly.

Gordon shook himself once as the knowledge settled in his chest. So, he hadn't imagined it. In the back of his mind, he wondered if he should be skeptical, but he dismissed the notion after mulling it over for less than a minute. He was qualified. He was great at his job. He had no wife or kids to keep him away from the office. But most importantly, he wanted the job more than he wanted anything—anyone— in the world.

"I'd take it, you know," he said.

He glanced at David anxiously, hoping that he hadn't ruined his chance by threatening the asshole's sentiments. His entire world could come crashing down around him if David told his father about the threats that he had been making. After all, even if they were true, David was his son.

"Well, that would be entirely your choice," David said, smiling. "I'm sure they'd offer you Partner."

Gordon nodded once, pleased that there didn't seem to be any residual tension in his colleague's cold eyes.

He briefly considered apologizing but thought better of it. That would be an acknowledgment of guilt. Better to just leave the matter be and pretend that they'd never interacted at all. Besides, if David did tell his father, then he could always use his slut girlfriend against him. He wondered how Michael Van den Berg would feel about the fact that his son's girlfriend was a prostitute.

So, instead, he nodded, tried to emulate the exact curt nod that Michael Van den Berg had used, and said, "David," right before turning on his heel and leaving the party.

He wasn't a stupid man. He knew when to take a win and exit with grace, and now, with a world of opportunity at his feet, he decided to do just that.

Michael watched Gordon Smith leave the party soon after he had made his deal, smiled when the door closed the idiot out of his son's house, and if he had anything to do with it, out of his son's life.

He saw David scan the room, knew the moment that his eyes had locked on him, and sighed when he moved towards him, parting the crowd with the ice in his eyes.

He also saw Ivy, her back to David, turn as if some invisible thread connected them, saw her eyes fill with concern when she saw David walking through the few remaining guests. He watched, fascinated, as she excused herself and, smiling through the crowd, came to stand in front of him at the exact same time that David did.

"What's wrong?" she asked, her voice trembling slightly, her large, emerald eyes cautious as she glanced from David to Michael.

"Why?"

He sighed. How did he begin to explain that forty years in the industry had given him hindsight, especially when his son's eyes were shuttered with hurt?

"I've been around a long time, David," he said.

He saw Ivy take his son's hand, even though she didn't know what was going on and knew that he had made the right decision. "You have your whole lives, your careers, everything ahead of you." When David didn't reply, he added, "I won't let you two stand alone in the chance that your news is taken well."

"We had a plan, Dad," David said.

"Let me guess. Find a way to tell everyone and pass it up as no big deal? A cute 'how we met' story?" He sighed. "Life doesn't work like that."

"No." David stared at him and Michael saw his jaw twitch in anger. "We were going to announce our engagement and hope that the news was enough to deter the asshole."

"Can someone tell me what's going on?" Ivy said, a slight edge to her voice.

"My father offered Gordon Smith a job with Selby Waters," David said, quietly.

He saw Ivy take the news, internalize it. He saw the smile that bloomed on her face and felt a swift kick of relief. She understood what he had done where his own son had been too offended to. "This is fantastic," she said. She looked at David, noticed the cold set of his eyes, and shook her head. "He bought him, David."

"And rewarded him for being a complete asshole."

"I promise you, David, this situation wouldn't have hurt Gordon at all, but it could have hurt you. Both of you. And I wasn't prepared to take that risk over offending your moral compass and potentially ruining your career."

"We could have handled it."

"I know," Michael said simply. He sighed when David frowned. "I know that you can handle anything, everything, by yourself," he said. "Your mother and I...whether we wanted to or not, we made sure that you had to and I'm sorry for that. But I want to help now," he said and met his son's doubtful eyes. "I want to help now, I want to help in the future...I want to help with everything."

When silence settled between them, he felt his heart constrict with fear. Had he been out of his son's life for so long that their relationship was unsalvageable? He saw Ivy look at David, noticed the small squeeze that she gave him. When David met her eyes, he saw the message pass between them and felt relief blossom.

"Thank you, Michael," Ivy said first. She reached for him and pulled him into her arms.

Michael blushed and patted her back awkwardly. "It was my pleasure."

David sighed and sent him a smile. "I am thankful that you're going to be keeping an eye on him," he said. "I'm more thankful that he's going to be out of my office and out of my hair."

"Keeping an eye on him?" Michael laughed. "I own him. You two have nothing to worry about where Gordon Smith is concerned."

"That's all very well," a voice said behind them. "But my question is: Why were you worried about him in the first place?"

Chapter 21

David felt his heart sink in his chest even before he turned around to face Bruce Standard. His boss, the man who could change his life forever with a single phone call, stood right behind their trio, looking up at them in curious silence, his face set in impassive calm.

When Michael cleared his throat, David held up his hand to silence him. "Thanks, Dad. We'll handle this."

He heard his father sigh before he walked away, shaking his head, and tried to steel himself against what was coming next.

He had to be honest.

It was his reputation at stake.

His career.

In the ensuing silence, David felt his chest constrict, felt all the fear that he'd harbored over the last few months unfurl in his throat, making it hard to breathe. Beside him, Ivy stood silently, her fingers wrapped stiffly around a flute of champagne.

Bruce watched them, a puzzled frown taking over his face, creasing his brow, and making him appear almost comical. "Is everything okay?" he finally asked, obviously sensing that they were having trouble getting started.

David took a deep breath, the words ready. He opened his mouth.

Nothing came out.

"Gordon found out how David and I met," Ivy said quietly, her voice coming out in a reedy whisper.

When she didn't say anything more, David looked at Bruce. He noticed the man looked at them with plain confusion. "I'm sorry," he said. "I'm struggling to see how that's relevant?"

"I…" Ivy faltered and turned to look at him.

David felt panic, hot and heavy, bubble through his stomach. *Say something, you idiot! Anything!* But try as he might, he couldn't seem to get the words past the ball of fear closing his throat.

"I'm sorry," Ivy said, looking at his face before her eyes darted towards the door. "I've made a mistake."

David snapped his head to her, saw the hurt and betrayal in her eyes as she looked around without meeting his gaze and felt his heart sink in his chest. He reached out a hand to touch her, but she took a single step back, out of his reach.

"Ivy?"

"This wasn't supposed to happen," she said quietly, clearly not wanting to draw attention to them. "I have to go. Excuse me."

Before he could say anything, she hurried past him, past Bruce Standard.

He watched as Damien and Louie peeled away from the remaining stragglers and joined her at the front door, saw them both flash a look of concern at him as she pulled open the door and stepped outside.

David started walking towards the door, then hesitated. Bruce Standard stood in the middle of his living room staring at him, clearly confused by what had just happened. He sighed and raked a hand through his hair before turning back to his boss.

"I met Ivy when I paid her to escort me to a work event," he said quickly as if by forcing the words out one after the other they'd be easier to say. "I fell in love with her. Gordon found out." Realizing that he wasn't exactly making sense, he shook his head. "I have to go find her. I'm sorry."

He turned away.

"Van den Berg," Bruce said from behind him.

David didn't turn around.

"My office. Eight a.m. Monday."

He nodded, his back still to Bruce, and moved towards the door, ignoring the few curious glances cast his way. No doubt people had seen Ivy leave already. He sighed and kept moving. It didn't matter anymore. He would almost certainly be fired. Worse, Ivy was pissed at him because he'd floundered. He'd failed to stand by her side as she'd tried to explain their situation to *his* boss.

He reached the door and grabbed his jacket off the hook, stuck his hand into the bowl that Ivy had placed on top of the Queen Anne table at the door, and pulled out his car keys. He slid them into his pocket and turned to reach for his wallet, his hand falling short when he noticed the glinting gold ring sitting in the bowl.

He felt his chest tighten. She had left it behind.

He felt his vision narrow with the swift punch of air that seemed to hit his stomach. He picked up the ring and curled his fist around it until the stone cut into his palm. She had left him. Just like that. She hadn't even waited for him to apologize or given him time to explain to Bruce. She'd just assumed that he'd fail her and decided to leave.

Somewhere beneath the anger, the realization that she was gone screamed through him in a single wave of grief. He could feel the doubt clinging to the corners of his mind. Maybe she would come back? Maybe if he went and found her, she'd let him explain? Maybe they could figure it out?

He sighed and pulled open the door, stepped into the cool night air, and ignored the fact that he was leaving the last of his guests alone in his house. He nearly turned back but decided against it. Camilla would make sure that everyone had some reason or another for believing that they'd left to tend to an emergency.

Once he'd hopped in his car, he revved the Porsche, felt it purr as if excited but, still, found no joy in it. Where was he headed? He didn't know where Ivy had gone. Worse, even if he did, would she want to see him?

He felt the ring that he'd given her, the one that she'd taken off and left behind, burn a hole in his left breast pocket. The betrayal left a bitter taste in his mouth.

Because he needed to think, David accelerated once he merged onto the freeway and cranked up the sound of AC/DC's Thunderstruck so that it was thrumming through his speakers. When the song brought images of Ivy singing along in his car, he turned off the music altogether, preferring the silence over the memory.

He'd head north to Santa Barbara, maybe stay with Meg, maybe avoid people altogether. He could book a hotel room, wake up and surf in the morning and then be back before his Monday eight a.m. meeting with Bruce Standard.

The thought left him feeling queasy, so he pushed it aside and focused on the road. He couldn't believe that he had spent all that time worrying and planning and hoping that everything would work out only to have it all explode in his face.

It had all been for nothing. In the end, he'd lost Ivy and his job. He'd ruined the one thing he'd worked his whole life for and pushed away the only person he'd ever wanted.

The realization that he had made a mistake didn't ease the fact that Ivy had left, chosen to break off their engagement and leave him over trying to work it out. But it did make him want to put his head through a wall. He was an idiot who had made a mistake. And now he'd be paying in full for the rest of his life.

She ignored the fact that both Damien and Louie were looking at her in weary silence and strummed her fingers against the door to distract herself from thinking about anything at all. Where only hours before she had felt love and hope, now she felt as if her heart had been put through a meat slicer and then taped back together. He was gone. She'd let him go.

Because the image of David, standing pale and silent at her side, forced its way into her memory, she closed her eyes and bit the inside of her cheek to stop from crying. God, he had been so scared, so…hesitant.

"Are you going to tell us what happened?" Damien asked, breaking the silence in the car as they drove towards Koreatown.

Ivy sighed and swiped at her face when the first tear streaked a line through her makeup. "His boss overheard us talking about Gordon, about…everything."

"No!" Louie gasped, genuinely horrified. "What did he say?"

Ivy shook her head, remembering all over again how David's mouth had opened and closed silently. "He asked for an explanation and David…God, he looked so scared, like his life was over…"

They lapsed into silence again.

A few minutes passed and Ivy couldn't help but feel that she'd done the right thing. If she wasn't in his life, then David wouldn't have to tell Bruce about how they'd met, he'd get to keep his job and get the Partner promotion. He'd have everything he'd ever wanted.

"So, you broke off your engagement?" Damien asked. "I'm so confused."

"You don't understand," Ivy said. "His world is…singular. Straightforward. *Conservative*," she said, hoping that the word would convey why it mattered to her liberal friends.

Louie turned in the front passenger seat of the car to look at her. "You think that you're doing him a favor? By leaving?"

"God, you're an idiot," Damien said loudly. He glanced at her while he drove. "Don't you think he should have a

285

say in the matter? Christ, Ivy! You were engaged like a minute ago!"

"Shh!" Louie ordered him.

He turned back a second time. "What did David say to his boss?"

"Nothing."

Damien and Louie exchanged a glance, a knowing look that instantly raised her hackles. "Stop it. I'm doing the right thing; I'm making sure that David has exactly what he wants, and you two are judging me? You're supposed to be *my* best friends."

Where Louie just raised an eyebrow at her, Damien chuckled. "Oh, hell no!" he said. "You do not get to claim the martyr card for breaking off your engagement because you're shit scared."

Ivy's head snapped up and she glared at Damien. "What did you say to me?"

"You heard me. You're terrified that this guy might take a bet on you and it scares the shit out of you."

"That's not true," she whispered, even as the first sliver of pain sliced through her. She didn't have to lie about the fact that she was terrified; she knew she was. Had admitted it countless times before. She'd never had to tell David that she was petrified of being with him, that being with him meant that, well, one day she could lose him. No, she *would* lose him. So, instead, she said, "I don't want him to lose everything because of me."

"*And* you're shit scared of commitment?" Louie asked, one eyebrow raised.

Ivy chuckled despite herself, despite the lead in her stomach. She gave a small nod, a single acknowledgment of what she couldn't say aloud. She was terrified of what he made her feel, terrified of the fact that he was prepared to give everything up for her. It made no sense. *Yet you're doing the same for him.* She ignored the voice in her head and focused on the road, of the quiet hum of the car.

It took them thirty minutes to get back to the apartment that she had shared with Damien only eight months earlier, the one he had since made a home in with Louie. Ivy, feeling the weariness in her bones, flopped face-down on Sally, and then when she couldn't hold her breath anymore against the thick, brown fabric, curled onto her side into the fetal position.

She glanced up when Damien brought her one of his old, comfy tee shirts, a towel, and a blanket, smiled when he reached down to touch her face. "As much as I think you're wrong, I'm really sorry that you're hurting."

She nodded and sat up so that she could pull off her dress and put the shirt on. It smelled like Damien and instead of being comforted by the familiar scent, Ivy felt hollowed out by the fact that he didn't smell like oak and leather. Like David.

"Let me know if you need anything," he said as he turned for his and Louie's bedroom.

Ivy lay back down and closed her eyes, ignoring the fact that she could feel her makeup caked on her face and pushing aside her OCD desire to go and wash it off. God, she just wanted to sleep. To forget.

Instead, she lay awake for hours with silent tears running down her face, thinking about David and how silent he'd been against Bruce Standard's potential judgment, about how she hadn't been able to say anything, about how she'd seen the door in her periphery vision, such a clear way to escape from all the fear. About how she'd left him.

She let the grief wash away any anger that she felt, let the hollow numbness fill her entire being until she fell into a dreamless, wide-eyed daze towards the early hours of the morning.

Chapter 22

David glanced at his watch and felt his stomach clench uncomfortably when he saw the time. He had thirty minutes left until he met with Bruce Standard, thirty minutes left to enjoy the privacy and safety of his office, thirty minutes left to be David Van den Berg, Managing Director at Black Finch Capital.

He exhaled on a long breath and, for the thousandth time in thirty-six hours, looked at his phone. Nothing. No text messages from Ivy. No calls. Not even an explanation for the fact that she'd broken off their engagement. *Because you didn't open your mouth to defend her*, the voice inside his head reminded him.

He dropped his head into his hands and ignored the heavy weight of his failure.

When a knock sounded on the door, he sat back in his chair, surprised that someone else was in the office this early. Leveling his voice, he said, "Come in."

When Bruce Standard pushed open his door, David stood and glanced at the clock on his wall. Bruce, obviously catching the gesture, waved him back into his seat and took the chair opposite him, crossing one ankle over the other knee. "I got in early. This thing with you and Ivy is driving me crazy."

David sat back down slowly. He took a few seconds to gather his thoughts. "I didn't anticipate falling for her; it just…happened."

Bruce sighed and rubbed his fingers under his glasses. "Start at the beginning."

So, he did. David told him everything. He told him about the night he and Ivy met and how they'd lied about dating to go to dinner with Bruce and Deborah; he told him about leaving her because she petrified him; he even told him about her father, the accident that had brought them back together, and finally, about Gordon's threats.

And thirty minutes later, when he was done, he pushed to his feet and added. "I'm such an idiot. I have to go and find her."

He felt numb inside just talking about her when he knew that he could have lost her. *You're a fucking moron*, he told himself. *You should never have let her leave in the first place.*

When Bruce chuckled, David glanced at him in surprise. The older man shrugged and glanced out of David's window at downtown Los Angeles. "And here I was thinking that I was such a good judge of character," he said.

David flushed. "Ivy is the best person I know," he said quietly, unwilling to defend his actions but prepared to argue for hers.

Bruce glanced at him. "Oh, I know. I'm talking about Gordon." He stood quickly and, tucking his hands into his pockets, started pacing the office. "I could ruin him," he mumbled. "The animal."

Even though he knew he had to leave, had to find Ivy, David sat down in his chair again and watched Bruce Standard walk the width of his office. He was talking about Gordon. "I…I don't understand."

Bruce stopped walking and frowned at him. "What?"

"You're not going to fire me?" he asked, feeling the force of the question burn in his mind.

"No! Where'd you get an idea like that? You're the highest-paid MD for a reason, David. Christ!"

"I thought that…once you found out about Ivy…"

"What?"

"The reputation of the firm," David started saying.

"Has nothing to do with our personal lives," he finished. "I mean, discretion is everything, but we're still human. Which is precisely why I'm disgusted by Gordon

Smith. Integrity is everything in this business." David watched as Bruce kept pacing and talking to himself, only the occasional word, including, "blackmail" and "illegal" reaching his ears.

David held his breath as Bruce came to a sudden stop. "I can't see a way around it. I'm going to have to fire him. He blackmailed a colleague. It's…inexcusable. Completely illegal."

"What about Ivy?"

"She was dating strange, probably creepy, old men—no offense—to pay for her terminal father's hospice care! She's done nothing wrong. Besides, escorting is legal." He sighed and shook his head, as if incredulous. "Quite frankly, David, I thought you two were close to getting engaged the night we all first met. I'd have lost money on the fact that you'd only met each other that night." He chuckled and slapped a hand to his leg. "I just realized I've known your fiancé for longer than you have!" He laughed, a deep rumble that filled the enclosed office.

"Actually," David said. "She called off the engagement."

"What?" For the first time that morning, Bruce looked shocked. "Why?"

"Because I didn't defend her when you asked about Gordon at the party."

"Why are you still here?"

"I thought you were going to fire me."

"What?"

David wasn't quite sure what he was supposed to say, so instead, he just nodded.

"No!" Bruce threw his hands in the air, letting his native New Yorker out the cage. "I heard the conversation about Gordon and needed to find out how you and Ivy had gotten wrapped up with him."

"Oh." David wasn't sure how he was supposed to react to that. He'd been preparing to get fired, go and track down

Ivy, grovel and beg for her to take him back, and then probably go home alone and drink himself to death when she said no. That had been his original plan anyway.

"I'll deal with Smith. You," he pointed at David, "better go convince that girl that you can't live without her."

David smiled and stood. He made his way to the door and paused, his hand hovering above the door handle. "Thank you, Sir."

When Bruce waved him away and continued pacing as he mumbled to himself, David trotted over to the elevator and pressed the button for the basement parking. He dialed Ivy's office. He'd ask her to meet him somewhere. The last thing he wanted to do was cause a scene at her work.

No answer.

When the elevator door pinged and opened to the basement, he hopped in his car and exited the garage, tried Ivy's cell, and, when it went straight to voicemail, tried Damien's.

"Hey!" Damien said. "I'm glad you called."

"Where is she?"

"She's sleeping on my sofa. Hasn't moved since Saturday night. If you tell her I told you, I'll deny it."

"Deal." David laughed despite himself and the nausea he felt sliding through his stomach at the possibility that she wouldn't take him back. "I'm coming over now."

He hung up the phone, accelerated through an orange traffic light, and sped the last few miles towards Koreatown.

He wasn't exactly sure what he'd say to her once he got there, but he knew that if he didn't try, he'd never forgive himself. He was nothing without her. She had swept in with her huge, green eyes, mane of hair, and legs to her armpits and he'd been a goner. And that had been before he'd gotten to know her, before he'd seen her cry when the SPCA ad played on the television, before he'd memorized the way her entire body curled against him while she slept, before he'd realized how funny, smart, and passionate she was.

She couldn't believe it was happening. I mean it was obvious to everyone that he belonged with Jessica, so why was he pretending to be in love with Amber, the pin-thin, big-boobed model from Idaho? Angered by the trash show drama currently unraveling on Damien's television, Ivy decided that the episode had been the director's choice and flicked her wrist to turn it off. She'd watch the final episode in four weeks so that she could miss all the frustration and just enjoy the reveal. When Garrett proposed to *Jessica*.

And that's all it took to have her eyes tearing up again. The word 'proposed'. *God, you're pathetic.*

She'd called in sick that morning because, well, she looked like shit from not having slept in nearly three days and didn't want her colleagues to have her committed when she started crying at random moments during the day.

At least she'd finally, at Damien's insistence, showered earlier that morning. She'd used the scrubbing brush from a toiletry kit that he'd bought her to scrub herself raw, hoping that she could somehow peel away thoughts of David, thoughts about how much she missed him.

It was a different feeling now, she realized, than when she missed him when he traveled for work. Now, instead of a dull ache with underlying anticipation for his return, she felt that every moment held some thought, or memory of him that would rush through her head and her heart like a pair of open scissors being swung by a demon toddler.

She wondered if it would ever go away.

When the door opened a moment later, she looked up, expecting to find that Damien had forgotten his lecture notes again. Instead, her heart shuddered to a stop, skipped a beat, and then continued at double the pace when she saw David standing in the doorway looking down at her.

He looks like shit too. Ivy blushed at the fact that the thought brought her a certain amount of relief, all the while ignoring the fact that her muscles were aching to run to him, her palms itching to touch him. Instead, she pulled the blanket up over her shoulders, trying to keep herself warm as much as she tried to keep herself from moving towards him, touching him, breathing in his scent.

He sighed and closed the door behind him before walking a few steps towards her and stopping. She looked up when his shoes came into the line of sight of her downcast eyes, tried to meet his eyes, and when she felt them burn with unshed tears, forced herself to look away. God, she'd never be the same now that she'd had him and lost him. Even her heart, the one thing that was supposed to be entirely for her, beat erratically in her chest, giving odd hops and skips with every step he moved closer.

"Ivy…"

She looked at him, this time meeting pale, blue eyes that were filled with pain.

"I tried calling but your phone went straight to voicemail," he said.

Despite how close he was, he didn't lean down and touch her, and, for that, Ivy was grateful. She might crumble if he touched her now.

"The battery died yesterday but I haven't needed it so didn't go buy another charger."

They fell silent again. For a moment he stayed that way, silently looking at her and shifting from one foot to another, his hands tucked into the pockets of his slacks. "I'm so sorry," he said finally, his voice breaking.

Ivy frowned and looked up at him, her heart tripping in her chest at the look of sorrow on his face. "I'm sorry that I didn't say anything to Bruce, that I didn't defend you," he continued. "I panicked and froze."

He took another step toward her and her whole body tightened at the proximity. "What I should have said was that an asshole was threatening my beautiful fiancé and if he didn't back off, I'd kill him. Baby…" he waited for her to

294

look at him, "I should have said so many things and I didn't. I'm so sorry."

"It's not your fault," she managed around the lump in her throat. Hearing him say the words brought a fresh slice of pain through her, but she knew that she had to explain to him, make him understand that it wasn't his fault. "I...I figured that you'd be better off without me. When I saw that you couldn't tell the truth, I realized that I didn't want to be the reason that you lost everything."

"Is that what you think?" he asked, a small snap of anger coming through the pain. "That I'd choose to lose you over a goddamn job?" He took a few steps back and then moved towards her again, as if he wanted to pace the room but couldn't bring himself to move too far. "And don't I get a say in all of this? You just thought that, what? You'd make up your mind for me?"

"You had your chance, David," she said quietly. "I gave you every opportunity and you didn't say anything. Worse, you didn't even try to stop me from leaving."

"I was panicking, Ivy!" he said, louder this time. "My boss was standing there, frowning at me and while I was trying to figure out a reasonable way to tell him everything in front of a house full of people, you decided to just walk out of my life! You didn't even wait to talk! You left your ring in the goddamn bowl!"

She felt the tears start again, hated that they betrayed her so easily, hated herself for the fact that she couldn't stay calm, stay reasonable when he was involved. She hated the fact that she was more scared of losing him in the future than loving him now. "I can't do it," she said finally, her voice low. Calm.

She looked up and noticed that he had paled. "Can't do what?"

"I can't lose you." When he frowned, confused, she sighed and added, "I'm petrified that loving you and...and being with you now will kill me when I lose you later."

"Why would you ever lose me?" he asked and, coming to sit beside her, reached a single warm hand to cover her cold ones. "Aside from you hating me for being an idiot and not sorting Gordon the minute he threatened us?"

She looked down at his hand, could easily acknowledge the little fires that had ignited in her skin the moment his wide palm had touched her. "I don't know," she said. "I just feel all this fear inside of me when I'm with you. Fear that you'll be taken from me."

"Fear that it won't last?" he asked.

"Fear that it won't always be like this," she added, bringing one of her hands to rest on top of his.

"I feel it too, Ivy. You scare me more than anything ever has before." He sighed and, looking at her, tucked a strand of hair behind her ear. "But I love you enough to take that risk and...I really hope that you do too."

She felt her heart tear in her chest, felt the panic claw its way into her throat. What was she supposed to say?

He sighed and dropped her hands before pushing to his feet. "I don't want to pressure you. I'll give you space, Ivy. But whatever you decide, it's done. We can't live like this anymore; this constant fear of failure and anticipation of loss is...it's killing us."

When he moved towards the door, she felt her world dimming around the edges; the panic that she'd felt only moments before filled her throat, making it hard to breathe. Watching him leave felt like physical pain, in her chest, in her head. God, she realized as she looked down at her hands, even they were trembling uncontrollably.

How could him leaving do this to her? How could such a small thing—him walking away for good—make her entire system revolt? Make her mind want to shut down and furl into itself?

Because you love him.

She knew that already, had known it for months but for the first time she realized the reason she was so scared. If

296

she had loved him any less, she wouldn't fear losing him as much as she did. She looked up and frowned at the empty room before jumping off the sofa and yanking open the door. He had gone. He had left and she hadn't even heard the door open.

Glancing down either side of the street, she didn't see the Porsche. Shit.

Ivy slammed the door and ran to Damien's room. She was going to have to borrow some pants.

Chapter 23

It had taken him three hours of driving around aimlessly to calm down enough to go back into work, but even the time hadn't done anything to relieve the anxiety underlying his decision. He'd given her an ultimatum, he realized. He'd told her that he wanted it all or nothing. Why the fuck had he done that? What if she chose nothing? Hours later, he still couldn't believe that he'd been so stupid because the truth was that he'd take whatever Ivy had to give. He loved her. He'd do anything for her.

Not even the chaos unraveling at work, the whispered rumblings about an emergency Partner meeting being called, had been enough to distract him from the fact that he might have just made the biggest mistake of his life. Not even seeing the most powerful men in the Black Finch LA office walk out of the conference room with unpleasant expressions was enough to pull him from his reverie, not even when more than one of them cast a glance his way as they filed past the open door to his office.

David stared at his computer screen at the same excel model he'd had open for three hours and, casting a glance at his watch, decided that one day of wasting time was enough. He'd go home, take a shower, pick up the ring that he'd left there and then he was going to go and bring Ivy home—for good.

Nobody asked him any questions as he walked out of the office earlier than he'd ever left before and David felt some relief. He'd hate to have to make small talk when all he could think about was finding his girl.

His girl.

His fiancé.

Hopefully.

It took him only forty minutes to get home, which was a miracle unto itself. He parked the Porsche in his driveway and made his way slowly up the stairs to the front door. The sleeplessness over the last few days had left his entire body, down to his bones, aching and weary. Even his mind, usually so sharp and focused, felt numb around the edges but, surprisingly, David didn't mind; if his fatigue stopped him from overthinking what would happen if Ivy said no to him, he'd welcome it.

Pushing open the door, he sighed as he entered the air-conditioned room and put his keys and his wallet in the bowl at the door. As he was about to move past, he stopped and frowned down at the bowl. The ring was gone. He'd specifically put it in there because putting it back in the box had felt like giving up, like admitting defeat. Shit.

I've been robbed.

His tired mind didn't stop to process that he'd just unlocked his door himself. With his head reeling, he pulled his phone from his pocket, thinking he'd call his parents; no doubt they knew someone at LAPD who could help.

When he heard a quiet thump from upstairs, he didn't think, he dropped the phone and bounded up the steps, taking two at a time.

Bursting into the room, he tried to stop himself as Ivy gave a small yelp of surprise right in front of him, right before he barreled into her where she stood just inside the door. When he felt them falling, he spun, taking her body weight on top of him as they crashed to the floor.

He gagged when her elbow landed on his diaphragm, lay still, his heart beating in his chest when she didn't move off him.

"Shit," she said, recovering from the shock of having his two-twenty frame accidentally tackle her to the ground. "David? Are you okay?"

He pushed up onto his elbows slowly, gently removed her elbow from his stomach, and then, before she could move away, pulled her from the floor into his lap. "I thought someone was robbing the house." He felt the familiar weight of her settle in his lap and breathed in her lily scent.

When he looked at her, she smiled and shook her head. "This is one of the safest neighborhoods in the County."

"It is?" he asked, ignoring the fact that they were both pretending as if nothing had changed.

She nodded. "I checked ages ago when you first mentioned kids. I want to live in a place where they can play outside safely, you know?"

His head snapped up and he noticed her smile, noticed that it reached her eyes, and made them seem impossibly green. "You're coming home?"

She nodded once. "I tried to stop you this morning, but you'd left before I got the chance." She paused for only a second before adding, "I'd rather die than willingly let you go."

"You're staying?" he asked again, wanting to make sure that he was hearing her right.

"For good."

He felt the relief bloom in his chest. Without saying anything, he shifted her, stood, and helped her to her feet, his hand grazing over a piece of jewelry that he'd know anywhere. He glanced down at her hand, felt a grin tug at the corners of his mouth.

"Thanks for leaving it out for me," she said.

"I left work early to come and pick it up before I tracked you down and brought you home."

"Really?"

"Really."

"It's a good thing I was already here then."

He chuckled and bent his head to graze his lips over hers. When she sighed and kissed him back, he felt his stomach drop, when her hands fluttered and came to rest on his chest, he felt his mind numb. She'd come back to him.

The knowledge scared him still, made him want to spend the rest of his life making sure that she was loved and safe. And that, he knew, he could do.

"Promise that was the last time that either of us ever leaves?" he asked. When she smiled, he added, "I don't think that I can lose you again."

"I never want to lose you either." She touched a hand to his cheek. "This isn't a fire drill anymore."

"Are you saying we're well in the weeds?" he asked.

"Hopelessly."

"Perfect." He bent down to kiss her again.

Epilogue

Ivy watched as Camilla repositioned her glasses on her nose and peered at the recipe book. She wanted to smile at the picture that her mother-in-law made, her perfectly made-up face emphasized by the spectacles that she had solidly refused to wear for the last twenty years, until a recent eye infection had made wearing her contacts too uncomfortable to bear.

"I think those glasses suit you, Camilla," Ivy teased gently, knowing full well that she hated them.

"Absolutely," Marnie, her own grandmother chimed in from where she stood by the sink next to Amanda, peeling potatoes for the Sunday roast—a tradition that Ivy and David had started after the wedding nearly a year earlier and which had somehow turned into a weekly host rotation.

"Hmph," Camilla returned noncommittally, her eyes never leaving the pages of the worn recipe book.

Marnie and Amanda exchanged quick grins and Ivy couldn't help but chuckle at the pair. They had quickly become two peas in a pod, and although Ike and her grandfather joked about their women leaving them to move in together, Ivy felt heartened by the fact that such a strong friendship could blossom so late in life.

"How is David's schedule now that he's made Partner?" Camilla asked, clearly trying to change the subject. "Especially with that idiot, Gordon, gone?" She opened the oven door and the smell of roasted lamb wafted into the kitchen, filling the air with gamey flavors of rosemary and meat.

Before Ivy could reply, she felt her stomach lurch and fall to her feet. Her mouth started watering and she hurriedly put down the vegetables that she had been dicing so that she could walk-run towards the upstairs bathroom in her and David's guest room. As soon as she was out of the kitchen, she ran, passing the boys coming in from the yard as she did so.

"Ivy?" She heard David's voice but didn't stop.

She made it with seconds to spare, throwing up in the toilet before she had a chance to even collapse onto the floor. *Oh, God, why now? Maybe it was the lamb? Maybe it was just time?* Sitting on the cold tile floor, she leaned her back against the wall and closed her eyes, hoping that the darkness would settle her stomach.

"Babe?" she heard David call as he opened the door to their room.

Unwilling to risk opening her mouth, Ivy sat quietly and waited for him to walk into the bathroom. When he did, he hurried over to her side and called her name before touching cool fingers to her face. "Are you okay?" he asked, his words laced with worry as he crouched down beside her. "Baby, what's wrong? Are you sick?"

She shook her head and slowly opened her eyes despite the nausea so that she could look at him. His ice-blue eyes were drawn in concern as he looked down at her, his hands cupping either side of her face. When her heart gave a small kick of acknowledgment, she smiled and touched a hand to one of his, cradling it against her cheek. "I'm fine," she said, quietly, trying to stay calm so that the sickness settled.

"You're clearly not fine," he said, pushing to his feet, his eyes focused. "I'm calling Dr. Trelawny." He pulled out his phone but when she held up a hand, he hesitated.

"Please, David. I'm going to be seeing a lot of her in the next few months and this is really not necessary."

"Why?" he asked, his voice coming out in a quiet croak.

She looked up at him then, felt hot tears burn her eyes when her pulse skipped under his gaze, just as it always did. "I wanted to wait a few more days to tell you," she said, touching a hand to her stomach, "but obviously our child has other plans."

"What?" he whispered, his face pale. He plopped down on the floor in front of her, his eyes never leaving her face. "What?"

She smiled and reached out a hand to take his. "I'm only eight weeks, so it's early…but the doctor is pretty adamant that everything will be fine."

She saw the moment that realization dawned, changing his eyes from a dark blue to azure. A wide grin broke through his look of wonder. "A baby?"

She nodded, felt amazement soar in her chest, slicing the ever-present panic that she'd felt since she'd taken the tests nearly four days earlier.

"We're having a baby?" he asked again, his tone far-away.

He was quiet for a moment, his eyes glazed and unfocused, so quiet that she raised a hand to his cheek. "David?"

Blue eyes snapped back to her and he blinked a few times as if coming out of a trance. Then, he sat down beside her and, wrapping an arm around her shoulders, pulled her close. "I honestly thought it would take longer, that we'd have more time to prepare."

Her heart thudded once in her chest. "I know. Me too."

They were silent for a moment and she couldn't help but wonder if he was as afraid as she was. A child. She'd never even been around a child other than Meg and James' twins and even then, that was for a few hours at a time. And it was always…overwhelming. She had no idea what the hell she was supposed to do. "Thank God we have three moms in the family," she said, voicing her concern.

He laughed softly. "Within a week of him being born, you're going to be begging them to leave us alone."

"Him?"

"Or her," he corrected. "I don't care. I'm just..." he shrugged, "happy."

"Me too."

"You're going to be amazing, baby," he said and rested a hand on her still-flat stomach. "Both of you."

Ivy sighed and covered his hand with hers, feeling content for the first time in days. "I'm sorry I didn't tell you right away. The doctor said that the first few weeks can be touch-and-go, especially for a first pregnancy...I didn't want to scare you. I'm already a basket case myself. Honestly," she looked at him, "even after three tests, I still thought there'd been a mistake."

He laughed, rubbed her stomach gently again. "You know I'm petrified, right?"

Leaning sideways, she kissed him on the cheek. "Yeah. Me too."

"Wait until I tell Camilla that she's going to be a grandma," he said. "She's going to be such a pain," he said with fondness.

"She'll be over the moon," Ivy confirmed.

"Amanda and Marnie too. Everyone will be ecstatic."

"Amanda and Marnie already know."

"You told them?"

She shook her head, no. "I saw them starting a pool with Ike and Grandpa and can only think that they're betting on the odds that I'm knocked up."

They giggled as they leaned back on against the wall, their heads together, their hands interlocked as they waited for the sickness to pass, each lost in their own wonder at the world and all it had to offer.

To My Readers

To all of my amazing readers,

Thank you so much for picking up a copy of *The Fire Drill*, and if you made it to this note, then thank you for powering through to the end. For those of you who enjoyed reading this book, please share your thoughts with the world by writing a review on Amazon, or drop me a line at hello@tess-shepherd.com. If you did not enjoy this book, try to stay with me over the next few years. I'm fledgling. But one day soon I'll surprise those of you who are my biggest critics.

Don't forget to follow my journey on Instagram, @author_tess.shepherd, or visit my website—www.tess-shepherd.com—for news and updates, including the release date of my next book, *Public Trust*, coming Winter 2020.

Love,

Tess

Printed in Great Britain
by Amazon